desert spring

MICHAEL CRAFT

desert spring

st. martin's minotaur ✹ new york

www.minotaurbooks.com

Library of Congress Cataloging-in-Publication Data

Craft, Michael, 1950-
    Desert spring / Michael Craft.—1st St. Martin's Minotaur ed.
        p. cm.
    ISBN 0-312-32080-9
    1. Gray, Claire (Fictitious character)—Fiction. 2. Motion picture producers and directors—Crimes against—Fiction. 3. Women theatrical producers and directors—Fiction. 4. Women college teachers—Fiction. 5. Palm Springs (Calif.)—Fiction. 6. College theater—Fiction. I. Title.

PS3553.R215D473 2004
813'.54—dc22

                                                                    2003058789

First Edition: March 2004

10 9 8 7 6 5 4 3 2 1

Mon dixième roman
commence encore pour Léon.

author's note

The novel *Desert Spring* and the stage play *Photo Flash* were conceived simultaneously as two versions of the same story, freely adapted to different media. Writing the play first, I received invaluable guidance with the script from Eric Margerum and Dean Yohnk, representing the theater departments of, respectively, Carthage College and the University of Wisconsin—Parkside, both in Kenosha, Wisconsin. Photographer Timm Bundies and Dr. Richard Borman offered generous assistance with various details of the novel's plot. As always, my agent, Mitchell Waters, and my editor, Keith Kahla, kept the momentum of both projects alive with their support and enthusiasm.

contents

PART ONE

photo flash

"Claire." The whisper came from behind, mouthed over my shoulder in the darkness. My name drifted forward on warm, stale breath with a thin cloak of mint. "It hasn't aged a bit—fresh as the day you wrote it."

"It" was a play titled *Traders.* I hadn't written it in a day, but over the course of several months, some five years earlier, when I had suspended my directing career on Broadway and retreated to my alma mater to spend a year as a visiting professor. That hiatus, during which I was tucked away in a sleepy college town in the foothills of the Berkshires, had been prompted by an itch to try my hand as a playwright. By all accounts, I succeeded. *Traders* enjoyed instant critical acclaim when I premiered it at Evans College that spring, and the show met subsequent success both on Broadway (under my own direction, of course) and in Hollywood, where the play was adapted to film. I snagged a Tony; the Oscar was a near miss.

History, in a sense, was now repeating itself. On a Saturday night in April, I sat in the darkened auditorium of a theater on a college campus, watching a performance of *Traders* that I had directed. But I was nowhere near the Berkshires; I was some three thousand miles southwest, in the Sonoran Desert, near Palm Springs, California, on the campus of Desert Arts College. And this time, I was not a visiting professor, but head of the theater department, a perma-

nent career shift that I had embarked upon the previous autumn.
At fifty-four, I was starting over.

"Claire," repeated Kiki, resting her fingers on my shoulder,
speaking into my ear, "you've outdone yourself. The role was *made*
for Tanner." Each whispered word ruffled a tuft of hair at my tem-
ple. I shuddered as a tickling sensation shot down my neck.

I acknowledged her praise mutely, reaching to pat her fingers.
Our silent touch conveyed an easy, wordless understanding rooted
in more than thirty years of friendship.

Kiki Jasper-Plunkett had attended Evans with me as a fellow
theater major. We'd graduated on the same day, then had gone our
separate ways, each on a quest for theatrical glory, mine in directing, hers in costuming. My path had led to New York, while Kiki's
had taken her back to Evanstown, where her decades of tenure as
head costumer would eventually entitle her to chair the department. Ah, the codified perks of academia.

A hand touched my other shoulder. "Bravo, Claire," whispered
another voice, drifting from behind on breath as stale as Kiki's—
we'd all been sitting in silence for over two hours, and I was
tempted to beg for one of Kiki's mint pellets. The voice, that of D.
Glenn Yeats, continued, "You've delivered more than I dreamed
possible." With my free hand, I patted his. Grateful for the cover of
darkness, I mused that anyone observing me at that moment would
have found my contortion ludicrous. With arms crossed high
against my chest, one hand touching Kiki's, the other touching
Glenn's, I seemed to mimic the stately repose of an embalmed
pharaoh. There I sat, fallen royalty.

Glenn Yeats, local royalty of our desert kingdom and very much
alive, had taken a backseat to me that evening—literally—sitting
behind me in the theater, next to Kiki. Glenn constantly told me
that this splendid new playhouse was "mine," but in truth, it was
his; he had built it for me, using it as bait to lure me from New

York. As founder and president of Desert Arts College, Glenn had built not only the theater, but the entire campus—his way of "giving back" to society after amassing billions as the brains behind his famed computer-software empire. He was a wealthy geek with a soft spot for the arts, particularly the dramatic arts. Lucky me.

But I digress. The focus of attention that April evening was not on me or on Glenn Yeats, but onstage, where the last scene of *Traders* had enthralled our closing-night audience, a many-headed mistress wooed by my cast, a faceless crowd sitting breathless in the dark, hanging on every word. I wish I could say that I alone, as author and director, was responsible for this enchantment, but theater is a collaborative art, with its magic dependent on the creative efforts of many. As *Traders* drew to its close, however, the audience doted not on the scenery, costumes, writing, or lighting, but solely on Tanner Griffin.

Starring in the central role of Jerome, my discovery and protégé was breathing new life into the role I had written. With a maturity of insight remarkable for his twenty-six years, Tanner had found a level of meaning in my script that had eluded even me. He'd captured his audience with a definitive performance that would be the topic of bragging for years to come. "I was *there*," they would effuse. "I saw Tanner Griffin play Jerome, live. What a night! He was virtually unknown back then, long before his first film."

Long before? Barely. Tanner was just on the verge of making his transition from stage to screen. The contracts had already been written and signed. He would soon become an image, an icon projected through a lens, ephemeral as flickering light. But tonight he was flesh and blood.

Visceral too was his interpretation of the monologue that ends my play. I heard my own words as if freshly coined by him. The thoughts I had committed to paper now spun from his lips as if they were his spontaneous creation. With everyone else, I sat agog as he uttered the final lines. His head slowly bowed as the curtain began to fall. The lights faded to black.

A moment of appreciative silence was followed by hesitation, then a burst of applause as the lights rose for curtain call. During the blackout, Tanner had left the stage, so the intensity of applause grew as each cast member entered from the wings. The audience understood that Tanner would be last to appear, and when he did, the crowd instantly, collectively rose to their feet—no laggards. Their tribute was punctuated by hoots, whistles, and a smattering of bravos.

Tanner had proven, in spades, that he could act, and his astounding good looks left everyone drooling, men and women alike. He seemed genuinely humbled by this reception, which only heightened his allure. In short, the audience adored him, just as I'd predicted.

What I had not predicted, and would have nixed had I foreseen it, was Tanner's subsequent gesture into the crowd—toward *me.* Rising from a bow, he extended both arms in my direction and began to clap with the others, inciting a chorus of "Author, author."

A spotlight swung in my direction, and I began to suspect that this impulsive tribute had been rehearsed. I wagged my hands as if to shush the needless hoo-ha, but the wave of adulation would not be quelled. Now the entire cast had joined Tanner in beckoning me to join them onstage. I placed my palm on my chest and shook my head demurely, signaling that while I appreciated the recognition, I had no intention of moving from my seat—which only exacerbated the crowd's raucous insistence that I take the stage.

"Good *God,* doll. I think you'd better go peaceably, or they're apt to hoist you overhead, mob-style, passing you from row to row, kicking and yelping." From the row in front of me, Grant Knoll winked, adding, "Not very ladylike." In the seven months since my move to California, Grant had become my closest friend. Not only did we find ourselves emotionally in sync, but the thrum of our lives had shared much in common. Most notably, although neither of us had ever married, we had both recently found romance. Not with each other. We both liked men.

"He's right, Claire," said Spencer Wallace, standing next to me, applauding warmly. A celebrity in his own right, Spencer was variously known as Megahit Wallace or Mr. Blockbuster. As Hollywood's reigning producer, his name was a household word, synonymous with movie-making. He had sat next to me in the theater that night because I had invited him to the closing performance of *Traders* and to the party at my home, which would follow. Four months earlier, I had invited him to the opening performance of *Laura,* my first production at the college, and he had discovered, as I was certain he would, that Tanner Griffin was blessed with star magnetism. Spencer had now signed Tanner to appear in his next film, and preproduction would begin the next week. Tonight, Tanner's brief period of study at Desert Arts College was drawing to a close.

"Yeah, Claire, go on. You're the *real* star tonight." Arnold Manley, standing at my other side, squeezed my arm and nudged me toward the aisle. Manny had been an earlier protégé of mine, an aspiring actor back in New York. I had cast him as Jerome in the Broadway premiere of *Traders,* and when the play was later adapted to film, Manny made the transition as well. Now in his mid-thirties, Arnold Manley had solidly established a career as one of Hollywood's most respected actors.

Manny's comment, that I was the real star tonight, seemed on the surface both flattering and modest, and I was willing to accept it as such. But a point of fact did not escape me. Tanner Griffin was the star tonight—not I—and, more pointedly, not Manny. So I couldn't help wondering if my earlier protégé now harbored a gnawing resentment of my younger discovery. Not that I'd ever known Manny to be conniving or petulant, but he had clearly been upstaged this evening in the role that had first brought him fame. What's more, although Manny was unquestionably attractive and photogenic, Tanner Griffin . . . well, Tanner still took my breath away every time my eyes fell upon him.

Setting these thoughts aside, I worked my way through the row of seats, brushing knees with patrons who scrunched back to let me pass. Many knew me, offering words of congratulation, a pat on the back, or a kiss on the cheek; all continued to applaud.

When at last I'd made my way to the aisle, I paused to straighten my dress and unrumple the wrinkles from my lap—in the white-hot glare of a follow spot. The aisle was carpeted in deep crimson, matching the velvet upholstery of the seats, which I had chosen. Would it be shamelessly vain to admit that I had decorated my theater to coordinate with my wardrobe? Don't get me wrong; my taste for red is not an all-consuming, self-defining passion. Though I generally wear at least a touch of red, I make a full-blown splash in that color only on special occasions. Tonight certainly qualified, and I wore a new nubby-silk suit of bloody scarlet. There was nothing subtle about it—talk about theatrical flair. As I strutted toward the stage in the spotlight, the audience roared its approval.

As if by magic (it *had* been rehearsed, I decided), a set of rehearsal stairs was rolled to the stage apron to accommodate my ascent from the auditorium floor. Tanner stepped forward to assist me, taking my hand. As he escorted me to center stage, I spoke into his ear, "This is punishable by death, you know."

"I'll risk it." Then he turned me to the audience, stepped back a pace, and joined the others in their sustained applause.

It would be disingenuous of me to claim I was embarrassed.

Having spent most of my life in theaters, I felt no discomfort in being the target of a thousand admiring eyes. As for the applause, well, perhaps it *was* a bit much—a surfeit of nourishment—but nourishment it was, like food or oxygen, the very lifeblood of theater, the payback, the bouquet tossed onstage by our many-headed mistress. I offered a simple but self-confident bow with the trace of a smile that told the crowd, My, I do admire your taste.

Surely, I thought, they now had what they wanted and we could all go home. But the ovation didn't dwindle in the least. So I turned to Tanner, offering my arms, and we indulged in a full embrace—prompting cheers—before joining hands with the rest of the cast for a long, last, deep bow.

As the curtain fell, the audience finally rested their reddened hands and broke into happy chatter. Purses snapped. Keys rattled. Cellophane crackled as mints found their way to dry mouths.

Backstage, emotions were equally high but colored with the bittersweet awareness that the pressure was off, the show was over. All those weeks of hard work had produced the intended effect—we had created a new reality for our audience, transporting them to another world for a few hours. But the theatrical experience, by nature, is fleeting. It's not like a movie, wound on a reel, stored in a can. Theater packs its punch, then vanishes.

So our laughter and backslapping was punctuated by sniffles and underlaid by the anxiety of losing something that, only moments earlier, had been tangible and living, something that was now slipping irreversibly into memory. I'd been doing this for over thirty years, shepherding hundreds of productions from start to finish, but it never got easier. While opening night always carried overtones of birth, the obverse metaphor also applied.

Parents and friends of the cast had begun to find their way backstage from the auditorium. Amid the squeals and giddy laughter, I stepped close to Tanner and held both of his hands. "You were magnificent," I told him softly. "Thank you."

"Thank *me*?" He shook his head; thick locks of sandy-blond hair, damp from the rigors of his performance, swung across his forehead. "I owe everything to you—the script, the training, the opportunity. I can't thank you enough."

"Then the gratitude is mutual. Each of us will have to endure the frustration of owing greater thanks than we feel we deserve in return."

Tanner cast his eyes upward, into the fly space above the stage, features pinched in thought. "I . . . I *guess* I follow that." He laughed.

"Miss Gray?"

I turned. Thad Quatrain, one of the younger members of our college troupe, had approached me from behind, still glowing with the excitement of our performance and the rush of our curtain call; I'd have sworn I could hear the kid's adrenaline pumping. I gave him a hug. "Good show, Thad. There'll be bigger things ahead for you next year." With Tanner leaving, I would need to start grooming other leading men.

"*Thank* you, Miss Gray," he gushed. "I don't know if I can *wait* till fall, though. Have you decided about the summer program?"

"Nothing's final yet, but I think I can pull it together. If I do, can you stay?"

He nodded eagerly. "Mark says it's up to me." He was speaking of his uncle and guardian, Mark Manning, a journalist from Wisconsin who was back at home now, having attended our opening, two weeks prior.

"Excellent. Knowing you're available, I'm that much closer to committing to the summer program. I'll let you know."

"Great."

"Hey, Thad," said Tanner, slinging an arm over the kid's shoulder, "let's get cleaned up. Party tonight."

"I'll see you there," I told them both as they headed offstage toward the dressing rooms. Tanner needed a shower, but even those actors who'd played less taxing roles needed to remove their makeup before leaving the theater—lest they break one of the many taboos that rule the art of Thespis.

"*There* you are, doll." Grant Knoll rushed toward me from the wings, a nice-looking man, not quite fifty, stylish in his linen slacks and silk blazer, both in muted desert tones. "I thought perhaps you'd ascended into the heavens, carried from our mortal midst on that wave of adulation. What a curtain call!" He flung his arms around me and offered a big, sloppy, congratulatory kiss.

I accepted it with pleasure. With a tsk, I dismissed the significance of the ovation, telling Grant, "It was all a bit much."

He shot me a skeptical look. "Nonsense. Milady loved it."

Under my breath, I told him, "Well, of *course* I did."

"Oh"—he remembered his manners—"have you met Brandi Bjerregaard yet?" He ushered from behind him the woman he'd escorted to the theater that night. She was younger than Grant by about ten years, attractive in a stark, urban sort of way.

"No, I haven't." I offered my hand to the woman.

She shook it—very businesslike—as Grant explained, "Brandi is a fellow real-estate broker and developer, working out of Los Angeles."

"Birds of a feather . . . ," she singsonged, referring to her and Grant's similar line of work.

"And, uh . . . ," I asked awkwardly, "where's Kane tonight?" For the last several months, Grant had been settling into a live-in relationship with a much younger man, Kane Richter, a graphic-design student at the college who also served as an office intern in the publicity department of the campus art museum. Despite the difference in their years, Grant and Kane struck me as the genuine item—probably the most "normal" and stable couple I knew—and indeed, they were making plans to host a formal commitment ceremony in the not-too-distant future. Yet, tonight, a Saturday, Kane was nowhere to be seen.

"He's in LA," said Grant. His matter-of-fact tone assured me that he wasn't concerned, so I reasoned that I needn't be either. Grant continued, "He'll be away for a few days, attending a seminar at the Getty Museum. Arts administration and promotion—or whatever." Grant whirled a hand.

"Ah." Turning my attention to Brandi, I noted, "So you and Kane are sort of trading places this weekend."

She lolled her head back and breathed a languid laugh. "Yes, Claire, I suppose we are."

"Claire, darling!" Kiki bustled toward me rattling two armloads of bracelets. "It was smashing. *You* were smashing. What a finale!" She planted a big kiss on my cheek. As I pecked back, she whispered in my ear, "Your new outfit looked *fab*-ulous under the lights. Did you plan it that way?"

I let the question pass. She was a fine one to hint that ulterior motives were lurking in my wardrobe. As a theatrical costumer, her own interest in clothes bordered on manic—well, *everything* about Kiki bordered on manic. But clothing was truly a fixation of hers. She changed outfits several times a day, and her style was anything but subtle. Tonight she wore peacock-blue palazzo pants and a gauzy peasant blouse covered with a sleeveless tunic of gold brocade. Nuzzling next to her huge hoop earring, I asked discreetly, "May I have a mint?"

"Of course, love." She ferreted through an enormous black vinyl bag, produced a tiny tin, extracted a pea-size mint, and popped it in my mouth. In her flowing robe, she conjured the bizarre image of a priestess in spike heels delivering a microscopic communion pill.

As my saliva met the mint, it seared my dry tongue.

A mob of other well-wishers spotted me and drew near. Leading the pack was Glenn Yeats. "Claire, dear," he said, stepping forward, offering a hug, "remember the first time we met? I flew to New York to tell you about my plans to build Desert Arts College. Then and there, I predicted you would become the crown jewel of my faculty. Tonight, dearest, you've proved once again that I have an uncanny knack for fulfilling my ambitions." He held me tight.

It escaped no one that his fulsome words were as much a reflection on his own talents as on mine. And while the others didn't realize it, his warm embrace conveyed more than affection. His hug was clinging and possessive, perhaps even desperate—revealing an insecure underside to the e-titan's armor of bravura.

He leaned to whisper in my ear, "We *do* make a handsome couple, don't you think?"

Other than the similarity of our ages—he was fifty-one, a few years younger than me—I'm not sure why he felt we were so well matched, but our pairing was a possibility he had promoted since the week of my arrival in California. "Not now, Glenn," I whispered through a smile, and he released his grip.

Spencer Wallace, the movie mogul, moved in. Ignoring Glenn, he grasped my hands and heaved a dramatic sigh, almost swooning. "Brava, Claire. Brava. It was spectacular, but then, I'd expect no less from *you,* dear lady." He bobbed his head deferentially, presenting an odd image. At sixty, Spencer was at the height of his career, known and respected by all within the film industry—and feared by many, he was that powerful. Still, this man of aggressive vigor had begun to look old for his years, almost frail. He patted my hand. "Claire, I'm honored beyond measure to call you a friend."

"Awww." I hugged him. "You've become more than a friend, Spencer." And I gave him a light kiss. He beamed. Was it just my imagination, or did the other mogul in our midst, D. Glenn Yeats, bristle at this exchange?

"I've brought a gift for you," Spencer told me. Then he added, "Not here—at the party."

"Oh? You shouldn't, Spencer."

"No," Glenn agreed with a flat, dull expression, "you shouldn't, Wallace."

Ignoring Glenn, Spencer told me, "It's nothing, really—a hostess gift, a token of our growing friendship."

Arnold Manley, who'd been spotted and surrounded by part of the backstage crowd, managed to break through the throng of starstruck fans and join my own little circle of admirers. "Gosh, Claire," he said, sweeping me into his arms, "I'd forgotten the excitement of working in your productions. I miss it."

I reminded Manny, "No one forced you to abandon the legitimate theater. The choice was yours." I tried to lighten my stern words with a tone of humor.

"Hollywood beckoned," he explained with a shrug. Then, with true concern, he asked, "Do you think less of me for it?"

"Of course not, dear." Despite my assurance, my peevishness on this point was a matter of record. I was known to be a tad defensive—in speech and in print—regarding the stature of "real" theater versus the lowest-common-denominator mentality of films, which are generally produced to serve no purpose beyond mass consumption. But we'll save that lecture. I told Manny, "I couldn't be prouder of everything you've accomplished."

Spencer noted, "And now Tanner Griffin is on his way as well—our next rising star. The industry always needs fresh blood."

I doubt if the comment was intended as an affront to Manny,

but I could understand if he interpreted it that way. Rather than openly question or rebut Spencer, which might have nasty consequences for Manny's movie career, he simply stepped aside, saying nothing.

"Ah, Miss Gray! There you are." A man with a notebook, wearing a press badge on his sport coat, edged through the crowd and introduced himself as Kemper Fahlstrom, an entertainment writer for the *Los Angeles Tribune.*

His name seemed familiar, and I greeted him cordially, but I didn't mention that I rarely saw his paper; for arts news, I still looked to New York.

"I'm wondering if you could spare a few minutes for an interview, Miss Gray. My editor is holding page one of the entertainment section, and I'd like to get something to him tonight. The show was wonderful, by the way."

"That's very flattering"—I hesitated—"but I'm sorry. There's a party at my home tonight, and I do need to rush along." I noticed that the backstage crowd was thinning; they would doubtless beat me to my own party.

"Claire," said Glenn, raising a finger, "perhaps you *should,* for the good of the school." He chortled. "Never turn away an opportunity for some page-one press—especially in LA."

I knew from previous discussions that Glenn had no particular enchantment with Los Angeles, but it happened to be the city where one of his two ex-wives, as well as his two grown children, now lived. He would waste no chance to demonstrate to them, preferably in print, that he had met unbridled success in his quest to reinvent his life by building, from the sand up, a world-class arts college in the desert.

"Glenn, really . . . ," I began to protest.

My friend Grant stepped forward to mediate. "Claire, if you'd like to stay and do the interview, why not? Everything is under control at the house—the catering staff has been there for hours. If you like, I'll scamper over and make sure everything's up to snuff."

I really wanted to leave. "Well . . ." At the same time, good publicity would be its own reward, and it was part of my job to promote the school and its theater program. Needing reassurance from Grant, I asked, "You'll play host till I arrive?"

"You bet, doll. Do your duty."

Glenn Yeats breathed a contented sigh. "There now—excellent—all worked out. We'll see you at the house, Claire."

And with that, my friends departed, as did the few remaining backstage stragglers who filed through a service door and headed out to the parking lot. With a reverberant thud, the big metal door closed, leaving me alone with the reporter.

I led him onto the set, suggesting we use the sofa at center stage. As we sat, he readied his pen and notebook.

"Now, then," I asked, "what would you like to know?"

2

Our interview didn't take long. I steered the conversation away from me and focused on praising others. I lauded the school and the efforts of its founder, D. Glenn Yeats; I confirmed that the D stood for *Dwight*, but assured the reporter that Glenn never used it. I complimented the entire cast of *Traders* and singled out Tanner Griffin for his extraordinary interpretation of the role of Jerome. I wished Tanner well in his fast-approaching Hollywood venture while commending Spencer Wallace for casting Tanner in the starring role of his new film, *Photo Flash*.

The reporter commented, "That'll leave quite a void in your theater program here at the college, won't it?"

"We'll muddle through, Mr. Fahlstrom." Under my breath, I added, "There ought to be a law against such thievery. Spencer Wallace deserves a public flogging—or *worse*." I playfully shook a knotted fist.

The reporter laughed. "You don't think much of movies, do you? Your loyalty to live theater is well known."

I hedged, "Films have their place in our culture. They can be highly entertaining." I was speaking in code, of course, meaning that most movies lack substance, but my slur was too subtle for the reporter, who slavishly scribed my words. We were finished within a half hour.

The night was warm as I whisked through the flat, open desert in my silver Beetle, heading toward home. Only the cleaning crew had remained at the theater, so I knew I would be last to arrive at the party I was hosting. When I turned off Country Club Drive, I saw cars lining both sides of the street in the quiet neighborhood where I now lived. Obligingly, the catering staff had cleared its trucks from the driveway, so I was able to slip into my garage and not have to worry about jockeying cars later.

When I cut the engine, I could hear the thump of music within the house; the party was in full swing without me. I entered through the kitchen, feeling lost in my own home. Total strangers—in jaunty uniforms from Coachella Catering—crowded my kitchen, talking over the music, banging trays, rattling barware.

"Ah, Miss Gray," one of the staffers recognized me; his name tag identified him as Thierry. Was he French? "Welcome back. Mr. Knoll told us you'd be late, but I'm sure you'll find everything is under control. Can I get you a drink?" He didn't sound French.

I had no idea who he was—probably the boss—but he'd asked the question I'd longed to hear, so I forwent the niceties of chitchat or introductions and accepted his offer with a grateful "Please."

"Uh, Erin!" he hailed a waitress from the living room. "Miss Gray is here. Could you take care of her?"

She popped through the kitchen doorway. "Happily. This way, Miss Gray." And she led me into the main room, where a makeshift bar had been set up on a pass-through countertop from the kitchen. She was pretty in a short, frilly maid's uniform, black with a white apron. Young, no more than twenty or so, she had blond-streaked hair in the modern fashion, looking more artful than natural. With a smile, she asked, "What can I get you?"

I hesitated. "Can you make a *very* dry martini, up?" I really did need liquor.

"Certainly." She set to it. While shaking my cocktail, she mentioned, "You have a wonderful home."

"Thank you, dear. I enjoy it." Surveying the room, I could tell my guests were enjoying the party's setting as well.

The house was still new to me—the *second* home I'd occupied since moving to the desert the previous fall. Originally, I'd bought a small condominium in a cozy six-unit development in nearby Palm Desert. That's how I'd come to befriend Grant Knoll; he'd sold me the condo and lived next door to me. But after a few months, I'd begun to feel cramped there. So Grant had found my current home in Rancho Mirage, nearer the DAC campus, declaring the new digs perfect for me.

At first, I was skeptical. The house was of vintage "desert modern" design, built sometime in the 1960s. These midcentury houses had suddenly become hot-again properties in the Palm Springs area, with a bold, distinctive style that scoffed at tradition and promoted a futuristic aesthetic straight out of *The Jetsons.*

On the day when Grant had first shown me the house, my jaw had dropped. For starters, the living room was triangular; in fact, there were virtually no right angles in the house. The living room ceiling, which was also sharply angled, continued outdoors and cantilevered over an expansive pool terrace, providing partial shade. Similarly, the stone floor of the interior continued through a wall of sliding glass to become the paving of the terrace. Though the building wasn't huge, its blending of indoors and out created a sense of spaciousness and easy living. The house was being sold with its main room furnished—no frumpy sofas or stuffed chairs, but sleek leather-cushioned benches, chrome and molded-plastic chairs, and a zooty coffee table shaped like a boomerang. Grant insisted it was all to-die-for, and I had to admit, I found the retro decorating oddly appealing. It seemed not dated, but fresh, in sympathy with my personal crusade to begin anew. So I bought it.

My old furniture, the threadbare junk I'd trucked from back East, wouldn't do at all; I pitched it in toto, as I should have done before packing and moving it cross-country. I trusted Grant's instincts and moved into my new quarters without changing a thing, with the exception of two minor additions to the living room.

First, on a stretch of wall above the long, low fireplace, I'd hung a new collection of framed black-and-white art photographs. The pictures, of various sizes and subjects, were partly my own work, representing a hobby I'd recently acquired—yet another aspect of the surprising new life I was building for myself. The photos that were not of my own making were the work of Spencer Wallace. The famed movie producer had long sought refuge in his home darkroom as a means of escaping the stresses of a high-pressure career. What's more, he'd nurtured a sentimental regard for black-and-white photography, telling me, "The medium harkens back to the golden age of the silver screen." For a hard-as-nails business-man, he had a poetic edge, mostly hidden, that surfaced in his pho-tographs. My interest in this visual pastime stemmed from Spencer's; he'd taught me the basics in his own darkroom, and through this shared interest, the two of us had nurtured our unlikely friendship. The fused collection of our photos over the mantel shared not only similar frames, but similar styles.

On a wall across from the fireplace, near the pass-through to the kitchen, was hung (incongruously, I admit) my other addition to the room's decor—a small oil painting, a bucolic landscape featur-ing a crude drawbridge, rendered in a pointillist style. The minor masterpiece, charmingly quaint, had been attributed to Per-Olof Östman, who was said to represent the finest flowering of an obscure school of Swedish neo-impressionist painters. But that's another story.

"*There* she is," said someone, snapping me back to the moment. With the realization that their hostess had arrived, my guests clustered around me with a chorus of greetings, making it difficult, though not impossible, for me to enjoy my first sip of Erin's icy, bone-dry martini. Where there's a will, there's a way.

"Claire! It's stunning," said Iesha Birch, director of the college art museum. I presumed she was referring to my new—but old—home, which she had not previously visited. She continued, "It's a pristine example of the postwar exuberance that immediately preceded the era of Cold War paranoia." She hugged herself, shaking the big toothlike beads of a primitive, painted necklace. "I adore it. It's such a statement."

"Isn't it, though," I agreed through a thin smile.

She ushered forward a man who was familiar, but I couldn't quite place him. Iesha asked, "Have you met I. T. Dirkman, the renowned architect?"

"Of course. Silly me." Taking care not to spill my drink, I extended my hand to shake his. I. T. Dirkman was currently one of the hottest "name" architects around. He had designed the entire campus of Desert Arts College—nothing but the best for Glenn Yeats. I had met with the designer several times during the early phase of planning my theater. "How nice to see you again, Mr. Dirkman. Welcome to my humble home." Since I had never heard what *I. T.* stood for, I felt at a loss when addressing him.

He glanced about our surroundings. "Not humble at all. It's splendid, Claire, splendid." I kept expecting him to add, Call me Ishmael—or perhaps Iggy or Ian—but he never did.

Glenn stepped up behind the architect, clapping an arm around his shoulder as if he owned the man. "Ah, I. T., it's like a dream come true. Who'd have thought, a year ago, before DAC opened its doors, that such an esteemed assemblage of talent could be gathered in one place?"

I noticed Spencer Wallace working his way toward the bar with an empty glass, so I seized the opportunity to introduce the producer to the architect, reinforcing Glenn's assertion that we were an arty crowd indeed. They greeted each other warmly, praising each other's work, but I noted that Glenn had backed off some, taking little interest in their conversation.

Stepping aside, I asked Glenn, "Is something wrong?"

He shrugged. "Somehow, I doubt if I. T., a true *artist* of the highest order, has much in common with Wallace, who's essentially a promoter." Sniff.

I might have reminded Glenn that he himself was essentially a computer nerd who'd hit the jackpot, but that seemed injudicious. Instead, I reminded him, "Spencer is the best in his field, as is Mr. Dirkman. From the look of it, they're getting along just fine." They were. I had no doubt that Glenn's offish behavior stemmed from his competitive nature, which sought to disparage Spencer's phenomenal success.

The crowd at the bar had grown thicker, so Erin slipped into the kitchen for a moment to replenish the ice and ask for help. She returned with another server, Carl, and together they took orders for drinks. Another waitress, Mindy, plied the crowd with a tray of appetizers, which were quickly snapped up, requiring a return visit to the kitchen.

Tapping his empty glass, Spencer excused himself from I. T. Dirkman and stepped to the bar. "Uh, Erin, might I have another Virgin Mary, please?"

"Of course, Mr. Wallace." She reached for a pitcher of tomato juice.

I knew most of the people present—they'd been involved with the show—but there were a good number of faces I didn't recognize, guests of guests and other hangers-on. There were easily fifty people present, probably far more, and my "spacious" new home was feeling crowded. As the April night was still warm and comfortable, some of my guests had drifted out to the terrace. Plucking a mushroom cap from a waiter's tray, I decided to join them.

It was a perfect, clear night in the desert, the sort of weather that prompts visitors to move here. One of the strongest selling points of the house I'd bought was the view from its back terrace. Clusters of palms framed a postcard vista of the ruddy Santa Rosa mountains, but tonight those features were merely black voids against the star-filled sky. A swimming pool—my own, what a rush—stretched along the far end of the terrace, its light casting blue ripples on the underside of the overhang from the house.

"Hi, doll. Glad you could make it." Grant Knoll stepped from the shadows with Brandi Bjerregaard, his companion for the evening.

I stepped toward him and gave him a friendly kiss. "Thanks for playing host till I arrived. You throw a perfect party."

"I'm gay," he said matter-of-factly, then sipped his drink.

Brandi caught my eye. "All the good ones are." She sighed.

I laughed, ate the mushroom, then plucked a cheese puff from a passing waiter's tray.

Tanner Griffin's voice caught my attention, and I turned to see him strolling outdoors with Spencer. Arnold Manley was with them as well, and I was pleased to note that there seemed to be no enmity between the two actors, my protégés, as they took turns scoring points with the powerful producer. When I greeted them with a wave, the threesome crossed the terrace to join me.

As they neared, Brandi said, "If you'll excuse us, Claire, I think we'll step inside." She nudged Grant. "It's getting chilly." It was at least seventy degrees.

I asked, "Wouldn't you care to meet everyone?" I doubted that Brandi had much interest in Spencer, but surely, I thought, she would be more than eager to hobnob with two hunky, young— and decidedly heterosexual—actors.

"Actually, we've met." Brandi headed indoors.

Grant guessed, "Must be the LA connection." And he followed Brandi into the living room. I interpreted this to mean that Brandi had encountered Spencer before, as his permanent home was in the Los Angeles area.

This testy interplay escaped Spencer, who seemed enthralled by the attentions of Tanner and Manny. It was almost as if Spencer harbored a prurient interest in them, but I found this unlikely. Not only was Spencer married, he had a solid reputation as a womanizer. He downed the last of his tomato juice, suppressed a belch, then grimaced.

I asked, "Sour stomach? Perhaps you should eat something. There's a late buffet supper; they're setting up for it now."

He smiled through a frown. "Thanks, Claire, but I'm just not hungry—no appetite lately."

With a touch of apprehension, I noted, "This has been going on for several weeks. Shouldn't you see someone?" By "someone," I meant "a doctor," but I didn't want my concern to sound inflated, and besides, I'd offered this advice before. Though I considered Spencer a friend, I doubted that he would appreciate the pestering of another "carping shrew"—the term he had often used to describe his wife.

"Yes, yes," he said, "all taken care of. It's nothing."

"Mr. Wallace," said Tanner, "can I get you some more tomato juice?"

"Why, *thank* you, Tanner—you'll go far in this business." Harhar. "It's a Virgin Mary. Just ask the young lady at the bar." He handed Tanner the glass.

"I'll take care of it." Tanner excused himself.

"Wait up," said Manny, following Tanner toward the doors to the living room. "I could use a refill myself."

Tanner asked his fellow actor, "Will you be staying in the desert long?"

"Afraid not," replied Manny as they stepped indoors. "I'm driving back to LA first thing in the morning . . ."

Watching them disappear into the crowd, Spencer said, "I must say, Claire, you certainly have a knack for sniffing out talent. You, too, could go far in this business."

Wryly, I told him, "I already have."

"I meant the *picture* business."

"I know what you meant."

"Ah!" Spencer poised a finger in the night air. "Speaking of pictures, did you find my gift?" His brows arched expectantly.

"Sorry. I've been distracted—the party and all."

"Of course. Let me show you." He offered his arm and escorted me toward the living room.

"It's a picture?"

"Another photo for your collection. Not very inventive of me, I admit."

Just as we reached the house, we encountered Kiki and another DAC faculty member, Lance Caldwell, coming out to the terrace. Seeing us, they stopped in their tracks.

Spencer eyed Kiki askew for a moment. "Good evening, Miss Jasper-Plunkett. I trust you're well."

"I am, thank you. Never better." Her tone was flat, almost cold. Conspicuously, she neglected to return the courtesy of wishing him well.

I had no reason to expect antagonism between Kiki and Spencer, but Kiki gave the clear impression she was miffed. Odd, I thought. So had Brandi Bjerregaard. So had Glenn Yeats.

Kiki brushed past us, out to the far edge of the terrace, jangling her bracelets as she strutted into the night, leaving us with Lance

Caldwell. A composer of great acclaim, he had lent luster and credibility to the music program at our fledgling college. Unfortunately, his talent was matched by his ego, which required constant stroking. I had done a fair job of this while cajoling him to compose the incidental music for our previous production, *Laura*. I had introduced him to Spencer at the show's opening, where they had greeted each other with words of mutual admiration.

"Caldwell," Spencer now greeted the composer with no enthusiasm.

"Wallace," the composer returned the frosty greeting. Then he nodded to me and whisked past us to join Kiki, who gazed into the swimming pool as if mesmerized by the soft, rippling light.

Was it my imagination, or was *everyone* miffed? As Spencer led me indoors, I asked, "What was *their* problem?"

He arched his brows innocently. "Was there a problem? I didn't notice."

I smirked. "I don't know how you could miss it."

His shoulders slumped. "Sorry, Claire. I'm not myself tonight. Feeling cranky."

"You've seemed out of sorts for weeks. You really ought to eat. You've been losing weight."

He shook his head. "Is there such a thing as male menopause? Everything seems different, and worse. Guess I'd better get used to it—old age—but I didn't think it would hit at *sixty*."

"You're *not* old," I assured him. I was only six years behind him, and I felt that I'd entered my best years.

With a tired smile, he asked, "Could we change the topic? It's depressing. Let me show you that photo."

"With pleasure." I took his arm as he led me to the fireplace.

Propped on the mantel near the other photos that hung on the wall was the framed picture he had brought as a hostess gift. Like the others, it was a black-and-white print with a white mat and a simple, black gallery-style frame. I hadn't noticed it when I'd first entered the room that evening because of the shifting crowd, but now, up close, I saw that the subject of this new image was a departure from the desert scenics that both he and I had been exploring. Setting my glass on the mantel, I lifted the frame and held the picture under the light of a nearby lamp. It was a panorama that had been shot from a large, lofty balcony looking out over the sea—clearly nowhere near Palm Springs. Spencer had doubtless snapped the photo either early or late in the day, as the shadows cast by the building, behind the viewer, sliced across the balcony at a sharp, dramatic angle. "Gorgeous," I told him. "I love the light and dark."

He nodded. "That's the beauty of black and white. It lends itself to such a simple, unvarnished way of seeing the world. A mere shadow can be breathtaking, while a shaft of light takes on a life of its own."

Returning the picture to the mantel, I asked, "Have you ever considered shooting a movie in black and white?"

"I've never had the guts. Can you imagine? Me, Spencer Wallace, afraid of my own roots as a cinematographer." He paused. "But I've been tempted, Claire. Seriously tempted. Especially now, with *Photo Flash.*"

"Say, that *is* an idea. The film is *about* a photographer, about photography itself. What better excuse—if you need one—to make an artistic statement." I took my glass from the mantel and sipped what was left of my martini, which was now warm. Maybe I would have another; my creative juices were flowing.

Spencer said, "It's an exciting notion, I admit. Tanner Griffin's film debut—in black and white. We'd get a double buzz."

"Huh?" a voice interrupted us. "You can't be serious, Spencer."

"Just thinking out loud," Spencer told our eavesdropper. Turning to me, Spencer asked, "You know Gabe Arlington, don't you, Claire?"

"My gosh"—I laughed—"I certainly know the name. What a pleasure, Mr. Arlington."

With a wide grin, he extended his hand. "If I may call you Claire, won't you please call me Gabe?"

"Of course, Gabe." I shook his hand. "Fellow directors."

Spencer amplified, "Fellow directors—across the great divide." He was alluding to my prejudice favoring theater over cinema. Gabe Arlington was a film director of long-standing reputation, though I hadn't heard much about him in recent years. He was older than I, about Spencer's age, looking rested and tan—and considerably more healthy than Spencer. A distinguished crop of blow-dried silver hair completed the image.

I told Gabe, "Tanner Griffin is eager to work with you. We were both pleasantly surprised when we learned that you'd be directing *Photo Flash*. I've been working with him on the script; he asked for help with several points of interpretation. Hope you don't mind."

"Hardly." He gave a jolly laugh. "Having my leading actor pre-coached by the great Claire Gray—what's to mind? It'll make *me* look all the better."

Spencer reminded him, "To say nothing of that screenplay—it's a winner. I can feel it in my bones."

I reminded Spencer, "Good thing. You wrote it."

He allowed, "I *am* proud of it. Objectively, it's a great story."

"It is," I granted. "And I must say, I've been impressed by your diligence in reworking the script."

"Great scripts, like great novels, aren't written; they're *re*-written." He raised his empty glass and toasted the truth of his pronouncement.

Gabe asked him, "You've been working on it here in the Springs?"

"I've really come to love the desert. My 'weekend retreat' in the old Movie Colony feels more like home every day. It's quiet—I can think and write—and I've got my darkroom right there. Plus, it puts two hours of interstate between me and Rebecca. What more could a man ask?"

"Huh. Your wife's not here?"

Spencer snorted. "Nobody's pining away, Gabe. Let's just call it a fragile détente. She's perfectly happy having the house in Brentwood to herself."

"Who wouldn't be?" Gabe laughed. "I've *seen* that house."

"She's welcome to it. I've got far more important things on my mind. To paraphrase the bard: the *film's* the thing. Everything set for next week?"

"All systems go. I'm returning to LA on Monday, and there's a preproduction meeting with the cast on Wednesday."

I sighed.

Both men turned to me, surprised by my wistful tone. With evident concern, Spencer asked, "Is something wrong, Claire?"

"Of course not." I mustered a smile. "The process is wonderful—isn't it?—nurturing a production, from start to finish."

Spencer wrapped an arm around me. "Postpartum blues? Sorry to draw the final curtain on *Traders*?"

With a feeble nod, I told him, "Something like that."

"How about another drink? That martini glass is woefully empty."

"Good idea."

Gabe said, "Claire, Spencer—if you'll excuse me." And he winked farewell, disappearing into the crowd, hailing some old acquaintance.

Walking me toward the bar, Spencer said, under his breath, "He's got a lot riding on this picture."

"So does Tanner; it's his big break. But Gabe is a veteran."

"Trust me, Claire—Gabe *needs* this picture. He hasn't directed a high-budget, high-profile production in nearly ten years. Sure, he had his glory days, way back when, but it takes only a flop or two to be dismissed as passé, and he's had more than his share. In the eyes of many, he was washed-up long ago. This business can be brutal. Signing him on for *Photo Flash* was a gamble, but I generally win."

I held Spencer's arm. "I hope you do win, for your sake—and Tanner's—and Gabe's."

When we arrived at the bar, the crowd had disappeared, having moved to the other side of the room, where the buffet supper was now being served. Thierry was just coming out of the kitchen. "Ah, Miss Gray," he said, "I hope everything has been to your satisfaction this evening."

"Yes, everything's lovely, thank you."

"It seems you need another drink?"

I eyed my glass as if I'd forgotten it was in my hand. "Why, yes, it seems I do."

Thierry cheerfully set about pouring and shaking a fresh martini. "And something for you, Mr. Wallace?"

"Another Virgin Mary."

"Yes, sir. Very good."

3

With dinner served, the focus of the party quickly shifted from drinks to food. The babble died down as people began eating; Tanner stepped to the stereo, switching to more tranquil music, inching down the volume. My guests settled into clumps of quiet conversation, gathering on furniture near the fireplace, sitting on the floor, or drifting out to the terrace. The catering crew moved back and forth from the kitchen, offering wine, clearing dishes, bringing out dessert plates. I moved among everyone, making sure all were happy, receiving nonstop compliments and thanks for a memorable evening.

Though it was Saturday night, the party wouldn't drag on indefinitely. By midnight or so, with everyone fed, my cast and crew's exhaustion had set in, and the revelry wound down fast. As soon as coffee was served, a few guests began getting up, carrying things to the kitchen, and circulating for a round of farewells. I stationed myself near the front door, and before long, everyone had gotten the message—it was time to go. Thierry dismissed the bartender and one of the servers; the remaining staff began packing their wares.

I wasn't keeping track of exactly who left—I was caught in a whirl of smooches and good-byes—but glancing over my shoulder into the living room, I noted that only Grant, Tanner, and the caterers remained. Abandoned glasses, napkins, cutlery, and dishes littered the room. Kiki was at the door with me, leaving with a last group of guests.

"Straight home now," I told her, wagging a finger in good-natured admonishment. "And drive safely."

"Of course, darling. Sober as a judge," she assured me.

"Steady as she goes!" said one of the other guests, someone I didn't know, stumbling out the door.

"Worry not," his buxom companion told me. "*I'm* driving." And she followed him to the street, rattling her keys.

Kiki asked, "Call me, Claire?"

"First thing in the morning, I promise."

"Well, not *too* early, I hope—tomorrow's Sunday."

I reminded her, "It's already Sunday."

"Incredible party," said one of the tech crew, slipping out. "Another *triumph* for Claire Gray."

"Yes, yes," I said, sounding bored, "yet another . . ."

"Good night, Claire," said someone else. "It was smashing."

"*Yes,* darling," echoed Kiki, "simply smashing. Ta-ta, love." She leaned to peck my cheek, then exited with a flourish.

Leaning through the door, I called after everyone, "Good night, all!" Then I turned back into the room and closed the door behind me, collapsing against it.

Grant was standing at the bar, pouring himself a last drink. He tapped the rim of an empty glass, telling me, "I think milady needs a nightcap."

I wagged a hand. Glancing about the room, I asked, "Where's Brandi? Did she abandon you?"

"Flew the coop, back to LA." He tapped the empty glass again. "Hmm?"

"No, thank you, dear. I've had enough."

Tanner asked, "Had enough music?" He was crouching near the bookcase that held the sound system, returning CDs to their cases.

He wore a simple outfit that night—dark dress slacks and a white cotton shirt with its collar open and sleeves rolled up. Lord, the sight of him.

"More than enough," I said with a laugh, referring to the music.

Tanner stood, punching a button on the stereo. The music stopped.

"Ahhh"—I stepped cautiously, on tiptoe, to the center of the room—"such blessed silence."

The words had no sooner left my mouth when a sharp crash came from the kitchen. It sounded as if a goblet had hit the tile floor. As we all turned, Erin popped up behind the pass-through bar, looking like a jack-in-the-box in a maid's uniform. With a sheepish grimace, she said, "Sorry, Miss Gray."

Apprehensively, I asked, "What was it?"

Thierry appeared in the kitchen doorway, wiping a glass with a dish towel. "It wasn't yours, Miss Gray. Just some barware from the catering company. We always expect some breakage." The brittle sounds of glass being swept into a metal dustpan affronted us from the kitchen. Thierry continued, "We're finished now, except for the final cleanup. Erin will stay to tidy up the living room and patio, but the rest of us will be going. I hope everything was to your satisfaction."

"Very much so, thank you. Everyone had a wonderful time. I'll be happy to call on you again."

Thierry bobbed his head. "I appreciate that, Miss Gray." Then he retreated into the kitchen, and I heard the sounds of whatnot being hauled out the back door.

Grant sipped his drink, telling Tanner and me, "One for the road."

"Careful," I warned.

"Bah—had plenty to eat tonight. Let's just call this a breath freshener." He sipped again.

Tanner moved to me from the bookcase, extending his arms. "How can I possibly begin to thank you?"

I growled suggestively. "As if you haven't thanked me a million times over. Tanner Griffin, how can *I* thank *you*?" And we embraced, sharing an easy kiss on the lips.

Grant strolled toward us, swirling the drink in his glass. He observed us for a moment, finger to chin. "My," he said, "isn't *this* a cozy picture? Not quite the typical teacher-student relationship."

Not quite, indeed. When I'd first met Tanner, just before classes had begun the previous fall, I'd recognized an attraction that was instant and mutual. I'd also recognized the questionable propriety of our rush toward intimacy, but ultimately, I'd been unable to resist it. By winter, he'd moved many of his things into my small-ish condo, spending most of his nights there—the primary motivation for my purchase of a larger house. Now, of course, the move may have seemed unwarranted, as Tanner would soon be leaving, but I was enjoying my new home and was glad to have had an excuse to buy it. Win some, lose some.

Grant clucked. "How old are you Tanner—*half* Claire's age?"

Focusing on me, Tanner paid little attention to Grant, answering, "Something like that, yes." More precisely, at twenty-six, he was *less* than half my age. Shame on me. Hell, lucky me.

Grant pattered on, "Though I must admit, Claire, I admire your taste in men."

I turned from Tanner, saying, "Thank you, Grant. And I've always admired *your* taste in men—to say nothing of your taste in real estate." I made a sweeping gesture that encompassed our surroundings.

Grant flopped a palm to his chest, humbled. "Why, thank you, doll. I'll take that as a compliment, coming from the illustrious Claire Gray—among the brightest lights in the American theater."

With a petite, ladylike snort, I sat at one end of the leather-cushioned bench that served as my sofa. "I'm a director, Grant, not a starlet. And now, I'm a *teacher*, of all things."

Tanner stepped to the bench, telling me, "I'll have to side with Grant."

Grant nodded—so there.

Tanner continued, "The name Claire Gray shines as bright as that of *any* star, onstage or off. When you left your career on Broadway and moved here to join the DAC faculty, you took a bold step that'll help to shape the next generation of American actors." He reached for my hands and brought me to my feet, adding, "And I, for one, am eternally grateful." He kissed me again, lightly.

I held his face in my hands. "Who'd have thought—certainly not I, not in my wildest dreams—that 'starting over' at fifty-four, I'd start over with the likes of Tanner Griffin?"

He exhaled a soft laugh of disbelief. With sincere modesty, he said, "I'm . . . I'm *no one*. You found me working in a body shop. I tinted your car windows."

I shook a finger in his face, dead serious. "I found a natural talent, a promising young actor who could help me develop my fledgling theater program. It didn't matter that you were a few years older than my other students; in fact, that was an advantage. I needed a leading man for our new troupe, and I found him."

From the side of his mouth, Grant said, "You also found a . . . uh, 'roommate.'" The lilt of his voice was heavy with insinuation.

"God, did I—in spades!" I felt silly and girlish referring in code to my lover as a roommate, but circumstances had dictated that Tanner and I needed to be discreet about our relationship. It was not quite a secret that we'd been living together, but we never discussed it publicly. Especially on campus or at social gatherings, we never behaved as a couple. First, to do so would lack professionalism. Second, and just as important, it would not be appreciated by

Glenn Yeats, who was not only my employer, but also a patient, would-be suitor. For the sake of appearances, Tanner had held on to his meager apartment in north Palm Springs.

My jubilant mood sagged as the full reality of Tanner's impending departure sank in. "I'm no fatalist," I said to no one in particular, "but it seems that all good things must in fact come to an end." I slumped onto the leather bench again.

Tanner sat next to me, taking my hand. His voice was tender. "It didn't need to end so quickly. This was all *your* doing, remember—recruiting me into your program last fall, casting me in the leading role of your first production, and inviting Spencer Wallace to the premiere."

Grant set down his drink and swooped behind us at the bench. "And the rest," he said with a broad flourish, "is theatrical history!" He recalled, with dramatic bravado, "It was one of those Hollywood fairy tales, the sort of catapult-to-overnight-fame that happens only in movies, rarely in real life. Spencer Wallace, Mr. Blockbuster himself, has signed our heartthrob-in-training to appear in his next major film." Grant kissed the top of Tanner's head, sniffing his tousled mop of sandy blond hair.

"Exactly as I'd intended." I tossed my hands, still conflicted over the results of my plan.

"Flash forward," said Grant. "It is now April, some four months after the powerful Mr. Wallace has discovered the hunky Mr. Griffin, and here we sit, among the debris and detritus of a *marvelous* cast party." Grant kissed the top of my head, but he didn't linger to sniff it.

As if on cue, Erin appeared from the kitchen with a tray, then set about clearing some of the "debris and detritus" Grant had mentioned. His description had conjured a picture of the ruinous aftermath of war, but in truth, my guests had been no more boorish than to leave a smattering of dirty dishes and half-drunk cocktails about the living room and outdoors on the terrace.

I sighed. "It wasn't just a cast party, you know. It was a farewell party for Tanner." I patted his hand.

"And a tribute to Spencer Wallace," he added. "Don't forget our guest of honor."

Grant strolled from behind the bench, retrieving his nightcap before Erin could snatch it and haul it to the kitchen with the other glasses she'd been plucking up. Grant swirled the last of his liquor and told me sincerely, "It was a fabulous evening, Claire. Memorable, too. Your guests will talk about this for *years* to come—wining and dining with the likes of Spencer Wallace, while sending Tanner on his way to begin the filming of *Photo Flash.*" Grant finished his drink, then mentioned, "I had a chance to gab with Wallace awhile. He has high hopes for this project—*loves* the script."

Tanner laughed. "He ought to. He wrote it."

"Inspired by his own hobby." Grant set down his glass and strolled toward the fireplace, telling me, "I see Wallace brought you yet another example of his work."

"Yes," I said, rising, joining Grant at the fireplace, "the one on the mantel is new. But some of those are mine, you know."

Studying the wall of pictures, he noted, "It seems your styles have merged."

"They have, haven't they? We've struck up a close friendship, Spencer and I. He's taught me a lot." With a quiet laugh, I stepped back to the bench, adding, "Everything has turned out perfectly— especially with regard to you, Tanner. I couldn't have plotted it better. Except, I had no idea it would happen so *fast.* And I had no idea *we'd* grow so attached."

Tanner stood and, without hesitation, suggested, "Just say the word, Claire, and I'll stay. I have far more to learn from you—right here. Hollywood can wait. Wallace can wait."

"Don't kid yourself." I shook my head decisively. "An opportunity like this knocks only once."

"Miss Gray?" said Erin as she made another pass through the room with her tray, gathering more glasses. "If you'll be sitting up for a while, would you like me to make a fresh pot of coffee?"

Looking from Tanner to Grant, who both expressed disinterest, I told the girl, "Thanks, that's good of you, but I think not. It's getting late."

She continued loading her tray, which was already heaped high.

"Too late for coffee . . . ," I thought aloud, strolling toward the bar. Then I turned to Grant. "Maybe a nightcap *is* in order."

"Of *course* it is." Grant joined me at the bar and poured a splash of cognac for each of us.

Tanner was standing near the coffee table, which Erin now cleared of a few more glasses. Noticing that her tray was loaded to capacity, Tanner asked, "Can I give you a hand with that?"

"I'll be fine. But thank you, Mr. Griffin." She squatted, picked up the tray, and hoisted it to shoulder level.

" 'Mr. Griffin'?" repeated Tanner with dismay—he was only three or four years older than the girl. He insisted, "It's Tanner."

"Yes, sir. I mean, I know, sir." She offered a quick, weak smile, then turned and crossed toward the kitchen.

Noting this interchange, Grant and I lifted our snifters to hide our grins.

With a confused laugh, Tanner followed Erin, asking, "Have we met? Do we know each other? We must."

Erin paused, blushing. "I'm sure we haven't met, sir." Then she scampered to the kitchen and disappeared.

Scratching behind an ear, Tanner called after her, "But you do seem familiar. And, please—don't call me 'sir.' "

Grant blurted a loud laugh. "Stop flirting, Tanner." Then, with a disapproving tsk, he told me from the corner of his mouth, "She's *far* too young for Tanner. He must be *twice* her age."

I gave Grant a dirty look, then downed a slug of my cognac. Tanner returned to the bookcase, where he put away the last of the CDs that were scattered about. "Tanner," I asked, "can we mix you something? Bar's still open."

He looked over his shoulder, shook his head. "Better not. Have to drive."

"Awww," I whined, setting my snifter on the coffee table as I crossed the room to him, "you don't *have* to, do you? Can't you stay *here* tonight? This has been 'home.' "

Finishing with the CDs, he turned to me. "Yes, this *has* been home for me. Well, a second home. But I never did completely move in—there wasn't time—and I never did let go of my old apartment. It isn't much, but I've got lots of stuff there, and the movers arrive first thing Monday. I haven't even begun packing, so I need to put in a busy day tomorrow—and I'll *never* get started if I wake up *here*. Sorry." He pecked my cheek.

"I know." Hangdog, I stubbed the toe of my shoe against the floor. "But tomorrow night?"

"I'll be here."

Brightening some, I asked, "And Monday night?"

"I'll be here."

"Then Tuesday—" The cloud descended.

"Tuesday, it's off to LA." Tanner tried, but he couldn't quite conceal his eagerness. When it comes to artifice, even an accomplished actor has his limits.

"Ugh, *please*," I said with a grand sigh. "Don't even *speak* of Tuesday."

Erin had returned from the kitchen with a bigger tray—a large, oval, silver serving tray—and continued to pick up around the living room. Though I found her presence intrusive, it beat the alternative, my waking up to the mess in the morning.

Tanner fingered my chin. "I thought that's what you wanted for me—a big break in pictures."

Peevishly, I acknowledged, "It is, it is."

"I thought you were proud of me."

"I am, I am."

Tanner wrapped me in a loose embrace. "Then it's time for this protégé to fly the nest—and a loving, miraculous nest it has been."

"I know, kiddo. You'll have to excuse me, but tonight, my emotions are mixed. And uncharacteristically fragile." I mustered a smile and patted his chest. "I couldn't be happier for you. Really."

"But . . . ?"

"But . . ." Pacing to the center of the room, I flung my arms in frustration and emitted a beastly growl. "Aarghh! I couldn't be happier for *you*, Tanner, but I could just *kill* Spencer Wallace for stealing you from me!"

Laughing, Tanner crossed to me and took me in his arms again.

Erin discreetly retreated to the kitchen.

"Oh, my," said Grant, swooping toward me from the bar. "Milady is indulging in a bit of melodrama this evening." Coyly, he added, "Not that I blame you." Grant stepped to Tanner, studied him for a moment, then languidly slid an arm behind his back, cupping Tanner's sandy-haired head in his palm. "If *I* had known the carnal pleasures of *this* stud-muffin, I'd be out for *blood*." As if putting a period on his threat, Grant planted a delicate kiss on Tanner's cheek.

"Shucks," said Tanner, not the least put off by Grant's advance, "I never knew you cared." Then he slipped away from Grant, crossed the room, and disappeared into a short hall that led to the bedrooms.

With a complacent sigh, I shook my head and sat again on the leather bench, telling Grant, "Thanks for reminding me how foolish and histrionic I can sound at times."

"Don't mention it, doll. You've had a lot on your mind lately."

Tanner returned from the hall carrying a light jacket. "I hate to break up what's left of the party, but I really do need to run. You'll be all right?"

I nodded. "Of course, dear. My nerves may be a bit frayed, but I'll survive. Always have." Rising, I walked Tanner to the front door.

He put his jacket on, telling me, "I'll call in the morning."

"Please do. Not too early, though. We could both use some rest."

With a sharp laugh, Grant interjected, "Just one more reason the boy *dare* not spend the night here. Milady would have him up till *all* hours—playing catch-me-catch-me."

"Do shut up," I told Grant without malice. Returning my attentions to Tanner, I said, "At the risk of repeating myself, love, you were superb tonight—and throughout the run." I straightened the collar of his jacket. "Now, then. Drive with care, get yourself tucked in, and we'll talk tomorrow—whenever you feel like taking a break from your packing."

Tanner hugged me. "It's a date."

"A phone date—but I'll take what I can get."

"Then, tomorrow night, the real thing."

I growled. "Now, *that's* a date."

"Night, Claire." Tanner gave me another quick kiss. "Night, Grant." Then he opened the door and left the house.

Grant called after him, "Nighty-night, hot stuff."

"Dormez bien," I added, watching him walk to his car. Then I closed the door and stood facing it for a long, silent moment.

Grant asked softly, "Claire?"

I turned. "Hmm?"

"He's such a special young man."

"With the emphasis on *young*?" I smirked.

"No, no. I mean it." Grant set his snifter next to mine on the coffee table, then moved to me. "The word sounds so threadbare, but Tanner is 'special' in every way."

"*I'll* tell the world."

"You won't have to, not now. Now that Tanner has been taken under wing by Spencer Wallace, *he'll* tell the world."

"Better Spencer than anyone else. He's the biggest and best producer in the business. I know that I've left Tanner's career in able hands." Ambling from the door to the center of the room, I gazed out the glass doors to the terrace, thinking aloud, "I've always prided myself as a practical, objective woman, not given to flights of fancy, thoroughly skeptical of the supernatural. I've never believed in destiny. But I must admit, from the moment when I first saw Tanner act, I understood that it was . . . well, preordained that the theater world would lose him to Hollywood. I have no doubt of his potential."

With a big sigh, Grant said, "Our loss, the hoi polloi's gain."

I turned to him. "Stop your pining. God knows, you've had a fair share of men in your life."

Matter-of-factly, he acknowledged, "Far too many." He added, "God knows, you've had men in *your* life, too."

Dryly, I acknowledged, "Far too few."

He led me to the coffee table, lifted both of our snifters, and handed me mine. "Come on, doll. Let's commiserate."

As we sipped the cognac together, Erin reappeared from the kitchen with her silver tray, this time heading out to the terrace, which had not yet been tidied up.

I swirled the heady brown liquor in my glass. "Ah, Grant," I said, looking into his eyes, "it seems I've known you forever."

He shared my smile. "But it's been only, what—six or seven months?"

I chuckled at the irony. "Moving out here, I'd never have guessed that my real-estate agent would become my best friend."

"Odder things have happened. I'm a broker and developer, not a porn star."

From the corner of my eye, I noticed Erin working her way across the terrace, toward the swimming pool. Her tray was already brimming with glasses and dishes. I laughed at Grant's comment. "A porn star? Don't flatter yourself, dear."

With mock umbrage, he retorted, "You're a fine one to talk—cradle robber."

"Shush." I lifted my glass. "To friendship."

He lifted his. "To friendship, and love, and . . . and men like Tanner who leave us weak in the knees."

"I'll drink to that." We touched glasses, then sipped.

Just as I was swallowing, Erin, outdoors, let loose with a horrific scream, dropping her metal tray and its load of glassware onto the stone terrace. Grant and I both choked. He managed not to drop his glass, but mine shattered at my feet.

Erin rushed to the sliding doors. "Miss Gray!" Breathless and shaking, she pointed to the far side of the terrace. "Someone's in the pool!"

Confused, I asked deadpan, "Swimming—at this hour?"

"No, Miss Gray. Sinking—facedown."

Grant and I exchanged a startled look, blinked as Erin's words registered, then rushed out to the terrace together, Grant tearing off his sport coat and tossing it aside. As the pool came into view, we both froze, gasping at the sight of a man in a business suit, a blurry black X beneath the rippling blue light.

Grant took a deep breath and tensed, preparing to dive. Then he paused, exhaled, and stooped to remove his gorgeous Italian loafers, handing them to Erin, who held them daintily with one hand. Grant took another deep breath, backed up a step—

"Mind the broken glass," I warned him.

—and he leaped into the pool with an awkward splash, adding a good amount of water to the cognac that had already spattered my new silk dress.

Erin joined me at the edge of the pool. We squealed, whimpered, and wrung our hands as Grant stroked his way to the bottom, then struggled to raise the body.

"Grant," I called, as if he could hear me, "do be careful!"

Standing next to me, Erin screamed again, a real bloodcurdler— I may have peed my pants. *"It's Spencer!"* she yelped.

Grant was just breaking the surface, gasping and sputtering, struggling to move the body, still facedown, to the steps at the shallow end of the pool. "Ugh. There . . . Jesus . . ."

I called, "Are you all right, Grant?"

He turned the body in the water. "Good God, Claire. It's . . . it's Spencer Wallace."

"No, it can't be . . ." With calm urgency, I pointed indoors to the phone on the bar, telling Erin, "Call nine-one-one."

"Yes, Miss Gray." Erin dropped Grant's shoes, darted inside, and dialed.

Grant was making a valiant attempt to revive the body. "Come on . . . come on . . . ," he huffed between long breaths.

I heard Erin babbling into the phone: "Yes, I'd like to report an accident at the home of Miss Claire Gray. It's located . . ."

I asked Grant, "Is he . . . ?"

Erin was saying, "We're not sure what happened, but it looks like someone drowned."

"Ugh, damn!" Grant heaved a groan of exhaustion. "Too late. Way too late."

"Oh, Lord," I mumbled.

"No," said Erin into the phone, "I'm not Miss Gray. I work for the catering company that served a party here tonight."

Grant looked from Spencer's body to me. "See if they can reach my brother."

With a finger snap, I told him, "That's *just* what I was thinking." I called to Erin, "Ask them to notify Grant's brother, Detective Larry Knoll of the Riverside County sheriff's department."

Erin nodded, then turned back to the phone. "Miss Gray wants to know if . . . oh, you heard? Wait, I'll ask." She put her hand over the mouthpiece and told me, "They need to know if it's an emergency, Miss Gray."

Flabbergasted, I marched indoors and grabbed the receiver.

"*Yes,* it's an emergency," I barked. "There's a corpse in my goddamn *swimming* pool!"

Well past midnight, instead of collapsing in bed after the party, I paced the living room, nursing the icy remains of a cocktail as a police investigation descended on my home. Red and blue flashers skimmed across the terrace as the medical examiner and his crew huddled near the pool.

Inside, the sheriff's detective sat on my leather bench, taking notes while questioning Erin, who sat primly in a three-legged chair near the dark fireplace. He asked, "And your full name, please?"

Her tone was shy but cooperative. "Erin Marie Donnelly," she recited with a touch of importance—her fifteen minutes of fame, I guess.

"You were working at a catered party here at the house tonight, correct?"

"Yes, sir. I'm employed by Coachella Catering. We do events all over the valley."

"Were you working alone?"

"Yes, sir." Erin hesitated. "Excuse me, sir. I'm not sure what I'm supposed to call you. Inspector? Officer?"

"Sorry," he replied with a soft laugh. "I'm Detective Larry Knoll, with the Riverside County sheriff's department. You can call me detective, if you like. Or 'sir' is fine." He didn't wear a uniform, but a dark, workaday business suit with a plain shirt and a loosely knotted tie—it was late. He smiled. "No need to stand on protocol, though. If it would make you feel more comfortable, just call me Larry."

"Oh, *no,* sir—I couldn't do that." Erin paused a moment, then asked, wide-eyed, "You're with the *sheriff's* department? This must be really serious."

He put down his notebook. "A suspicious death is never taken lightly, Erin, but I'm here tonight because some of the smaller desert cities contract their police services with the county sheriff. In neighboring Palm Springs, they have their own police force. Here in Rancho Mirage, you're stuck with me."

I moved between them, telling Erin, "We're hardly 'stuck' with Detective Knoll. He happens to be the brother of my friend Grant, so Larry is also a friend. He's the best on the force; I've seen him at work before."

Larry told Erin, "Miss Gray is exaggerating. I'm just a cop doing a job." He turned to me. "By the way, where *is* my waggish brother?"

I gestured toward the hall to the bedrooms. "Changing. He jumped in with most of his clothes on." Under my breath, I added, "Hope they're not ruined."

"Drip-dry fabrics have never been Grant's style. I'm afraid silk and cashmere don't take well to chlorinated pool water." Larry picked up his notes again, returning his attention to Erin. "Now, then. You were working here alone tonight?"

She nodded. "Yes, sir." Then she shook her head. "I mean, *no,* not at first. There was a cook and a bartender, Thierry was in charge, and there were several other servers. But they left after the buffet supper was finished, along with most of the guests. I stayed behind for cleanup."

"Can I get contact information for the other staff?"

"I'm sure the office will provide it." She gave Larry the phone number.

"Claire," he said, "how many guests did you have?"

I stepped to the bench and sat next to him. "At least fifty. It was a cast party, so the actors and crew were all here, some faculty and friends, plus a few *friends* of friends. The party was also a send-off for Tanner, who's about to launch his film career. Gabe Arlington, the director, attended. So did Spencer Wallace, the producer."

Larry tapped his notes. "The victim."

With a sober nod, I told him, "I'm still stunned."

He turned a page, asking Erin, "Can you tell me how you discovered the body?"

She described how she'd been cleaning up after the party, taking everything to the kitchen. "I'd finished here in the living room, so I went outside to the terrace. I started at that end"—she pointed—"then worked my way toward the pool. That's when I saw . . . this, like, *man* in the water, and I dropped the—"

Larry interrupted, "Was he faceup or facedown?"

"Face*down,* sir," she said decisively. "Near the bottom, as far as I could tell. I was so surprised, I dropped the tray I was carrying and . . . *screamed.* Then I—"

"*Marvelous* scream, by the way," I told her. It would have been perfect for the stage.

"Thank you, Miss Gray," she said, befuddled but grateful for the compliment. To Larry, she continued, "Then I ran back to the living room and alerted Miss Gray and your brother. He jumped in the pool and tried to save the poor guy, but I guess it was too late."

"Uh-huh." Larry studied his notes for a moment. "Did you yourself serve anything to Mr. Wallace tonight?"

She nodded. "Virgin Marys."

"Tomato juice?"

"Basically. Bloody Mary mix with garnish, no booze. He drank quite a few, but that's all he wanted—no food, no alcohol. If you ask me, he seemed sort of sick. Not in his party mood at all."

Suddenly curious, I beat Larry to the question: "You knew Spencer Wallace?"

Erin clasped her palms to her chest. "Gosh, *no,* Miss Gray. I mean, not personally. But I've worked a few parties at his house, so I knew who he was."

"Ah." Larry wrote something on his pad. "And he normally did eat and drink at his own parties?"

Erin rolled her eyes. "And how."

"Well . . . ?" Booming and throaty, Grant's voice sounded from the bedroom hallway. All eyes turned as he entered the living room, asking, "How do I look?"

Pausing for effect in the doorway to the hall, he wore a lavish, red silk robe with a marabou collar—mine, of course. Incongruously, he also wore heavy, rumpled, gray boot socks, the sort with a red stripe around the tops—no shoes. Strutting like a model on a runway, he passed in front of us, crossing the room. Larry shook his head with good humor; Erin tittered; I laughed openly.

Arriving near the front door, Grant twirled to face us. With a grand toss of his arms, he declared, "Works for me!"

I stood, still laughing. "Grant, I must admit, you do seem to make a 'statement,' whatever you wear."

"It's not *what* one wears," he lectured, "but *how* one wears it."

With hands on hips, I asked, "But why on earth did you raid *my* closet? Tanner has *lots* of clothes here, you know."

Grant aped my posture, hands on hips. "I doubt that Tanner would appreciate knowing I'd fingered through his underwear." Twitching his brows, he added, "Not that I didn't."

"And I'm supposed to be thrilled that you've fingered through *mine*?"

He clutched the collar of the robe high against his throat, as if for warmth. With a feigned whimper, he asked, "You really mind?"

I flicked a wrist. "Of course not. Have fun."

"Well"—Grant paused—"the socks *are* Tanner's. Oooooh. Think I can keep them?"

I scowled. "Don't be perverse, Grant dear." Then I grinned. "Well, why not? It seems like scant reward for your heroics tonight."

He shook his head woefully. "It takes very little to tickle my fancy, now that I've entered my dotage."

"You're forty-nine."

"See?"

Larry stood, crossed to his brother, and patted his back. "Well, Grant, I hear you rose to the occasion tonight. For whatever it's worth, I'm proud of you."

"Thanks, bro. Too bad it was for naught. I tried to revive him, but he was already gone."

"Yeah," said Larry with a slow shake of his head, "so I've heard."

Erin stood, asking tentatively, "Detective?"

Larry turned to her.

"I was wondering—have you finished talking to me?"

He stepped toward her. "Yes, for now. But I may need to reach you again later."

"Of course, sir. I'd like to finish up in the kitchen. Can I make everyone some coffee?"

Grant and I exchanged a frown of disinterest—the hour was late.

But Larry answered, "Sure, Erin, that'd be great. No telling how long we'll be here."

Grant and I groaned as Erin left for the kitchen.

Larry, oblivious to our bedraggled state, retrieved his notebook from the coffee table and continued his questioning. "Let's see, now," he said to me. "Do you recall when Spencer Wallace arrived tonight?"

I crossed to one of the chairs near the fireplace and sat. "Sorry, Larry. Everyone arrived at once, right after the show. I was detained at the theater, and by the time I got home, most of the guests were already here."

"Was Wallace with anyone?"

"Don't think so." I asked Grant, "He was alone tonight, wasn't he?"

"Not exactly." Grant strolled to the bench and sat, crossing his legs. "While I was talking to him about the new movie, he implied he was with *you* tonight."

I clucked. "I'm sure you're mistaken."

"Perhaps Wallace was mistaken, but I'm sure *I'm* not. He referred to himself as—get this—your 'consort.'"

I stood, blurting, "That's nuts!"

"Tell *him* that." Grant blinked. "Oops—too late."

"Oh, Lord." I plopped myself into the chair again.

Larry cleared his throat. "Pardon a blunt question, Claire, but were you two, uh . . . involved?"

"Of course not. I've had my hands quite full with Tanner, thank you. As for Spencer, the man's *married,* for cry-eye."

"*Was* married," Grant corrected me, "till tonight, and not very happily, I might add. The man's philandering is—*was*—legendary."

Larry asked, "Any idea where his wife was this evening?"

Grant shrugged. "LA, I imagine."

I explained, "The wife stays at the main house near Los Angeles, in Brentwood, I believe. They also have a weekend home in Palm Springs—the old Movie Colony, in fact. Lately, Spencer was here most of the time. He was polishing his script for *Photo Flash,* at least when he wasn't in the darkroom."

Larry looked up from his notes. "Darkroom?"

"His photo lab. Spencer was an avid hobbyist, specializing in black and white—said it harkened back to 'the golden age of the silver screen.' He got *me* interested in it, too." I pointed to the collection of framed photos above the mantel. "Those are some of the prints we processed together at his home."

Larry stepped to the fireplace and studied the pictures for a moment. "Not bad. Then you *were* close, the two of you."

"We were friends. I admired his professional accomplishments—who wouldn't?—and he seemed to admire mine. We came to enjoy a hobby together. But that was the extent of it." I sat back in the chair, slumping. "I'll save you the trouble of asking: No, we were never intimate."

Larry grinned, wrote a note, then turned from the photos to face me again. "Tonight, at the party, didn't you find it strange that he disappeared at some point?"

"Not at all. People came and went all evening. Frankly, I never *did* notice that Spencer was no longer around."

" 'Scuse me. Detective?"

We turned toward the back of the living room. A sheriff's deputy in a tan uniform had entered from the terrace.

Gesturing outdoors toward the pool, he asked Larry, "Can the ME have a word with you?"

Larry told us, "The medical examiner may have some initial findings. Back in a minute." And he went outdoors with the deputy, disappearing into a clump of other officers and technicians.

I rose from my chair with an exasperated sigh. "Ughh, what a night." Crossing to the bar, I was tempted to pour another drink, but decided against it, shoving my glass aside. I plucked a plastic swizzle stick from a bunch near the ice bucket and twiddled it in my fingers.

Grant pulled his legs up onto the bench and lay on his side, adjusting the folds of my silk robe. Propping himself on an elbow, he intoned grandly, " 'Theater is my life.' How many times have I heard milady say it?"

"More than once, I admit."

"If that's truly the case—your life is theater—I should think that tonight's *dramatic* developments would constitute 'just another evening at home.' Ho hum." He patted his mouth.

Stepping to the bench, I nudged Grant's legs and sat near his knees, pondering the swizzle stick. My tone was matter-of-fact. "You know very well that unexpected death, however dramatic, plays no role whatever in my day-to-day life."

"Hmmm." Grant considered my words for a moment. "And yet," he noted, "tonight, I had to fish a corpse out of your pool."

Ignoring his remark, I thought aloud, " 'Theater is my life.' Such a simple statement, it verges on hackneyed. But it's true, Grant. My dreams have been ambitious and direct, and I've attained them— I've established a solid reputation in the theater world. And now, well into my middle years, I've grasped at the opportunity to start over in a new direction, in a new locale, as if rebuilding my life from scratch." Looking at Grant, I concluded, "I've devoted myself to theater, and my goals have served me well."

Grant moved his feet to the floor and sat up, scooting close to me. Softly, he said, "Those goals have been strictly professional, Claire. Well done—you've proved your point and climbed to the top. I salute you as the *prima donna assoluta* of the American theater world. But what about . . . the woman within?"

With a touch of humor, I asked, "You're saying I'm shallow?" I was avoiding the real issue, and Grant knew it.

"Hardly." He touched my arm. "You know only too well what I'm really asking: Where's the man in your life?"

Fidgeting with the swizzle stick, I told him, "I've just never had time for that. We've been through this before, Grant—I'm happily independent. It may sound lame, but I've been wed to my work."

The swizzle stick snapped in my fingers. Flustered, I set the pieces on the coffee table.

"What about . . . Tanner?"

"Ah." I slumped next to Grant, drained of tension, but my words were tinged with melancholy. "Tanner's been glorious. I've needed him badly." With a feeble laugh, I added, "What woman wouldn't?"

Grant paused. "And now he's gone, almost."

I nodded. "Almost."

Grant rose. "I must say, doll—you're taking it better than I expected."

"I knew it was coming. It was inevitable. In a sense, I planned it this way."

"Hmm?" Concern colored Grant's voice.

I rose from the bench and crossed toward the front door, where I had last seen Tanner, leaving my home that night. Contemplating the door, I spoke more to myself than to Grant. "Tanner and I were drawn together by a force that's hard to define. How can I justify a romantic relationship with a man half my age—and a student, no less? I can't, not sanely." My voice took on a quiet intensity as I explained, "But the attraction was there, and it was mutual. What's more, we each had something to offer the other, something beyond sex. *He* had the innate talent, the promise for greatness that was simply lacking in the younger students at DAC. *He* could help me put our theater program on the map. And we did. Meanwhile, *I* had the experience and influence that could mold Tanner's raw potential into the actor he is today—and launch him to true stardom. Which we've done. He's on his way."

I turned from the door to face Grant, telling him, "So I knew all along this wasn't for keeps. I could look beyond the jowl-wagging and the disapproving gossip because it didn't matter. Tanner and I were part of a larger plan. We've brought it full circle. It's complete."

"And now," said Grant, moving to me, "you're losing him."

I shook my head with a wan smile. "I never really 'had' him. I may be largely inexperienced in affairs of the heart, but I'm not naive. I do love Tanner, and I have no doubt that he has loved me. But a lifelong, live-in relationship?" Through a soft laugh, I concluded, "It was never in the cards."

Our conversation was interrupted—thank God—by Larry, who appeared again outside the open terrace doors. "Thanks, Doc," he called to someone near the pool. "Talk to you in the morning." As Larry walked inside, the police flashers stopped, darkening the terrace, and a few moments later, several vehicles revved their engines and drove off.

"Well," said Larry, notes in hand, all business, "Wallace drowned. That's all we know."

Grant moved to a chair near the fireplace and sat. "So it was just an accident?"

"A horrible accident," I corrected him, crossing to stand near him.

Larry said, "Too soon to tell. Like any suspicious death, this one requires a complete medical-legal autopsy. Unfortunately, of the many possible causes of death, drowning presents the greatest obstacle to a definitive report."

Trying to follow, I mumbled, "I'm afraid I don't understand."

"Death by drowning cannot, in fact, be 'proven' by an autopsy. Drowning is known as a diagnosis of *exclusion*. If circumstances point to drowning—like a body, facedown, at the bottom of a swimming pool—drowning is logically presumed the cause of death."

I posited, "But that leaves the possibility that a dead or dying person either fell or was pushed into the water."

"Exactly."

Twirling a hand, Grant wondered, "Wouldn't you find water in the lungs if the person actually drowned?"

"Usually," said Larry, "but not always. There's a phenomenon known as dry drowning, by which the victim suffocates as the result of sudden laryngospasm—closure of the airway—caused by water in the throat. Either way, if water filled the lungs or not, the operative word is *suffocation*. It's an agonizing death."

All the more sobered by this insight into my friend's demise, I tried to remain unemotional and objective. "Do you know yet if there was water in Spencer's lungs?"

"We do. There was. But aside from circumstantial evidence, it's nearly impossible to tell whether we're dealing with an accident, which is reasonable; a suicide, which seems unlikely; or murder."

Larry's last word hung in the air for a moment before I asked, "Do the circumstances strike you as suspicious?"

The detective sat on the bench, facing Grant and me near the fireplace. Setting his notes on the table, he said, "This wasn't a pool party. Wallace didn't suffer a mishap while swimming; he was fully clothed. That might not seem remarkable if he'd been drinking heavily tonight—accidental drownings often result from alcohol abuse—but we know he was *not* drinking. Therefore, if he ended up in the water by accident, it was fluky at best." He summarized, "Do I find all this suspicious? You bet."

"Sorry to interrupt," said Erin, stepping from the kitchen with a tray. She paused uncertainly in the doorway, explaining, "The coffee's ready."

"Excellent," said Larry, waving her in. "I could use some."

As Erin moved to the coffee table with her tray, I sat in the chair next to Grant, who told the girl, "Just half a cup, please." I seconded, "Yes, a splash for me as well." Erin began pouring for us.

Grant asked Larry, "So, then, was it a freak accident? Or murder?"

"The investigation has just begun. But you've asked the central question."

I couldn't help musing, "All the elements of a neatly convoluted plot . . ."

"Uh-oh," said Grant. "Milady sniffs a tantalizing whodunit."

"Nonsense. It's a regrettable tragedy."

Grant told Larry, "I don't know if you're prepared to take on a sidekick, O brother mine, but I have a hunch the great Claire Gray is willing to assist the investigation. As you already know, she has a uniquely *theatrical* perspective on perplexing death."

"Oh, shush," I told him.

Erin was offering cream and sugar to each of us. Larry and I declined, but Grant fussed—pouring, spooning, stirring.

Rhetorically, Larry said, "If it was murder, there had to be a motive."

"And a means." I nodded. "And an opportunity."

"Of course," agreed Larry, who had already drunk his coffee, setting down the empty cup, "but the motive tells all. I'll need to look into Wallace's family background, his business dealings, the works. You two were friendly, Claire. Off the top of your head, do you know if he had any conspicuous enemies? Perhaps a rival with an ax to grind?"

Erin refilled his cup, then peeped into the smallish coffeepot. Deciding a refill was needed, she put things in order on the tray, then took the pot and stepped toward the kitchen.

I told Larry, "Spencer Wallace was wealthy and powerful. He could—and did—make and break careers. Over the years, I think it's safe to say he made plenty of enemies. And there was no short-age of jealous rivals. But would anyone stoop to *kill* the man— here, tonight, in *my* home? I can't imagine that anyone felt an animosity toward him that was sufficient to provoke murder."

Erin, I noticed, had paused at the kitchen doorway, turning to watch me as I spoke. When my eyes met hers, she bit her lip and slipped out of the room. What, I wondered, was that all about?

Larry was perusing his notes again. Without looking up, he asked, "Can you get me a complete list of everyone who was here tonight?"

I rose, cup in hand. "I'll try, Larry, but there were quite a few unfamiliar faces. I'll pull together my guest list and get it to you tomorrow." Crossing to the bar, I set down my cup and made a note to myself on a pad near the phone.

Grant swallowed the last of his coffee, then said to his brother, "Don't tell me you suspect *everyone* at the party."

With a menacing frown, Larry replied, "Anyone and everyone." Then he laughed, explaining, "It's a start. Every guest tonight presumably had the *opportunity* to engage in deadly mischief. The sooner I start eliminating those who had no conceivable *motive,* the sooner I can zero in on serious suspects."

Grant yawned, rose, and stretched a kink from his shoulders. He reminded Larry, "There were fifty guests. You'll have your hands full." An idle glance led his eyes to the photos over the mantel, and he stepped to the fireplace to study them.

"That's the grunt work of police work," Larry said vacantly, immersed in his notes and his thoughts.

Immersed in my own thoughts, I strolled toward the bench where Larry was seated. "The killer's motive—if there was a killer—is a total mystery. But what do we know about the victim?"

"Good question. Let's review." Larry flipped back through his notebook, reciting, "Spencer Wallace, a famed movie producer, aged sixty, died of apparent drowning under suspicious circumstances. He had nothing to eat tonight, and though he was known to drink heavily sometimes, tonight he drank only tomato juice.

The caterer's maid who served him said his mood seemed off, and she described him as sickly. The victim's permanent residence is near Los Angeles, but he'd lately spent most of his time at a second home in Palm Springs . . ."

Grant turned and caught my eye as we simultaneously recognized that details of Larry's summary were beginning to sound familiar. Then we both swung our gaze to the wall of photos.

Larry continued, "Wallace was working on a movie script that will soon go into production. He was also spending considerable time in his home darkroom, working on his hobby, black-and-white photography."

Grant and I interrupted him with a shared gasp.

"Good God," said Grant.

I blurted, "Photography!"

Larry rose from the bench, bewildered. "What about it?"

"*Photo Flash*. The script," I told him, stepping to his left side.

Flanking Larry on the right, Grant explained, "Wallace's screenplay was inspired by his hobby."

I added, "The plot focuses on the murder of a renowned photographer."

Larry's head ping-ponged as Grant picked up the story again: "He was poisoned slowly, over time, in his darkroom."

I leaned close to tell Larry, "By cadmium poisoning."

Larry blinked. "Cadmium?" He began taking notes.

"An extremely toxic element," said Grant. "But cadmium also has legitimate industrial uses."

I elaborated, "It's one of the major toxins in fluorescent lighting tubes, for instance. More to the point, cadmium compounds are widely used in photographic materials."

"Hold on a minute," said Larry with a disbelieving chortle. "How do you two *know* all this?"

"It's in the script!" we both told him.

Grant continued, "In his screenplay, Wallace spells out exactly how the photographer was poisoned—with cadmium chloride—and exactly how the crime evaded detection."

"It was all *meticulously* researched," I assured Larry. "Spencer Wallace knew as well as anyone: when it comes to details, you can't bluff a mystery audience."

With a touch of skepticism, Larry said, "I gather, then, you've both read the script."

"Of course." I explained, "Tanner will be starring in the film. He asked me to read the script and sought my advice on various points of interpretation."

Grant told his brother, "I've read it too, here at Claire's. Since Tanner needs to memorize the script, I've helped him by running lines, feeding him cues."

Larry nodded, making note of all this, then asked me, "Do you have a spare copy?"

"I think so, yes." Enticingly, I added, "Care to borrow it?"

"Please. It seems I have some brushing up to do with regard to cadmium poisoning. I'll alert the coroner's office to test for it at once."

My brow wrinkled. "Doesn't it take *weeks* to get results of tox- icology?"

"Usually, yes. But that's when you don't know what you're looking for. If we know we're looking for cadmium, the testing is straightforward." He sat again. "If you'll excuse me for a moment, I need to make notes on all this while it's fresh."

"Sure, Larry. Let me try to find that script for you." I headed toward the bedroom hallway.

"Uh, Claire?" said Grant, following me a step or two.

I turned. "Yes, dear?"

He fingered the marabou collar of his—rather, my—robe. "I hate to impose, but I wonder if I might spend the night here. My clothes are wet, it's late, and—"

"Of *course*, Grant. Not another word. In fact, I'd rather not be alone tonight. I'm sure you're bushed; God knows *I* am. Let's get you fixed up in the guest room." I led him down the hall.

"Thanks, doll," he told me when we reached the extra bedroom. He paused outside the door to give me a good-night kiss. "If I wake up early, I'll try not to disturb you."

"I appreciate that, but somehow, I have an inkling I won't be sleeping late tomorrow morning."

He breathed a little sigh of understanding. "Just try to get some rest." Then he retreated into the bedroom, closing the door behind him.

Stepping to the next door, I entered my own room, the one I'd shared with Tanner for several months. Tonight, I realized, the room seemed suddenly, depressingly empty. Ignoring that issue, I crossed to the dresser and opened one of the drawers. I found Tanner's copy of the bound screenplay at once; it was dog-eared from repeated handling, with his lines marked in yellow highlighter. Digging deeper, I found a second copy of the script, the one I'd studied. Taking the script, I closed the drawer and stepped across the bedroom toward the hall. Near the door, I caught a glimpse of myself in a dressing mirror and realized, with sagging spirits, that my new red dress was probably ruined by the cognac I'd spilled from chest to knee.

Ah, well, I thought. An excuse to shop.

Walking the hall from the bedroom to the living room, I heard Larry's voice and thought he might be using his cell phone. Not exactly eavesdropping, I slowed my pace—the better to hear—when I realized he was conversing with Erin.

"Sure, thanks," he said.

"Cream or sugar?" she asked, leading me to conclude she was serving more coffee.

"No, black, please."

For some reason, I stopped, delaying my return to the living room. At this point, I concede, I was indeed eavesdropping.

There was a long moment of silence, then Larry told Erin, "They're finished."

"Hmm?" Her voice had a vacant air.

"Miss Gray and my brother—I'm sure they're finished with their coffee." I heard him set down his cup, mumbling, "It *is* late."

There was another pause. Then Erin said with a tone of resolve, "I wonder if I might have a word with you, Detective." She set down the pot with a decisive clack.

"Certainly. That's why I'm here. What is it?"

"It's about . . . it's about Miss Gray."

Needless to say, I was now on full alert. I may have stopped breathing, for fear of detection.

"Yes?" asked Larry, intrigued.

"Earlier, when I first brought out the coffee, you were all discussing what happened tonight. You were talking about possible motives, and you asked Miss Gray if she knew of anyone who might've had a reason to kill Mr. Wallace."

Larry riffled through the pages of his notebook. "And she replied that while Wallace had both enemies and rivals, she doubted that any of them would stoop to murder."

"I, uh . . . I think Miss Gray neglected to tell you something."

"Something"—his footsteps approached her as his voice lowered—"something like what?"

"At the party tonight, after most of the guests had left, I was cleaning up—here, in this room—and Miss Gray was talking to Mr. Griffin."

Larry clarified, "Tanner? Miss Gray's . . . 'friend'?"

"Yes. They were discussing his move to Hollywood, and Miss Gray was getting all worked up."

Oh, no, I thought. Should I interrupt this? Or should I stay put so Larry could react candidly? Though tempted, I didn't move.

Larry asked, "She was angry?"

"When Mr. Griffin said it was time for him to 'fly the nest,' Miss Gray sort of flipped. I mean, she was like—"

I heard Erin stomping across the room, and I could easily visualize her flinging her arms, exactly as I had done.

"—she was like, 'Aarghh! I could *kill* Spencer Wallace for stealing you from me!'"

Screwed, I thought, shaking my head. Screwed as screwed can be.

Larry asked, "Was she just being . . . dramatic? Or did you get the impression she was serious? Sometimes people exaggerate."

"Well," allowed Erin, "Mr. Griffin and your brother laughed, so *they* didn't think she was serious. But they're not *women,* Detective. I don't think they fully understand what Miss Gray has been going through."

A primal instinct shot down my spine and put my feet in motion. Suddenly I was emerging from the hall into the living room, waving the movie script with triumph. "Well, I found it!"

Larry and Erin turned to me in silence.

I explained, "The screenplay. *Photo Flash.*"

But still they remained mute. Their embarrassed look would have struck me as funny had I not known the topic of the discussion I'd interrupted.

With a lighthearted laugh, I asked, "What in God's name is going on here?"

Brightly, I added, "What'd I miss?"

Sunday morning was not the time of serenity and solitude I'd been hoping to enjoy. My gay friend and former neighbor had spent the night, and his brother the detective now suspected me of murder.

"That's nuts," Grant told me when I voiced these concerns. "Larry would never seriously suspect you of *any* crime, let alone murder." Grant revved the engine of his Mercedes as it began the trek up a steep mountainside road that led to the Regal Palms Hotel. He was treating me to a luxe champagne brunch to help get my mind off the disturbing developments of the previous night.

I stared blankly out the windshield as palms and tall, colorful grasses whisked by. "Somehow," I mused, "your brother strikes me as the consummate professional. I doubt that he would let his objectivity be clouded by friendship."

Grant tsked. "I *heard* your so-called threat against Spencer Wallace. No one in his right mind would take it seriously."

"The catering gal did."

"Obviously befuddled—probably a crack baby." He turned into the hotel driveway and coasted to a stop beneath the massive portico.

A pair of smartly uniformed parking valets helped us from the car. Absorbing the genteel surroundings, I felt instantly calmed. As Grant escorted me through the doors to the lobby, I turned to get a good look at him. "I'm amazed," I said. "I was sure your clothes would be ruined."

He tossed his head with a laugh. "My ensemble may not look fresh-off-the-rack, but hell, linen is *supposed* to be worn rumpled." His loafers, now sockless, clacked on the marble floor as he strutted across the lobby with me at his side. His bare ankles revealed perhaps an extra inch of leg below the cuffs of his pants, which had shrunk under the iron earlier that morning during a futile attempt to restore their creases.

"Ah, good morning, Mr. Knoll," said a spiffed-up hostess as we approached the main door to the dining room. "I have your usual table on the terrace if you'd care to dine alfresco today."

Grant turned to me, deferring to my wishes. "Too breezy? Too warm?"

"Not at all. Let's enjoy the weather." April in the desert already hinted at summer, with daytime highs pushing ninety. But at mid-morning, the valley still basked under a sun that felt warm and welcoming, not hot. I had gazed out upon the spectacular view from Grant's regular terrace table many times and was eager to do so again.

Within moments, we were seated and champagne was being poured. I don't make a habit of boozing in the morning, but the prospect of bubbles on my tongue seemed oddly appealing, and the consequent light-headedness would be its own reward, so I made no effort to signal the waiter to cut short his pouring. He filled my crystal flute to the rim, then backed away with a subtle bow.

Grant raised his glass. "To a quick resolution to the events of last night."

"I'll drink to that." And I did. The champagne was bone-dry and ice-cold. I swallowed the first sip with rapture, then indulged in a few more, as did Grant.

During this lull in our conversation, I glanced about the other tables on the terrace. People gabbed, laughed, and ate. Laid-back and casually dressed but conspicuously accessorized in all manner of designer whatnot, most were Angelinos on a weekend's retreat from the smoggy metropolis. Sunday papers were folded on the tables or scattered on the stone floor. I glimpsed headlines from New York and Los Angeles and the local *Desert Sun*. There was no mention of Spencer Wallace; news of his drowning was too late for the overnight deadline. As far as the trendy brunch crowd was concerned, this was just another peaceful morning in paradise.

One table, at the far end of the terrace, was getting raucous. Their giddy hoots and loud repartee lent a disagreeable note to the elegant surroundings. Perhaps they had tarried too long with their champagne before moving on to the eggs Benedict and lobster soufflé. I assumed a hotel manager would soon stop by to politely, but firmly, shush them.

Grant followed my stare. "Who *are* they?" he wondered, appalled. There were five or six of them at the circular table. One of them, a man with his back to us, brayed at the sky, handing his newspaper to the woman sitting next to him.

I conjectured, "Perhaps they don't know better—or simply don't care."

"Well, they're *old* enough to know better." Grant jerked his head in the direction of the unruly table. "Those aren't kids. In fact, Laughing Boy looks older than *us.*"

"We're hardly ancient," I said with mild umbrage. But Grant's comment was apt; Laughing Boy was no moppet. From behind, his silvery hair gave him a grandfatherly air. What's more, he looked familiar, but the back of his head was an insufficient clue to his identity, and I was at a loss to place him.

"Shall we get something to eat?" asked Grant. "I'm starved."

"Sure. Let's graze."

So Grant rose, helped me from my chair, and walked indoors with me to the lavish buffet, leaving the rowdy table behind.

It was all too much—the food, that is. An omelette chef stood at the ready to concoct fresh, frothy egg dishes of any description. Baskets brimmed with breads and buns. A sculpted cornucopia of ice spilled heaps of shrimp and crab onto silver platters. Sausage and bacon and little breakfast steaks hissed in flame-licked chafing dishes. Boats of jams and sauces and syrup littered the long table in festive confusion. Though it was my intention to "just pick," a waiter stepped forward to hand me a fresh plate, offering to carry my first plate, now loaded high, back to the table for me. I gratefully accepted his offer, returning, unencumbered, to my frenzied foraging.

So engrossed had I become in the task of food-gathering (as if I might starve), I failed to notice that the table of revelers had stepped indoors to do the same. When I returned to the terrace with Grant, the lofty setting seemed eerily quiet. It was not till I seated myself, scraping the metal chair legs on the limestone pavers, that I realized Laughing Boy and his cohorts had ditched their bubbly and hit the trough. "Ah," I said with a dainty snap of my oversize damask napkin, "that's better."

Poising a silver fork, I focused on the task at hand. Generous chunks of lobster disappeared from my plate as fast as I could drag them through a buttery, opalescent pool of hollandaise.

Grant and I spoke very little—our mouths were busy. At some point, Laughing Boy's table returned, but I took little note of them, as they too had grown quiet, engrossed in the magnificent brunch. Though I had found their behavior boorish, even they understood that, ultimately, fine dining is no laughing matter. We were one in our appreciation of the moment, the food, and the setting.

From the corner of my eye, I watched a quail scamper across the apron of the hotel swimming pool and disappear beneath the fronds of a tiny, precious sago palm. Our mountaintop, that morning, was a peaceable kingdom.

But I could not completely brush aside, even momentarily, the vexing questions that had arisen with the discovery of a corpse in my own swimming pool. Ah, well, I told myself with a pensive sigh, at least the mystery of Spencer Wallace's death had allowed me to sidestep the issue of Tanner's departure.

As if reading my thoughts, Grant put down his fork, dabbed his lips, and asked quietly, "What's wrong, doll?"

"Well"—I whirled my fork—"everything. I mean, Spencer, of course. It was ghastly."

"The case is in good hands. Larry usually manages to get to the bottom of these things. Yet milady seems vexed. Are you sure it isn't Tanner?"

Exhaling noisily, I allowed, "Perhaps it is. I was so sure I would be stolid. Intellectually, I've known that I'm losing Tanner to bigger things, to another calling, one that I helped him achieve, so I've been congratulating myself on the success of my plans for him. Still . . ."

"Still," Grant concluded my thought, "he's leaving. You're losing him."

My shoulders slumped. "God, Grant, I wish you wouldn't put it quite that way." With an inelegant little snort, I forced back a tear.

Ashen, Grant rose from his chair and scooted to sit directly next to me, on the low wall that surrounded the terrace. He reached for my hands and leaned close. "Sorry, doll. I'm such a lout, being so blunt."

"You?" I laughed quietly. "A lout? Never, Grant. You're the perfect gentleman—and my best friend." I raised his hand to my lips and kissed it.

He gave me a hug. "Would you like some more champagne?"

My glass was almost empty, and the little wine that remained in it was warm and flat. I considered, but declined, "Better not. The day is young, and there's no telling what might follow."

"Most meals are followed by dessert." Grant twitched a brow.

I groaned. I'd gotten a quick look at the dessert table while filling my first two plates. It was all too tempting, but I had already overindulged. In fact, I could barely breathe. With a soft shake of my head, I told Grant, "Thanks, love, but I'll have to pass."

"Aw, come on," he said rising, offering his hand. "A little sweet taste is just what the doctor ordered to cut through this savory repast. Perhaps just a dollop of sorbet?" Seductively, he added, "I spied mango."

Hmm. There was little point in resisting, so I rose. Walking indoors with Grant, I told him under my breath, "You *are* wicked."

"Yes," he agreed. *"C'est moi—une tentatrice extraordinaire."*

No sooner had we arrived at the dessert table (a dollop of mango sorbet, my eye) when Laughing Boy and his companions came in from the terrace as well. Sated by their meal, as well as the champagne, they were again becoming too jovial; they sounded even louder indoors than when I had first noticed them outside. As logistics would have it, I still could see only the back of Laughing Boy's head, its silvery locks shaking as he regaled his party with an observation unheard by me but found *terribly* amusing by the others.

"Good God," he continued as I slid a litchi nut onto my plate, where it mingled with an assortment of other sweet delicacies, "who'd have thought it? It seems Spencer finally met his match."

The others agreed merrily with a chorus of inane right-ons.

I froze momentarily, not only in reaction to the cold humor and the unseemly topic, but also in recognition of Laughing Boy's voice. It was Gabe Arlington, director of *Photo Flash*. I considered turning my back to the group and wandering nearer, the better to listen, but common courtesy demanded that I should make my presence known and forestall the future embarrassment of discovery at an awkward moment.

Someone said, "I wonder if Claire Gray has read the paper yet."

Shocked into action, I asked brightly, "Did I hear my name?"

Heads—including Gabe's silvery mop top—turned. It seemed the entire crowded room was caught in suspended animation for an interminable span of several seconds while everyone tried to assess what had been said, heard, and meant. Even the background clatter of plates and cutlery hushed.

"Good *heavens*," said Gabe, getting a good look at me, smiling too broadly, "what a pleasant coincidence. Good morning, Claire." Then his look instantly sobered as he stepped to me at the dessert table and offered a hug.

I managed to return the gesture without spilling my slippery litchi nut.

"You must be devastated," said Gabe, patting my back.

Confused, I asked, "It's in the papers already? The police didn't arrive till after midnight."

"Uh, no," he said, equally confused, "at least I didn't notice it in the paper. But it was all over the TV news this morning."

"Ahhh." I should have known, but I rarely thought about television, and it would never even occur to me to switch it on in the morning.

Grant was standing nearby with his mango sorbet, which was beginning to melt, sliding lazily across the waxy surface of a banana leaf that garnished his plate. Cocking his head, he asked anyone, "Then why were you wondering if Claire had read the paper?"

In sheepish silence, Gabe's companions abandoned him, retreating to their table on the terrace.

Gabe asked me, "Then you didn't see it?"

"See *what*?" My confusion was now tinged with annoyance.

"The *Los Angeles Tribune*. Your interview."

"Oh. I'd totally forgotten . . ."

"Kemper Fahlstrom apparently caught you after the show closed last night."

Nodding, I recounted, "We spent a few minutes talking on the set before I headed home for the party." My brow wrinkled. "Hope I didn't come across like a blabbering idiot."

Gabe didn't answer.

"God," I asked, "*did* I?"

"No, no," said Gabe through a soothing laugh, "not at all, Claire. You were marvelously articulate. It's just that, well, one of your quotes struck a somewhat prophetic note—in light of what's happened." He cleared his throat with a nervous cough.

"What on earth . . . ?"

Grant took my arm. "Let's have a look at that paper."

Gabe offered, "I have a copy." He led us back to the terrace.

Grant and I followed with our dessert plates, setting them down at our table as Gabe stepped over to his own table, mumbled something to his group, then returned with the folded copy of the *Tribune,* which was not on the ground, but had been passed around by his guests.

"They gave you great coverage," he said lamely while handing me the paper.

Taking it, sitting, I recalled, "The reporter said his editor was holding page one." Then I unfolded the entertainment section and saw, with a gasp, that the editor had been true to his word. Splashed across the front page, above the fold, was Kemper Fahlstrom's interview. There was no photo, but the headline alone was sufficient to grab my eye. "Oh, Lord," I groaned.

"What's wrong, Claire?" Grant moved around the table and stood behind me.

The headline trumpeted: SPENCER WALLACE DESERVES PUBLIC

FLOGGING—OR WORSE! An italic subhead attributed my words: *Claire Gray accuses megahit producer of stealing her star.*

My eyes bugged as I skimmed the article. It was a verbatim account of my conversation with the reporter the previous night. Everything was in context and factually correct, even the observation: "Miss Gray playfully shook her fist while lamenting, 'There ought to be a law against such thievery.'"

"Uh-oh," said Grant beneath his breath. "Considering the developments later that night . . ." He didn't need to finish.

I shook my head. "What rotten timing. If the headline writer hadn't had a field day with my quote, it might've gone unnoticed."

"No such luck," said Gabe, sitting in Grant's empty chair. "That headline—coupled with the news that broke on television this morning—well, let's just say that tongues are wagging. I'm sorry, Claire." His look of genuine sympathy had the unintended effect of making me feel all the more concerned.

"It's nothing," Grant tried to assure me. "It'll all blow over by tomorrow." His words were unconvincing.

"Christ," I muttered, "if your brother didn't already see me in a suspicious light, he will now." I set the newspaper on the table and tapped the bold headline, smudging the tip of my index finger with black ink.

"Hmm?" asked Gabe, having no idea who Grant's brother was.

"Nothing," I dismissed the question with a blithe smile. "I'm just out of sorts this morning."

Gabe commiserated, "It's all been very trying, I'm sure."

"Hasn't it, though?" Shifting focus, I asked the movie director, "You'll still be heading back to Los Angeles tomorrow?"

"Far as I know. I'm not sure what impact, if any, Spencer's death will have on production of *Photo Flash*." Gabe stood, shrugged. "The show must go on."

"Indeed." A new worry: *Would* the show go on? Or, as the result of the producer's untimely death, would Tanner's budding film career be nipped before take one?

Gabe stepped to where I sat and leaned to give me a hug. "Hang in there, Claire. I need to get back to my guests." And he retreated to his table.

I turned to Grant. "Do you have your cell phone?"

"Always." He patted a lump in his jacket pocket.

"If you don't mind, I'd like to phone Tanner." I hadn't called his apartment earlier that morning, thinking he needed his sleep. But if he'd switched on the television, he'd heard the awful news, and I assumed he would want to talk to me.

"Sure, doll. Let me power it up for you." He punched a button on the handset, explaining, "I *always* switch it off at restaurants."

"You're a breath of civility in a barbaric world."

"I try." Then he noticed something on the phone's readout. "Oops. I have a voice mail waiting from Larry."

" 'Oops' isn't quite the expression I'd use for that discovery. Wonder what he wants—do you suppose he saw the *Tribune*?"

"One way to find out." Grant punched in the number. Within seconds, his brother answered. "Hi, Larry," said Grant. "What's up?"

I writhed in silent, inquisitive agony as Grant listened, nodding, grunting occasional uh-huhs. At last he said, "I'll tell her. Thanks, Larry. We'll be there." And he snapped the phone shut.

My pleading expression asked, Well . . . ?

"Well, Larry didn't see the *Tribune*—at least he didn't mention it. But he's been in touch with Spencer's widow, Rebecca Wallace, and she and her attorney are driving to the desert from LA this morning to meet with Larry."

With a measure of relief, I noted, "Standard procedure, I should think."

"But according to Larry, the widow wants to see, with her own eyes, where it happened."

"Peachy." I rolled my eyes. "Company's coming. When?"

"High noon." Grant glanced at his watch.

I did likewise; the morning was slipping away. "That doesn't give us much time."

"Always time for mango sorbet," he countered, then sat again across from me at the table.

Grant spooned the slurpy ice from his banana leaf.

I pondered my litchi nut.

6

When Grant's car had descended the mountain and began crossing the flat valley floor, I asked, "Do we have time for a detour?"

"Depends. Where? How far?" With a sharp laugh, he added, "As if I couldn't guess."

"How insightful of you. Yes, I'd like to swing past Tanner's apartment in Palm Springs."

"Oh, I forgot—you wanted to phone him." Steering with one hand, Grant fished in a pocket with the other. The car swerved, but the Sunday morning traffic was nil, so neither of us flinched.

"I've had second thoughts about that. If he's learned what's happened to Spencer, I might seem to be trivializing the tragedy if I tell him about it by phone—as if it were morning-after gossip. Better to discuss this face-to-face."

"As milady wishes." Grant slowed the car at the next intersection and turned up valley.

With Grant's well-tuned engine, heavy foot, and an open roadway, we made good time, arriving within minutes at a drab little apartment complex near the edge of town. It looked like a run-down motel, and for all I knew, in former years it may have been just that. These were the humble quarters that Tanner had called home before our lives had merged. In recent months, he had viewed the apartment as little more than storage space.

"Looks pretty quiet," said Grant, pulling off the road and braking his car on the barren plot of sand that served as a front yard. A neighbor's dog, napping in the shade of a peppertree, looked up for a moment, then dropped his snout to his paws, drifting off again. Grant surmised, "I don't think anyone's here."

I didn't see Tanner's black Jeep, but it may have been parked in back, especially if he was loading things. "We've come this far," I said. "I'll try the door."

Grant cut the engine and, getting out of the car, accompanied me to Tanner's door. The dog didn't bother lifting an eyelid.

I knocked, then waited. Listening for any action within, I heard only the whisper of traffic drifting across the sands from Interstate 10, perhaps a mile away. I knocked again, louder.

Grant said, "He must have gone out."

"But he was so insistent that he had to be *here* this morning—packing."

Lamely, Grant suggested, "Maybe he ran out of boxes."

"I think I have a key. I want to look inside." Snapping open my purse, I dug to the bottom, but the only keys there were mine.

"Allow me," said Grant, choosing a key from the others on his ring.

"If you intended to tantalize me, you have. Okay, I'll bite: What on earth are you doing with Tanner's key?"

Grant paused. "Jealous?"

I paused, considering the question. "Maybe."

"Why? You *never* tire of reminding me that Tanner is straight—period."

Grant was right; I had lorded Tanner's heterosexuality over my gay friend with such satisfaction that my attitude had verged on gloating. Yet, there stood Grant, displaying between his thumb and index finger my lover's house key. It glinted in the sunlight like a forbidden jewel. As Grant had adroitly shifted the topic from his reason for having the key to my reasons for feeling insecure in an unlikely relationship, I decided to sidestep both issues. Jerking my head toward the locked door, I ordered, "Give it a try."

Grant stepped forward and gave a perfunctory knock—just in case—then slipped the key into the lock, turned it, and cracked the door open a few inches. "Tanner?" he called inside.

Hearing no response, he opened the door wider, and we both stepped in.

The apartment consisted of only two small rooms and a bath, so it was plain to see that no one was home. Glancing through a window, I also saw that Tanner's Jeep was not parked in back. I wondered aloud, "Where *is* he?"

Grant checked the answering machine on the kitchen counter. "No messages."

Boxes gaped open, empty, from the corners of the main room. Clothes, books, dishes, and such were stacked here and there on the floor. Surveying the general disarray, I mentioned, "He hasn't gotten much packing done."

Grant added, "It's hard to tell if he even slept here last night."

With a touch of annoyance, I asked, "Where *else* would he have slept last night?"

Indeed.

Riding with Grant back to my house in Rancho Mirage, I fretted over Tanner's whereabouts while trying not to let my questions fester into vague, groundless suspicions. After all, Tanner was not accountable to me for his every move, and I had no reason to think that he had not driven directly home from my party the previous night. Still, it was a quiet ride.

"You know, doll," Grant said softly, sensing my consternation, "the only reason I happened to have Tanner's key is that he asked me to bring in his mail now and then. Since moving in with you, he hardly ever gets out to the apartment, but my work takes me all over the valley, and I'm out that way every few days. Just doing a favor for a friend."

I reached across the car's center console and patted his hand.

When we turned off Country Club Drive onto my side street, the sight of Tanner's Jeep in my driveway prompted a ditsy laugh of relief. I told Grant, "He's probably beside himself, wondering where the hell *I've* been."

Spotting a second car in the driveway, Grant noted, "Kiki's here too. Word spreads fast."

Walking through the front door with Grant, I found Tanner and Kiki at the pass-through from the kitchen, helping themselves to an impromptu breakfast they'd set up on the bar—juice, coffee, a plate of pastries. At the sound of the door, they turned, abandoned the food, and rushed toward me.

"Claire, *darling,*" gasped Kiki, "what a perfectly horrid way to end a party!" She wrapped me in a fierce hug, jangling her bracelets.

"Claire," said Tanner, trailing behind Kiki, "I came over the minute I heard. Kiki phoned me this morning, but no one could reach *you.*"

Kiki explained, "I heard it on the news. I thought maybe you'd gone to Tanner's, so I phoned him at the apartment, but he hadn't heard from you. Needless to say, he was shocked to learn what had happened."

"Shocked," he repeated, nodding.

Grant to the rescue: "It was my fault entirely, the lack of communication. We assumed the news hadn't spread yet, so I took Claire out for a quiet breakfast. She didn't want to disturb anyone so early on a Sunday."

I added, "Especially you, Tanner—what with your packing and all."

"Yeah, I was in the middle of it." Clearly, he'd been busy. He was looking rugged and butch that morning, wearing olive-colored cargo shorts, a sweat-splotched gray T-shirt, and tan work shoes. The sight of him was enough to make me swoon, even under such vexing circumstances. He cut in on Kiki's hug, planting a light kiss on my lips. "So considerate," he said, "finding yourself at the center of a murder investigation and worrying about interrupting my packing."

Vacantly, I protested, "I'm not quite at the *center* of the investigation."

"I only meant that Wallace died here, at your home."

"Oh."

Grant asked Tanner, "Then you haven't heard the corker?"

"*Corker?*" blurted Kiki. "There's a corker?"

I explained how the catering maid had overheard my exaggerated threat against Spencer at the party and had later reported it to Larry Knoll.

"Oh, dear," said Kiki, fingering her lips. Leaning close, she asked, "You didn't *do* it, did you?"

With a laugh, Tanner answered for me, "Of course not, Kiki. Last night, when Claire said she 'could kill Spencer Wallace,' she was speaking to me—I remember those words verbatim. I recall their tone as well. It was obviously an empty threat."

"Hey!" said Grant. "Maybe the *maid* did it." His tone was jocular.

But he'd raised a valid point. "Maybe she did," I allowed. "Or the cook, or one of the other servers—or anyone else who was here last night. Point is, the threatening words were *mine,* and in retrospect, they *are* highly incriminating. Larry made note of them."

Tanner said, "It's a good thing Grant's brother is on the case. He knows you too well to suspect you of foul play."

"Let's hope so," I said under my breath.

"And with any luck," said Grant, "he'll wrap this up fast."

Kiki nodded, telling Grant, "When you said 'corker,' I assumed you meant the headline in this morning's *Trib*." She pointed to a copy of the Los Angeles paper that she'd brought over. It was on my coffee table, spread open to the interview.

With slumped shoulders, I noted, "There were *two* corkers."

"By the way, Kiki," said Grant, trying to sound an upbeat note, "you're looking resplendent this morning. As usual."

"Oh, *pish,* darling." She tittered. "But thank you—I do try. Sometimes I fear I *almost* overdo it." That morning, she had almost overdone it in a bizarre outfit that resembled a transparent choir robe over zebra-print leotards—her Sunday look, perhaps. "It's a curse," she added, "my *penchant* for costuming."

"Hardly a curse," Tanner told her. He then asked any of us, "Can I get you something to drink?" He returned to the pass-through and picked up the glass he'd poured for himself.

Kiki eyed his glass, horrified. "What *are* you drinking?"

"Tomato juice. Can I get you some?"

Slyly, she asked, "Nothing stronger?"

"Everything's put away from last night."

I offered, "I can find you something."

"Ugh!" said Kiki grandly. "Never mind. Don't bother, love." To Tanner, she added, "A shot of orange juice would be splendid, thank you."

He poured it, then handed it to Kiki, asking over his shoulder, "Claire? Grant? Something for you?"

I declined.

Grant told Tanner, "No, thanks. Not much appetite this morning." He failed to mention that he and I had already gorged ourselves at the Regal Palms.

Shaking his head, Tanner commiserated, "I'm sure. Rough

night, huh? I understand you played the would-be hero. Good going, Grant."

"Shucks, doll-cakes, it was nothing." With exaggerated humility, Grant joined his hands in the fig-leaf position. "Duty called; I answered. Unfortunately, the poor devil died." He heaved a big sigh. "If you'll all excuse me, I want to make sure I didn't forget anything in the guest room." And he took his leave, crossing the living room to the bedroom hall.

A brief silence fell over us. Kiki sat on the leather bench at the center of the room. Then, pensively, she muttered, "Murder . . ."

"For all we know," said Tanner with a carefree shrug, "maybe it was just a freak accident." He sipped his tomato juice.

I eyed him with curiosity. "I must say, Tanner—you don't seem terribly distraught by Spencer's death."

"Sorry. Didn't mean to sound glib. But the truth is, Spencer Wallace was *not* the most likable of men."

"How very diplomatic of you," said Kiki.

Tanner asked her, "You've had encounters with him?"

"That's one way of putting it."

"All set!" said Grant, returning from the guest room. "Just wanted to make sure I didn't leave my toothbrush on the sink."

I reminded him, "You didn't *bring* a toothbrush."

"Ah. I suppose you're right." He patted the patch pocket of his sport coat, which bulged with more than his slim cell phone.

As he passed me on his way to the breakfast bar, I got a glimpse of red-striped wool protruding from his pocket. Good God—I suppressed a laugh—he had stolen Tanner's boot socks. "Don't tell me you're hungry," I said, my voice laced with innuendo.

"Just thought I'd browse some." Then Grant stopped short. Picking up something from the plate of pastries, he examined it curiously. "Oh? What's this?"

Tanner told him, "That's a protein bar. Try it—they're great."

"Yechhh!" Recoiling, Grant dropped the bar on the plate. It sounded like metal hitting glass.

Suddenly energized, Kiki rose from the bench and rushed to Grant. "Darling, darling—no, no, no—you've got it all wrong!"

Baffled, Grant asked, "You, uh . . . *eat* this stuff?"

"Of course not," she said impatiently. "But you've got it all wrong—the *delivery*, I mean." She picked up the protein bar as Grant had, telling him, "You said, 'Oh? What's this?'"

Grant eyed her warily. "Yes . . . ?"

"But that's so flat, so uninspired. My *dear*, it's *the* classic discovery line from every BBC mystery that's *ever* been produced. Just when things seem most perplexing, dark, and hopeless, our intrepid sleuth is examining the contents of the desk of the deceased. Then, from the corner of his eye, he notes a shred of paper, not fully burned, among the dying embers in the cold hearth. Stooping to pluck this scrap of evidence from the ashes"—Kiki demonstrated with the protein bar—"he examines it at arm's length, like Hamlet contemplating Yorik's skull. Finally, drawing it near, noting the few cryptic words scrawled upon it in the dead man's hand, he wonders aloud, and I quote, 'Aowww? Hwat's this?'"

Having hung on Kiki's every word, Grant declared, "I like it."

Matter-of-factly, Kiki told him, "Of course you do, darling. It's fabulous. Now, give it a try."

Grant cleared his throat. He took the protein bar from Kiki and gazed upon it as if studying Yorik's skull. "Aow? What's this?"

"Yes, yes. Much better," Kiki encouraged him. "After me: Aowww . . . ?"

He tried it again. "Aowww . . . ?"

"That's it, darling," she said rapidly. "Think of a cat, a sickly cat: Aowww . . . ?"

"Aowww . . . ?"

"Yes!" She flailed her arms. "Perfect! Now the rest: Hwat's this?"

Grant cleared his throat again. "What's this?"

Kiki shook her head and wagged a finger. "No, pet. Not 'what,' but 'hwat.' Hear the difference? You have to invert the *w* and the *h*. Very British, don't you know—*very* theatrical. Put the *h* first: hwat. Try it now, very crisply: Hwat's this?"

Grant paused. Then: "Hwat's this?"

"*Yes, yes, yes, yes, YES!*" Kiki twirled ecstatically.

With bravura, Grant asked, "Aowww? Hwat's this?"

Dryly, Tanner told me, "I think he's got it."

"By *George,* he's got it!" Kiki grabbed Grant and flung him through a quick, elaborate swing-style dance step.

With crossed arms, I noted, "Not quite the scene I expected to find in my living room on the morning after a murder." I sat on the bench.

The others turned to me, instantly sobered. Kiki dumped Grant, midstride, and moved to me. "Sorry, Claire. Guess we got carried away." She sat next to me on the bench. "But cheer up, darling. I mean, we don't actually *know* that Wallace was murdered, do we?"

Staring at a void on the opposite wall, I said, "The circumstances of his death are highly suspicious, at best. And let's not forget—that mousy maid overheard me tell Tanner that I 'could kill Spencer Wallace.' Ugh."

"But you didn't," Kiki said flatly.

"I might as well have. The words, in retrospect, *are* highly incriminating—Larry made note of them. Topping things off, I was quoted with a similar threat in this morning's paper."

My grim summation cast a momentary pall over my friends. Noticing that Tanner's glass was empty, I rose and, with a soft smile, told him, "Let me get you some more juice."

"I'm fine." He set down the glass and crossed to me. "But I'm concerned about *you*, Claire. We all are."

"Of course, love," said Kiki.

Grant chimed, "We're here for you."

"Look," I said reasonably, "it's been upsetting, but I'll deal with it." Then a frown colored my expression. I took Tanner's hand. "I just remembered—your movie."

"What of it?"

"I do hope Spencer's death doesn't throw a wrench in things. This picture is important to you; it'll launch your career."

Tanner's tone was distinctly carefree as he recounted, "The screenplay is finished. All the production contracts are complete, and I've heard that the funding is secure. Wallace wasn't *directing*, you know—that's Gabe Arlington's job. As far as I know, filming of *Photo Flash* will begin next week, on schedule."

I recalled Gabe's comment from earlier that morning—"the show must go on." Apparently he and Tanner were similarly philosophical and unruffled by Spencer's death. Neither seemed to be mourning the loss.

"In fact," Tanner continued with a trace of laughter, "the buzz about the murder is bound to heighten publicity. So don't worry about my career. The untimely death of Spencer Wallace can only *help* it, not hurt it."

The same, I thought, could be said for Gabe Arlington's career.

"Ahhh," said Grant wistfully, strolling from the breakfast bar to the bench, "the silver lining."

I turned to him. "That seems rather cold."

"Sorry." His offhand apology lacked any depth of contrition.

Tanner added, "Just trying to be practical."

Then Kiki: "As we were just saying, dear—Spencer Wallace was *not* a particularly likable person." She punctuated her statement with a sharp, knowing nod, to which both Grant and Tanner responded with nods of agreement.

"Well, *I* liked him." Crossing to the fireplace, I studied the framed photos that hung above the mantel. "He taught me things—and showed me new insights—and shared his knowledge. He was a friend."

Grant stepped up behind me. Coyly, he asked, "Like me?"

"No, Grant," I told him through a soft laugh, "not at all like you. You're my *best* friend."

Kiki stood. "I thought *I* was your best friend." Her tone conveyed humor, but a touch of offense as well.

"Well . . . ," I answered sweetly, sincerely, "you're my *oldest* friend."

"Thanks," she said, her voice dry as sand. Then she crossed toward the kitchen with her glass of orange juice.

I asked, "Need something?"

"Yes." She turned from the kitchen doorway. "A *real* drink." And she disappeared in search of alcohol.

Tanner stepped to me at the fireplace, then took my hands, studying me. "You'll be okay?"

"I certainly hope so." My tone was pragmatic, with no sense of foreboding.

"Then I think I'll run along. Just wanted to check in on you, but I've got *lots* to do today."

"I know you do." Taking his arm, I walked him to the front door. "It was sweet of you to pop over. Will I see you tonight—as promised?"

"Of course—as promised." Arriving at the door, he gave me a kiss. "Will that hold you for a while?"

"Mm-hm." I sounded like a woozy, doe-eyed schoolgirl. "Bye, love."

"Bye." He opened the door, but turned back to tell Grant, "See you later."

Grant beamed. "So long, Tanner. Don't work too hard." Suggestively, he added, "If you need any help, you *know* how to reach me."

Ignoring Grant, Tanner called to the kitchen, "I'm leaving, Kiki. Have a good day."

"Farewell, darling," she warbled from the other room. "Toodle-oo!" Her voice wafted over the sounds of stirring, pouring, and the clanging of ice.

Tanner paused to tweak my cheek, then left. I closed the door behind him.

"He's *such* a delight," said Grant, moving from the fireplace. Noticing Kiki's purse on the bench, he sat down, picked up the purse, and fingered the latch.

I agreed with a smile, "Isn't he?" Then I frowned. "I just wish Tanner felt a *smidgen* of remorse over Spencer's death. He's an actor—he could fake it."

"He's a man—men *can't* fake it." Grant peeped inside the purse, reacting with mock horror.

I thought aloud, "But Spencer gave Tanner his big break."

"No, Claire dear," said Kiki, entering from the kitchen with a sizable pink-hued cocktail. It looked like a cosmopolitan, lavishly garnished with fruit and such—she'd even found a paper umbrella in the back of a drawer, something the previous owner of the house had neglected to throw away. Stopping behind Grant at the bench, she told me, "*You* gave Tanner his big break. You found him; you taught him; you introduced him to the all-powerful Spencer Wallace."

"May he rest in peace," said Grant with sarcastic humor, turning to look at Kiki over his shoulder. He'd been pulling things from her purse—keys, makeup, breath spray.

"Yeah, *right*," agreed Kiki with a cynical snort. Seeing but not caring that Grant was rifling her purse, she crossed to the fireplace and stood elegantly with her drink at the mantel.

Sitting on the bench, I began taking things from Grant and returning them to Kiki's purse. I told both of them, "I really do think you should try to muster at least a pretense of respect for the man's memory."

"Very well, darling," said Kiki, practicing her pose, "as you wish." One arm rested on the mantel with her drink. Her other hand was poised languidly in the air, fingers splayed, as if holding a cigarette. "Oh, God," she said, noting her empty hand with disgust, "I should *never* have quit smoking."

"That"—Grant barked with delight—"and a few *other* bad habits!"

"Yeah, yeah . . ." Kiki slurped her cocktail.

With kindly admonition, I told her, "Easy on the booze, love. It's early."

"It's the *one* vice I have left." She slurped again. Then she sighed and set her glass on the mantel. Glancing at the photos, she found something of interest and turned to examine them more closely.

"Your life is better now." Earnestly, I added, "Much better."

"Yes, dear. You're right, of course." Her vacant tone conveyed that she was barely listening.

Grant told her, "Didn't mean to be flippant, Keeks. We're proud of you."

"I'm sure you are, dear, but don't be patronizing. It's so—" She stopped short, picking up the one framed photo that was not hung on the wall, but propped on the mantel. "Aowww? Hwat's this?"

Grant and I exchanged a glance, then rose from the bench and joined Kiki at the fireplace, flanking her. Bewildered, Grant asked, "Hwat?"

Kiki displayed the photo for us. "This picture—do you know what it is?"

"It was a gift," I said. "Spencer brought it to the party last night."

"Yes, darling. But I'm asking if you recognize what's *depicted* in the photo."

"Can't say I do."

Grant studied it. "Well, it's a seaside setting—looks rather tropical—as seen from a lofty balcony." Holding it at arm's length, he babbled, "Lovely composition, by the way. The black and white adds an unexpected dimension, lacking the garish postcard hues typically associated with such a vista."

"Look closer," said Kiki with a kittenish lilt. "Check the *shadows* on the balcony."

"Aha." I had a flash of insight.

"What?" asked Grant. "I see nothing."

I told him, "Artfully concealed in the shadows is a reclining female figure. Nude, if I'm not mistaken."

"Oh." He saw it. Unimpressed, he gave a grimace of disapproval.

I asked Kiki, "Am I connecting dots that don't exist, or does this photo hold some special meaning for you?"

She tossed a shoulder. "Well, I don't know that I'd call it 'special,' but yes, I do recognize the setting. It's a vacation home owned by Spencer Wallace—in Cabo San Lucas. I've been there."

"Huh?" asked Grant. "I thought his vacation home was *here,* in Palm Springs."

Kiki explained, "He had several, darling; he was *filthy* rich. This one's in Mexico—'a bit farther away from *Mrs.* Wallace,' as he liked to describe it." Kiki returned the photo to the mantel, strolled back to the bench, and sat.

"And you were there." Each word of Grant's flat statement was peppered with insinuation.

"Mm-hm." With perfect nonchalance, Kiki dug a tube of lipstick out of her purse and began touching up.

Sitting in one of the three-legged chairs by the fireplace, I explained to Grant, "Kiki first met Spencer when he attended the opening of *Laura* last December. It seems there was a mite of chemistry. They had a brief fling."

"*Very* brief," Kiki stressed. "A flingette."

"I see." Enjoying himself, Grant crossed to the bench, musing, "But not *so* brief a flingette that you didn't have time for a little travel, eh?"

Gloating some, Kiki replied, "I'd prefer to call it a lost weekend, a *sordid* lost weekend in the dusty, torrid Baja." Then her mood deflated. "But he was a jerk, a true asshole, if you'll pardon my expletive. And *that*"—she snapped her purse shut—"was *that*."

Grant eyed her askance. "So who's the babe on the balcony?"

Kiki primped. "Need you ask?"

Grant stepped back to the fireplace and peered at the photo. Skeptically, he asked, "It's *you*?" He handed the picture to me and looked over my shoulder as I perused it.

Kiki whirled a hand. "I admit, I don't *recall* him taking the picture. But I did sunbathe on the terrace—nude, obviously—and I know I fell asleep because the terrace was in shadow when I awoke. He must have snapped me as I napped." Mustering some indignation, she added, under her breath, "The filthy bugger."

"Well," said Grant, "if you *squint* at it . . . I suppose . . . the dark hair." Though Kiki's hair was now black, she changed its color almost as frequently as she changed clothes, a point that eluded Grant. He took the photo from me and returned it to the mantel.

"I will say this," said Kiki, pleased as punch. "He knew his craft. He certainly chose a flattering . . . angle, or lens, or whatever."

Dryly, I agreed, "Didn't he, though?"

The doorbell rang. Perhaps out of whimsy, perhaps in deference to the futuristic design of the house, its previous owner had installed door chimes that played the opening notes of the theme from *The Jetsons.* "I really *must* have that changed," I thought aloud as I moved to the front door, turned the knob, and swung it wide.

"Morning, Claire," said Detective Larry Knoll, stepping in. "Sorry to trouble you on a Sunday." He wore no tie today, but a pale blue polo shirt under his suit jacket. Also under his jacket was the glint of a polished leather shoulder holster. Another holster, on his belt, carried a cell phone.

Closing the door, I told him, "In light of last night, I'd be surprised if you *didn't* come calling."

Spotting his brother, Larry said, "Hey, Grant. Nice outfit."

Lolling at the mantel, Grant lifted a foot to display the bare ankle beneath his rumpled slacks. "You *would* notice."

"And Miss Jasper-Plunkett," said Larry, moving to the bench where Kiki still sat. "Nice to see you again, even under difficult circumstances."

She extended her hand like royalty. "*Please,* Detective. It's Kiki. How delightful to see *you* again." When he leaned forward to shake her hand, she yanked him near, asking, "Is it true? I hate to be indiscreet, but is Claire in trouble? Is she really a suspect? I mean the threat, the interview, and all. I highly *doubt* that she did it, you know."

"Kiki!" said Grant and I in unison, each moving a pace in her direction.

Larry stage-whispered to Kiki, "I'll let you in on something. I, too, highly doubt that Claire would stoop to murder—at a party, in her own home, no less—while vowing to throttle the guest of honor."

I stepped to the detective and patted his back. "Thank you, Larry. It's all very disturbing, and I spent a restless night. You have no idea how grateful I am that you recognize my empty threat for what it was—dramatic hyperbole."

He nodded. "Exactly. You're a friend, and I've come to know—and enjoy—your 'dramatic' style." Hesitating, he added, "Of course, I *am* a cop first, and I need to remain objective."

From the corner of her mouth, Kiki said, "*That* sounds ominous."

Grant glared at her. "Do shush, Kiki."

Perfectly at ease, I told Larry, "I understand your position. And I'll help any way I can."

"I ought to have some crucial issues cleared up soon—at least as far as you're concerned, Claire. The coroner is completing his initial exam, and he knows to test for cadmium. If those results are positive, then we know we're dealing with homicide, and the killer could have been anyone at the party last night—or anyone who's had access to Wallace's darkroom."

Grimly, I asked, "That would leave me on your suspect list, wouldn't it?"

"Actually, it would. But the point is, I'm *not* expecting the coroner to find cadmium. It's too much like the screenplay; I've read it. Murder isn't generally so neat and tidy, with the clues laid out, point by point, in a manuscript left by the deceased. So if I'm right and Wallace tests negative for cadmium, the investigation goes back to square one. But *you'd* be in the clear."

With supreme understatement, I said, "Glad to hear it."

"Anyway, the reason I'm here." He checked his watch. "It's nearly noon. I thought Wallace's widow and her attorney might already be here. I assume they'll arrive any minute."

"Oops," said Kiki, rising. "I *just* heard my exit cue."

With playful cynicism, Grant asked, "Aww, Kiki, gotta rush?"

"Yes, darling, I do 'gotta rush.'" She crossed to the fireplace and plucked her cocktail glass from the mantel. "I'm less than eager to meet the bereaved Mrs. Wallace." And she whisked into the kitchen.

With feigned naiveté and a finger to his chin, Grant said, "I wonder why . . ."

Kiki instantly returned from the kitchen without her glass. Snatching her purse from the bench, she headed for the front door. "It's been a stitch, everyone. Claire? Call me later. Maybe lunch tomorrow." She blew me a kiss and opened the door. "Ta, duckies." And she left with a flourish, closing the door behind her.

Larry shook his head, as if clearing a fog. "What was *that* all about?"

I shrugged. "With Kiki, one never knows."

Enjoying himself, Grant tattled to his brother, "Kiki had a flingette with the deceased."

With arched brows, Larry theorized, "So she doesn't care to meet the wife."

Grant laughed. "Well, duh." As the late morning was getting warm, he removed his sport coat and draped it over one of the chairs near the fireplace. The red stripe of Tanner's sock peeped from the pocket.

Changing the topic, I asked, "Won't you sit down, Larry?"

"Thanks." He sat on the leather bench and pulled a notebook from his inside breast pocket.

"Can we get you some coffee?" I offered, removing the open copy of the *Tribune* from the coffee table, folding it, and setting it aside with some magazines.

"No, thanks, all set. Claire, I wonder if I might review a few facts of the case with you."

Sitting in the chair nearest him, I replied brightly, perhaps too eagerly, "With pleasure."

"Uh-oh." Grant laughed, drifting to the bar to pour himself some orange juice. "Milady *is* wheedling her way into the investigation. I warned you last night, bro. You've got a sidekick."

I piped in, "Stop that, Grant." I was embarrassed to realize that his puckish words carried a kernel of truth.

"Well," said Larry, "to be perfectly honest, I'm not sure I mind. Claire seems to have known the victim as well as anyone, and I'm impressed by her ability to recall details and conversations."

With self-satisfaction, I noted, "All those years of theatrical training must have paid off. Memorization is part of the craft." Then my tone turned thoughtful. "I must admit, the riddle intrigues me. How and why did Spencer Wallace die? Was he murdered? And if so, who killed him? It's not unlike a baffling, nicely twisted stage play. I've been directing plays for over thirty years, so I suppose that qualifies me as a passable expert when it comes to analyzing character, motivation, and plot. If you find those skills useful, I offer them freely."

Larry had studied me as I spoke. Now, with a pensive nod, apparently satisfied that I could help, he said, "Let's talk about the victim." He set his open notebook on the coffee table. "Specifically, I'm intrigued by his recent health history. The maid said he appeared sickly last night."

I nodded. "He did. He even mentioned it to me, dismissing his complaints as the ravages of advancing years. But that struck a false note—he was only sixty."

"What were his specific symptoms?"

"Well"—my eyes searched the ceiling as I thought—"last night he complained of a sour stomach. But he'd been out of sorts for weeks, plagued by a whole array of unpleasant symptoms. For instance, he was irritable. He often found himself apologizing for his behavior, and no doubt about it, he was always on edge and testy. He was losing weight, but claimed not to be dieting, and he said he felt generally sluggish or anemic. He even complained that he couldn't get his teeth really clean, and in fact, I noticed that they seemed too yellow."

Grant stepped toward us from the bar, swallowing a sip of juice. "Did he smoke?"

"He did. Heavily at times." With a feeble laugh, I added, "But his oddest complaint was *here*"—I tapped my nose. "He thought he was losing his sense of smell. Naturally, I encouraged him to see a doctor. Last night, he implied that he had done so. He dismissed the results as 'nothing.'"

Larry underlined something in his notes. "He did see a doctor, last Wednesday. We found out he visited a walk-in clinic in Palm Desert. After hearing his complaints, they took chest X rays, which led to a tentative diagnosis of bronchial pneumonia. But now"— Larry hesitated—"well, I'm not so sure."

Concerned by his tone, I asked, "What do you mean?"

But the doorbell rang before Larry could answer. "That's probably Mrs. Wallace," he said, rising, taking his notebook from the table.

"God," I said, rising with him and crossing the room toward the front door, "I hate to imagine what *she's* going through."

Grant set down his glass. "I'd better leave," he said, sounding suddenly rushed. "These *clothes*—hardly presentable. I'll just duck out through the terrace. Bye, kids!" And he stepped to the rear wall of the room, sliding open the glass doors that led out to the pool.

I exchanged a quizzical look with Larry while reaching to open the door. As I did so, Grant stopped in his tracks. "Forgot my jacket," he explained, rushing back into the living room and grabbing his sport coat from the chair near the fireplace.

Ignoring Grant's antics, I turned to the guests outside my door.

"Good morning," I said with a peculiar mixture of sobriety and warmth. "Mrs. Wallace, I presume."

She stepped inside with her companion. "Yes, Rebecca Wallace. And this is my attorney, Bryce Ballantyne."

I was distracted by Grant, who had retrieved his jacket and was now darting through the room toward the pool.

Larry called after him, "So long, Grant."

I turned briefly from my guests. "Call me later, Grant."

"Later!" was his sole word of parting. And he was gone.

Returning my attention to my visitors, I said, "Please accept my condolences, Mrs. Wallace. I'm Claire Gray. I was proud to call your late husband a friend." I shook Rebecca's hand, then closed the door behind her. I told her lawyer, "Thank you for coming, Mr. Ballantyne."

"My pleasure, Miss Gray." He shook my hand mechanically.

They stepped into the room, and Larry moved forward to greet them. "I'm Detective Larry Knoll," he told them, offering his hand. "Thanks so much for driving over on such short notice."

While they exchanged a predictable round of pleasantries and sympathies, I spent a moment observing the new arrivals. I judged Rebecca to be about fifty years old, some ten years younger than her late husband. Bryce, her attorney, was younger still, under forty. Their clothes were dressy and stylish, marked by urban sophistication, which struck me as a bit "too much" for a Sunday morning. Both Rebecca's dress and Bryce's suit were dark, signaling they were not local, as desert residents rarely wear dark colors by day. Still, neither outfit was black, signaling that neither of my visitors wished to make a show of mourning. Rebecca was unquestionably attractive for her years, but icy. Bryce looked athletic and fit, but his manner and bearing were reserved. He carried a slim, elegant attaché case, which he set on the floor near the coffee table as Rebecca and Larry got down to business.

"Where did it happen, Detective?" Rebecca jerked her head toward the terrace. "Out there?"

"Yes," said Larry, "the pool's just outside."

She stepped toward the open sliding doors, then stopped, turning to her lawyer. She spoke to him in a clipped tone. "It was a long drive, Bryce. Could I have some water?"

Bryce nodded and moved toward the kitchen.

I rushed forward. "I'm so sorry. How clumsy of me. Would you prefer some juice, Rebecca? Or perhaps coffee?"

"Water's fine. Bryce can get it." She gave him a steely look, and he slipped into the kitchen. Then she walked out to the terrace and turned, staring at the swimming pool without expression.

With an eye on Rebecca, I moved to Larry's side and asked, "Is it my imagination, or is this gal a piece of work?"

"Try not to judge," he said gently. "People react to sudden loss differently. In my line of work, I've seen the entire gamut of grief."

Watching the woman, I was skeptical of Larry's charitable words. "Maybe," I said, "but something tells me Rebecca has shed few, if any, tears."

"Give her a moment; then we'll try to draw her out."

Bryce returned from the kitchen with a glass of water, stepped outdoors to Rebecca, and handed it to her. She drank a swallow or two, still staring at the pool. They exchanged a discreet squeeze of arms.

Then Bryce came back into the living room. "Thank you for your patience," he told Larry and me. Though his manner was courteous, it was evident that he found the situation awkward. He tried explaining, "Rebecca needed to, uh . . . 'connect' with the tragedy."

Soberly, I assured him, "I'm happy to be of any help whatever. I'm so very sorry for your loss."

"Thank you, but the fact is, I didn't know Mr. Wallace very well."

Larry asked, "Weren't you his lawyer?"

Bryce shook his head. "I've been in the employ of *Mrs.* Wallace for some years now. She has her own financial interests, and I've helped manage her portion of the estate."

Rebecca stepped in from the terrace just then and handed him the empty glass without looking at him. "Thank you, Bryce." He took the glass, backed off a step, then went to the kitchen. Rebecca heaved a tired sigh, telling Larry and me, "Spencer always had a flair for the theatrical." With grim humor, she added, "Talk about a dramatic exit . . ."

I shook my head. "It was terrible. I'm still stunned."

She looked me in the eye. "Trust me, Claire. You'll get over it."

Larry cleared his throat. "If you feel up to it, Mrs. Wallace, could we sit down and discuss a few things?"

"I've come all this way. Why not?" She settled primly on the leather bench.

As Larry sat in the chair nearest Rebecca and paged through his notebook, Bryce returned from the kitchen and sat next to Rebecca on the bench, within reach of his briefcase. I took the chair next to Larry.

Looking up from his notes, Larry said, "I don't mean to be impertinent, Mrs. Wallace, but your attitude toward your husband's death is rather puzzling."

"Then you didn't know my husband, Detective. He was not a likable man."

Quietly, I mentioned, "I keep hearing that."

"It's true," Rebecca assured me. "His business methods were ruthless. His ego was boundless. His film-production empire was all that mattered—God knows, I didn't."

"And yet," I said, "he was a genius."

"I keep hearing *that*." Rebecca exhaled a derisive snort. "But genius, in the arts or otherwise, is often just an excuse for bad behavior. And believe me, Spencer could behave *very* badly. He seemed to feel self-indulgence was his birthright—just because he'd figured out how to sell movie tickets, and lots of them."

I paused, weighing her words. "Rebecca, I confess to being bewildered. The Spencer Wallace *I* knew was a perfect gentleman."

"Then he must have respected you. Good for you, Claire. But the Spencer Wallace *I* knew was a perfect prick." With a crooked smile, she asked, "Am I sorry he's dead? Not one bit. And, uh . . . I *did* inherit everything. Correct, Bryce?"

"Yes, Rebecca." The attorney set his briefcase on the coffee table, snapped it open, and pulled out a few folders. "Spencer may have tried, but he couldn't evade California's community-property laws."

Larry asked, "He tried?"

"I'm sure he did," Rebecca answered offhandedly. "He had no use for me, but he was afraid to divorce me—far too costly. So he led *his* life; I led *mine*."

"You lived apart?"

"By and large. I stayed at the main house in Brentwood; he was spending more and more time here in this godforsaken desert. There are other homes, most notably his little getaway in Cabo." She jerked her head toward the photo that faced her squarely from the mantel.

"Ah," I said, following her glance. "You recognize it."

She stood, moving to the mantel. "Oh, yes. I've been there— once. Did he take *you* there, Claire?"

"Well, *no*," I said, flustered.

She picked up the photo, studying it. "He took *many* women

there—chippies and whores, mostly—and a few men, too. His appetites were voracious, and the house in Cabo was his playpen." Setting the picture back on the mantel, she noted with distaste, "Nude sunbathing—*really*. Thank God no one would mistake *this* one for *me*." She patted her frosty, ash-blond hair.

Larry asked, "How do you know he took women to Cabo?"

Returning to the bench and sitting, she explained, "He *bragged* about it, for Christ's sake. Not only did he *entertain* there; he had a quack Mexican doctor on call to help him out of his 'little fixes.' That was his stock euphemism for knocking up yet another nubile young popsy. Can you believe it? More than once, he gloated to me— *me!*—that he'd just gotten out of 'another little fix.'" She fumed.

I mumbled, "I admit, it's amazing."

"Mrs. Wallace," Larry said with a squint of confusion, "you said that your husband also took men to his place in Mexico. What for?"

"What do you *think*?" she blurted. "Spencer's appetites swung *both* ways, Detective. Oh, sure, he preferred women to men, but if he encountered a choice, studly specimen, he just couldn't help himself. And of course, as a producer, he was always on the lookout for fresh talent, which, in turn, was only too eager to please *him*. He bragged about that, as well—called it 'executive privilege' or the 'casting-couch syndrome.'"

Bryce stifled a leering laugh. When Rebecca's eyes slid in his direction, he coughed, muttering, "Sorry."

Rebecca leaned forward to Larry and me. "Did you hear about his latest conquest?" she asked with an eager, gossipy inflection. "Or should I say '*non*-conquest'? Spencer had been putting the finishing touches on his latest script, a movie called *Photo Flash*. There's a hot new discovery playing the lead. Tanner Griffin—ever heard of him?"

Suddenly very uncomfortable, I told Rebecca, "It happens that I know him quite well. In fact, your husband first saw Tanner in a play I directed last winter."

"Ah," she said, as if recalling a paltry detail, "now that you mention it, that does ring a bell. Then you *know,* my dear, what a tempting morsel the young Mr. Griffin is. Spencer couldn't stop *talking* about him. He boasted that he'd 'bag that boy' eventually, and I'm sure he tried—Spencer could be *very* aggressive. But now, alas, Spencer is gone, and the sensational Mr. Griffin, God love him, will forever be 'the one that got away.' " She laughed merrily.

Distressed by this story, I rose and stood behind Larry at the fireplace, looking outdoors, immersed in thought.

Larry said to Rebecca, "You mentioned *Photo Flash.* Have you read the script?"

"Indeed I have."

"So have I," said Bryce, producing a copy of the screenplay from his briefcase.

Larry told Rebecca, "Then you know that it was inspired by your husband's photography hobby. The plot focuses on a murder by cadmium poisoning."

Rebecca nodded. "Specifically, cadmium chloride was the toxic compound, if I'm not mistaken."

"Correct," said Larry. "I myself read the script overnight. Are you aware that your husband, prior to his death, was suffering from some health conditions that might suggest cadmium poisoning?"

"He had some complaints—said he was getting old—but how does that relate to cadmium?"

Larry explained, "Claire and I were reviewing some of his symptoms with my brother just before you got here, and it struck me that—"

"Detective Knoll," said Bryce, "excuse me. The man who was leaving when we arrived—that was your bother? You called him Grant."

"Right," said Larry. "Grant Knoll is my brother."

"So *that* was Grant Knoll," said Bryce with dawning insight. "I knew he lived in the desert, but I hardly expected to see him *here* this morning."

With my interest drawn back to the conversation, I asked the lawyer, "How do you know of Grant?"

Rebecca turned sideways on the leather bench. "Yes, Bryce. Whatever are you talking about?"

Meaningfully, Bryce reminded her, "The *deal*."

"Ohhhh . . ." She nodded.

With pen poised, Larry asked, "Deal?"

"It's history now," said Bryce, tossing papers back into his brief-case. "Water under the bridge. Since Rebecca needed to sign off on any of Spencer's real-estate dealings that could affect her portion of the estate, a fair amount of paperwork crossed my desk. Earlier this spring, after Spencer began spending so much of his time out here, he struck up an acquaintance with your brother, and—"

Interrupting, I explained, "I introduced them."

"Oh?" said Bryce. "That makes sense. Well, it seems Spencer was feeling more and more at home in the desert. He was always on the lookout for a promising investment, and Grant made him aware of a proposal for a mountainside golf-course project that he himself was investing in. It was a risky venture, due to opposition from an environmental group concerned about an endangered sheep species, but on the upside, it was potentially lucrative. Spencer wanted *in,* and—well, to make a long story short—he later pulled *out* at the wrong moment. When word got around, the whole deal collapsed. Spencer was shrewd, I'll hand him that. He walked away unscathed. But unless I'm mistaken, Grant took a bath."

I turned to tell Larry, "He never mentioned it to *me*."

Larry's brow was pinched in thought. Then, with a weak smile, which seemed forced, he told me, "Grant must've been embarrassed. Who knows?"

Rebecca stood, smoothing wrinkles from the lap of her skirt. "Detective, if you don't mind, I'd really like to be going. This has been a tiring morning, and much as I hate to admit it, news of Spencer's sudden demise is indeed unsettling."

"I'm sure it is, Mrs. Wallace." Larry stood also. "I'll probably need to see you again tomorrow, if you'll be around. And I'd like to take a look at your late husband's darkroom in the Palm Springs house."

"Of course, Detective. Bryce and I will be staying for a few days, I'm sure." Her attorney had been fussing with his attaché case, locking it. He now stood as Rebecca continued, "I need to start sorting through Spencer's things. You can reach me at the house." She and Bryce moved toward the door.

Larry and I followed. He pulled a business card from his pocket and handed it to Rebecca at the door, telling her, "Be sure to call if you need me, and I'll stay in touch as well. Rest assured, we'll get to the bottom of this."

"Thank you, Detective."

As they were shaking hands, the cell phone on Larry's belt warbled. He turned aside to answer it, asking his caller, "Can you hold, please?" Then he told Rebecca, "If you'll excuse me, I need to take this call. Thanks again for your cooperation." He flashed Rebecca a smile, gave Bryce a quick handshake, then stepped out to the terrace, out of earshot, where he conversed on the phone in the shade of an umbrella table near the pool.

Turning to my guests, I said, "Before you leave, Rebecca, I was just wondering—when Spencer began working on a new screenplay or film project, did he ever discuss plotting issues with you?"

Through a twisted smile, she answered, "We had very few heart-to-hearts, Claire."

"I understand. But you did read the script of *Photo Flash*. Bryce has one too."

"Yes, but that's not typical. Spencer seemed especially proud of this one. He had high expectations for it."

"Let's hope his expectations prove justified. It'll make a fitting final tribute."

"Perhaps," she said, unsure of her own feelings.

I patted her hand. "Try to get some rest."

"I will." With a weak smile, she added, "I need it."

I told her attorney, "Good to meet you, Bryce. Take care."

"Sure thing, Miss Gray." He opened the door. "Good day."

They left. I watched them walk together toward the street. Then I closed the door with a light, uncertain sigh.

Larry seemed to be finishing on the phone—he was returning his notes to his pocket—so I strolled out to join him on the terrace, hoping for an update. The noontide sun had turned hot. As I arrived, Larry snapped the phone shut and clipped it to his belt.

"That was the coroner," he said.

Trying not to sound too eager, I prompted, "And . . . ?"

"The autopsy is complete," he informed me, "and the medical examiner has some initial findings. I was wrong, Claire, and your hunch was correct. Wallace tested positive for cadmium. What's more, he had severe kidney and liver damage, which is consistent with chronic cadmium poisoning, as are *all* the symptoms we discussed earlier—weight loss, anemia, irritability, yellow-stained teeth, even his loss of the sense of smell. He was a heavy smoker, which increases the toxic effect of cadmium. It could have been inhaled as fumes from his photo baths, which may have been spiked with cadmium chloride. Or the lethal compound could also have been dissolved in something acidic, then ingested—he was drinking tomato juice last night, which would do the trick." Larry paused before concluding, "In short, this investigation has entered a new phase."

I spoke the words slowly: "It was murder."

"Yes."

"And the killer was someone who either had access to Spencer's darkroom or attended last night's party. Or both."

Larry nodded. "Yes."

"Which means"—hoping for a rebuttal, I needed to voice the unthinkable—"which means, I'm a suspect."

Larry eyed me with an odd expression for a moment. When he spoke, his voice cracked. "I don't . . . I don't mean to alarm you, but by any objective measure . . ." He hesitated. "Yes, Claire, you are indeed a suspect."

Was it my imagination, or had the earth stopped spinning?

Birds hushed. The breeze died.

The sun glared, its intensity magnified by its reflection in the pool.

Not a single ripple broke the mirror of the water's flat surface.

PART TWO

developments

7

"Good God, Claire," gasped D. Glenn Yeats over the phone, "you must be beside yourself. Such a dreadful turn of events."

It was Sunday afternoon, shortly after Larry Knoll had left my home. Glenn had just gotten word of Spencer Wallace's death and had called to talk about it. Frankly, I'd been expecting to hear from the computer tycoon and college founder since sunrise, but apparently he hadn't turned on a television that morning, and none of his underlings had been willing to deliver the unwelcome news that the head of his theater department had, once again, been thrust by circumstance into a police investigation.

He continued, "Let's hope it was all just an unfortunate accident. Sometimes, suspicious death is mere happenstance, a peevish twist of fate."

I hated to disillusion him. "Sorry, Glenn. The coroner has already determined that *this* suspicious death was no mishap; it was murder. Spencer didn't die because he was drunk and stumbled into my pool. No, he was the victim of chronic cadmium poisoning. The drowning merely finished him off."

As soon as I'd said the words, I realized that my phrasing had been too blunt. Perhaps I had already been jaded by the facts of the case, but to Glenn's ears, my hard-boiled pronouncements must have sounded cold and uncaring. I myself was taken aback by my seemingly callous tone.

"Claire," said Glenn, at a temporary loss for words, "let's not discuss this on the phone. I'd like to see you. Soon."

Pleading fatigue—true enough—I managed to fend off an afternoon meeting, but I was unable to defer his requested rendez-vous for more than a few hours, so I agreed to join him for dinner at his home that night.

I had insisted that we make it an early evening. Shortly after six, I passed the gatehouse and revved the engine of my Beetle, preparing for the steep ascent of the winding roadway that led up past the Regal Palms Hotel and onward to Nirvana, the exclusive community of mountainside estates that Glenn Yeats called home. My ears plugged as I neared the top; when I swallowed, they popped. Rounding a final curve in the road, I saw the dramatic lines of Glenn's sanctuary appear from the uppermost terrace of the development.

During the seven months since I had moved to the desert, I had been a frequent visitor to Nirvana, but the sheer power of wealth displayed there never failed to impress. I was as agog that Sunday evening as I had been the previous September when I had first set eyes upon Glenn's magnificent dwelling. Like the college campus he had built, his house was also the work of the famed architect I. T. Dirkman, and it was no less a contemporary masterpiece.

Tonight, though, was different from most of my previous visits because I was not to be one of scores of guests invited to a party. Glenn had a habit of opening his home for all manner of events—from faculty get-togethers to memorial services—but tonight's gathering would be decidedly more intimate. I was to be the single guest at a dinner for two.

Pulling into Glenn's driveway, I found no parking valet waiting to whisk away my car—we were indeed roughing it tonight. I wondered wryly if Glenn would press me into duty washing dishes after our meal.

At the sound of my car (or had the gatehouse guard alerted him?), Glenn stepped out to the courtyard to greet me. He wore a casual but expensive-looking outfit—silk shirt and gabardine slacks—giving the unfortunate impression of a rich nerd out of his element. Behind him, from the house, a huge, modern, asymmetrical chandelier glowed with warm, yellow light in a front hall big enough to be aptly described as a lobby. Outdoors, overhead, the sky shone with cool, blue twilight. The sun had just begun to slip behind the peaks of neighboring mountains, which jutted from the horizon as saw-toothed, abstract silhouettes.

Crossing the courtyard toward each other, we met midway and paused to embrace. "Good evening, Claire. Welcome."

"Glenn," I said, taking his arm, strolling toward the house, "you're the perfect host. Once again, you've arranged for a perfect night in a perfect setting."

"This could all be yours," he reminded me. His tone was so offhanded, he might have been offering me a drink or a Kleenex, not half his empire.

We had not explicitly discussed marriage; I had never let the conversation go that far. But I had no doubt that the subtext of Glenn's patient, persistent wooing was matrimonial. He had previously set his sights on snagging me from Broadway to chair the theater department at his fledgling college, and he had won. He had now set his sights on snagging me as the third Mrs. Yeats, and he intended, as always, to win.

The prospect of immense wealth was appealing, naturally, but the prospect of losing my independence was not. After all, I had evaded the altar for fifty-four years. Had I felt the need to be kept or protected, I'd have tied a knot at a more knot-tying age.

Now such a commitment struck me as silly and pointless.

Now I was winding down a live-in tryst with Tanner Griffin. What possible interest would I have in bedding D. Glenn Yeats, who could not begin to compete with Tanner at a raw, physical level?

Still, Glenn had many other sterling attributes that made him an enviable potential partner. To his credit, he had shown the longsightedness to let me sort through my jumbled feelings. To my discredit, I had been unable or unwilling to weigh his advances seriously.

". . . every bit of it," he was saying. "It could all be yours."

"Not now," I said softly, pausing at the entry to his home. Patting his hand, I added, "It's been a hellish day. I can barely think straight."

"Let's get you a drink."

"Now, *there's* an offer I needn't consider twice."

Glenn laughed. "Come on in." He led me into the house, through the hall, and directly back to the pool terrace, where a table for two awaited. A cocktail cart stood at the ready, stocked with ice, liquor, glassware, and a tall, silver martini shaker—he didn't even need to ask. Wordlessly, he set about fixing my drink.

Since moving from the condo into a house, I had come to appreciate the sybaritic pleasures of having my own swimming pool. It seemed I now *lived* on my terrace, enjoying a nude dip whenever a free moment allowed. Landscaping and a garden wall assured total privacy, an incredible luxury to this transplanted New Yorker.

But my delightful new circumstances paled to the splendor of Glenn's outdoor living area. Not only was it bigger than mine—considerably so—but both its setting and its design set it apart as one in a million. For starters, Glenn's privacy was established not by walls or plantings, but by sheer, open space. He overlooked the entire valley some thousand feet below, with only a low stone parapet separating his terrace from the granite slopes beneath. The pool itself was black, of seemingly infinite depth; at its sleek edges, water met the stone paving in a perfect plane. A gargantuan fireplace, the twin of another indoors, lent a finishing touch of fantasy. This evening, it was still too warm and not yet dark enough to warrant a fire, but the massive hearth felt homey and comforting beneath the endless expanse of sky. A pair of planets glimmered near the rising crescent moon.

"I would never leave this spot," I said with breathless awe, taking it all in.

"You needn't." He winked at me, destroying the sublime moment, though the icy martini he passed to me soon restored my sense of peace.

We sat and sipped, and I realized I was grateful for his invitation that night. "It feels good to relax," I said.

His gaze moved from the distant airport, below, to me, at his side. With a tone of genuine concern, he asked, "How bad *is* it?" The question was vaguely worded, but Glenn's meaning was clear. He wondered how deeply I'd gotten tangled in the investigation.

"Pretty bad," I admitted. "I'm an active suspect."

Glenn nearly choked on his drink. "*What?* You can't be serious."

"Afraid so." I summarized, "Not only did Spencer Wallace die in my swimming pool, but I'd made threats against him that evening, twice—once at the party, in the presence of the catering staff, and earlier, to a reporter, the one you foisted on me, by the way."

Glenn groaned. "Sorry. I was thinking of the school, but I should have realized you were tired."

I hadn't been tired; the curtain call had left me with an adrenaline rush. But that was beside the point. "What's more," I continued, "Larry Knoll has since determined that Spencer was being slowly poisoned by cadmium, a possibility that I myself suggested, having read Spencer's screenplay, in which he seemed to spell out the recipe for his own undoing. The killer may have poisoned Spencer at the party or in his home darkroom—or both. In either case, I was there. So I had ample *opportunity* to do the deed, and my knowledge of the script gave me the *means*."

"But, Claire"—Glenn set his glass down—"Detective Knoll is surely aware that you had no conceivable *motive* to kill Wallace."

"Didn't I? Not to play devil's advocate, but you can't just dismiss my threats. Sure, they were empty; they were merely dramatic exaggeration, easily understood as such when I spoke them. But now, with Spencer murdered, it looks as if I was hell-bent on paying him back for stealing Tanner from DAC's theater program."

"That's absurd," Glenn burbled. "You *invited* Spencer Wallace to our opening production at the college. You *knew* he was scouting for talent. And Tanner's rise to stardom will be a *credit* to the school."

"*We* know that, but anyone else might draw the conclusion that I'm a scheming, vengeful, murderous bitch."

"You, Claire?" He laughed. "Never."

I took his hand. "I appreciate the vote of confidence, but objectively speaking, I had a motive." I might have pointed out that I'd had a double motive. Whisking Tanner off to Hollywood, Spencer had raided not only my program, but also my bed. It seemed injudicious, however, to share this latter consideration with Glenn.

With his free hand, Glenn swirled his drink. "What does Larry think of your, uh, 'motive'?"

I let go of Glenn's hand and sat back, mulling over my predicament. "Larry is professional enough to realize that he can't ignore suspicious circumstances. Obviously, the best way to clear *me* of suspicion is to name someone else as the real killer. I was disposed to help him do that even before I had a direct interest in the case."

Glenn cringed. "Oh, God, Claire—not again."

In the few months since my arrival, I had already gotten

involved with two other murder investigations, and Glenn had made no secret of his disapproval. His claims of fearing for my safety had only strengthened my resolve to assist the police; his protective instincts had also diminished any appeal I might have found in his overtures to romance. The whole issue had grown even more touchy when, to Larry's satisfaction and to Glenn's chagrin, my help on those earlier cases had proved valuable and productive.

Sidestepping past quibbles, I told Glenn with a meaningful stare, "This time, it's different."

"Oh?" His tone conveyed not only skepticism, but a hint of condescension. If he was trying to jeopardize what affection I felt for him, he was succeeding.

Resisting the temptation to debate matters that would only antagonize him, I stayed the course, explaining in terms he would readily understand, "This time, my own good name is at stake, as is the reputation of the school."

He seemed to catch his breath for a moment as my logic led him to the very conclusion he had hoped to avoid. "Then, uh"—his features twisted—"if Detective Knoll can make use of your assistance, perhaps you should provide it."

"I intend to."

Once Glenn had given his blessing (not that I thought I needed it), we both sensed that a fragile stasis had been achieved, so our conversation drifted to safer, less contentious topics, mainly those involving the school and my plans for the theater department. When I mentioned that I was giving serious thought to conducting a summer workshop, Glenn beamed like a child who'd been handed an unexpected gift adorned with a frilly bow.

"I'm surprised you'd even consider it," he told me. "After finishing your first season, I should think you'd want to take a break."

"I would," I admitted, "but with Tanner leaving the program, I need to start grooming other actors as leading men. We have an ambitious slate of productions ahead of us next year."

"Excellent," he bubbled, rubbing his hands together. "I like your thinking—*and* your dedication." Christ, he was easy.

Without further discord, cocktails led to dinner. Glenn had called upon staff from the nearby hotel to prepare and serve our meal. When the evening had waned and dusk had turned the sky an inky shade of indigo, a tuxedoed waiter appeared with candles for our little table, followed by another who brought out the appetizer course. It was delicious, as one would expect, considering its source, but in truth, I had no idea what I was eating. With no menu to guide me, I was at a loss to identify whether the sauced, flaky crust on my plate concealed fish, fowl, or cheese. Though generally not reticent by nature, I was nonetheless unwilling to ask crudely, What's this? While Glenn prattled on about something, I recalled Kiki's discourse earlier that day regarding the proper delivery of the query—Aowww? Hwat's this?

Glenn just wouldn't get it, so I covered my grin with my large damask napkin. I recognized that it, too, had come from the Regal Palms.

During the main course (I didn't need to ask—it was duck—well, maybe goose), Glenn set down his fork, swallowed, and sat back in his chair, thinking. Exhaling a quiet, wistful noise, he said, "Maybe it's for the best."

"Hmm?" My mouth was full.

"Wallace," he said with a note of disapprobation, shaking his head. "He won't be missed. Maybe it's for the best."

"*Glenn,*" I said, shocked by his comment. "Spencer Wallace was *murdered*. How could that possibly be 'for the best'?"

He gave me a shushing gesture with both hands—did he fear I'd disturb the coyotes in the craggy slopes below? "Perhaps that was too harsh of me," he allowed. "It's just that, let's face it, Wallace was *not* the most likable of men."

"So I've heard."

"He'd made many enemies, Claire. I'm afraid he reaped what he'd sown."

"Are you saying he *deserved* to die—in *my* swimming pool?"

With remarkable indifference, Glenn explained, "I'm not condoning murder. I'm merely making the observation that someone antagonized by Wallace must have felt that he deserved to die." Picking up his fork, he sampled another bite of our dinner, chewing contentedly. Dabbing his lips, he said, "The saddle of rabbit is outstanding, don't you think?"

"Best ever." I'd have sworn I'd seen a wing on my plate, but by now it was reduced to bones and sauce.

We ate in silence, Glenn relishing the rabbit, me pondering his attitude toward Spencer's death. Glenn's blasé justification of the murder—what goes around comes around—was troublesome, to say the least. It was almost enough to cast Glenn himself in a suspicious light.

The e-titan and the movie mogul had not been direct competitors, so I had no reason to feel that Glenn was among the legion of enemies who he claimed had been irked by Spencer. While the two men shared no business concerns, they did, however, share certain traits. To their credit, both were successful, intelligent, powerful, and wealthy. On the negative side, each felt boundless esteem for his own role in the world. I'd always noted that their interaction had been colored by an undertone of disdain, if not outright sniping—as in "This valley ain't big enough for the both of us."

Sitting there, picking at my rabbit, watching Glenn lick his fingertips, I realized with a start that if I myself had had a plausible motive to kill Spencer, so had Glenn. Spencer had "stolen" Tanner

Griffin from my theater program, which was, after all, Glenn's creation. Indeed, the theater department was the raison d'être of the entire school; Glenn had built Desert Arts College first and foremost to advance the dramatic arts. Was he now stewing over the loss of Tanner as much as I was? More so?

It was a tempting thought that Glenn's support of my efforts at the school was so obsessive that he'd turned murderously vengeful when Spencer's recruitment of Tanner seemed to thwart my mission. What's more, I considered, Glenn had been at Saturday's party before Spencer was found dead. But then I recalled that I'd previously entertained suspicions about the darker side of D. Glenn Yeats, only to be proven laughably off base. Was my theatrical perspective on crime solving again taking a turn toward the melodramatic? Plucking the olive from the bottom of my martini glass, I popped it in my mouth and rolled it over my tongue, chiding myself for nurturing such shady doubts about my generous mentor and benefactor.

Light, friendly conversation peppered the remainder of our meal.

As we were finishing dessert (I can say with certainty only that it was sweet; beyond that, I'll hazard no guess), Glenn checked his watch and said, "It's early. Can't you spend the evening? We could watch a movie, perhaps, or simply share each other's company." He reached across the table and placed his fingers on my hand. "I know no greater pleasure, Claire, than being with you."

"I'm touched, Glenn." My weak smile was more of a pout. "But I just can't stay, not tonight. It's been *such* an ordeal. I'm exhausted."

"Of course, my dear. I understand."

He did not understand, but I gave him a grateful nod.

And I took no pleasure in lying to him.

8

Although I was indeed exhausted that night, my reluctance to linger with Glenn had nothing to do with fatigue.

After strolling with Glenn through the house to the parking court, bidding a winsome farewell, and exchanging a solid if not heated kiss on the lips, I hopped into my Beetle and roared down the mountain road that would lead me home to Tanner. By plan, he was coming over to spend the night after his day of packing. I had wanted to share a meal with him—one of our last—but Glenn had scuttled those intentions with his urgent plea for our dinner meeting. When I had phoned to explain my predicament to Tanner, he hadn't minded at all, saying it would give him more time to finish at his apartment. He would shower and change there, then drive over, letting himself in with his key.

Turning off Country Club onto my side street, I held my breath for a moment, wondering if he had arrived yet, hoping I wouldn't need to spend another minute without him. A smile spread across my face as the boxy form of his black Jeep appeared from the shadow of my garage.

I pulled in, got out of the car, and fairly ran into the house. The lights were on; something soft and jazzy was playing on the stereo. But I didn't see Tanner in the living room or the adjacent kitchen. Was he waiting for me in the bedroom? An enticing prospect, to be sure, but it was still too early for the climax of the boudoir—better to prolong our penultimate night together.

Rushing through the hall to the bedroom, I saw that he had been there, as evidenced by a large nylon gym bag on the bed; he'd begun removing a few things from my dresser drawers. With a bittersweet grin, I wondered if he'd missed the pair of boot socks Grant had pilfered. Stepping over to the bag, I reached inside and took out one of his neatly folded T-shirts. Lifting it reverently, I then buried my face in it, inhaling the intoxicating smells of detergent and fabric softener and Tanner himself.

So it's come to this, I told myself. Though I meant to feel ashamed—reduced to sniffing my young lover's underwear—I felt only the rush of excitement and intimacy. Digging deeper in his bag, I found a jockstrap and, dropping any pretense of ladylike behavior, made an absolute pig of myself.

"There you are!" I said, walking outdoors from the living room to the terrace. There was a distinct lilt to my voice and bounce to my step as I discovered Tanner lounging in the shallow end of the pool, sans swimwear. Eerie blue ripples from the underwater light distorted his body beneath his chest.

He broke into a broad smile at the sound of my voice. "I didn't hear you come in." With a hint of apology, he added, "The music . . ."

"Glad you made yourself at home."

"The water's great." He raised a dripping hand from the surface and beckoned me with his index finger.

It took me all of twenty seconds to slip out of my clothes and pad barefoot to the corner of the pool. Tanner stood on one of the steps that ascended from the water, then offered me a hand as I dipped my feet in next to him, submerging my legs to the knees. In contrast to the cool night air, the water felt warm, so I eased myself in to the neck.

He sat next to me, wrapping an arm around my shoulder. "You're especially beautiful tonight."

"You're not so bad yourself." I tried to mask the extreme understatement in my infatuated tone. Tanner Griffin was, as always, a sight to behold. "You look none the worse from the rigors of your day of labor."

"It wasn't so bad, just time-consuming. I mean, I wasn't moving grand pianos; I was packing clothes and books."

"And the kitchen," I added. "Pots and pans are heavy."

He laughed. "Not the aluminum junk from *my* kitchen. If I were smart, I'd just throw it all out."

Considering that I had moved a truckload of worthless furniture from New York, only to trash it a few months later, I allowed, "It might save some effort."

"It's already packed," he said with a shrug, sending soft ripples across the length of the pool.

Then he took my hand and strolled me away from the steps, wrapping me in his arms when the water deepened to chest height. We held each other, chins hooked over each other's shoulders, moving woozily together, swaying to the music that drifted from the living room.

I felt the nudge of his arousal against my belly. "You're a born dancer," I said, deadpan. "Such technique."

"Just follow my lead." He humped me playfully, backing me to the wall of the pool, where he slid himself between my legs and mimicked penetration. This wasn't sex, not even foreplay; we both understood that that could wait. Rather, this was a frolic—pure, simple, and pleasurable. I gladly endured his gentle pummeling while, from behind, one of the pool's jets splashed against the nape of my neck.

After a minute or so, Tanner said, "I'd better stop." His voice had gotten throaty.

"It's your call," I said with airy indifference. He could keep it up all night, for all I cared.

"It'll be better for you later," he promised.

"Then you'd better stop."

He took a step away from me and, with a kick, pushed himself toward the deep end of the pool, floating on his back. His penis gave a friendly salute, waving proud and tall in the night air. I laughed.

"What's so funny?" he asked, speaking to the black sky.

"Nothing at all. Just enjoying myself."

He scrunched himself into a ball, sank a few feet, then spun himself facedown, swimming to the bottom of the pool with long, strong strokes. A moment later, he shot to the top, breaking the surface like a manly dolphin. His cold spray drenched me. I yelped.

"Sorry," he called, dropping back into the water. Treading it, he barely cleared his mouth. "C'mon," he said, inviting me to join him at the deep end.

This scene was not a new one; in fact, it was a familiar routine. These nighttime escapades often provided the perfect, relaxing finale to a stressful day. Our high jinks in deep water had become a delightful ritual.

So I waded in his direction, and when the bottom of the pool dropped away from my feet, I swam. As I drew near Tanner, he dove again, sliding noiselessly deeper and deeper. When he reached bottom, he flung all four limbs, drifting, at peace with the living body of water.

And in that instant, I saw Spencer Wallace. His lifeless body was a blurry X beneath the surface, broken by the shifting waves of light. I gasped, inhaling some water. Then I coughed loudly, spitting it out. Repelled by the sight of Tanner as Spencer, I paddled to the side of the pool and grabbed the stone apron.

"Hey! What's wrong?" asked Tanner, breaking the surface, swimming toward me. "I heard"—he sputtered through the water—"I heard you scream."

Had I screamed? "I was coughing. I sort of choked."

There must have been a wild look in my eye. Tanner glided up to me and grasped both of my hands. Alarmed, he asked, "Are you all right?"

"Of *course* I am." I forced a laugh.

"But . . . but what happened?"

I was tempted to fudge my answer and dismiss my morbid vision, inventing some innocuous reason for my outburst and my abrupt change of mood. But I had already lied outright to Glenn Yeats that evening, and this was not a pattern I wished to establish with Tanner. In the months I had known him, we had been scrupulous in hiding nothing from each other.

"My imagination got away from me," I explained. "When you dove to the bottom of the pool—and stayed there—I had a memory flash of last night when we found Spencer Wallace." I jerked my head toward the deep end.

"Oh, gosh." Tanner cradled me in his warm, slippery arms. "How awful for you. And how thoughtless of *me*."

I shook my head. "Not at all. You couldn't possibly have known what I saw last night or how I'd react tonight."

The carefree spirit of our skinny-dipping interlude had evaporated. Tanner asked, "Would you like to get out of the water?"

Insipidly, I answered, "Thank you for understanding." I pecked his lips.

We sloshed our way to the shallow end of the pool and lumbered up the steps. Water fell from our bodies; the dripping sound seemed magnified in the still night. Padding across the terrace to a pair of chaise longues, we left shiny black tracks on the stone paving.

"Don't get your clothes wet," said Tanner, grabbing his T-shirt from one of the chaises and helping me wiggle into it. As the neck hole popped past my head, I drank in his smells. Though not burly, Tanner's build was considerably bigger than mine, and he liked wearing loose, roomy T-shirts, so the makeshift cover of soft, white cotton hung from me like a smock. He then stepped into a pair of khaki shorts and zipped up, asking, "Want to go indoors?"

"Nah. It's a lovely night. Let's stay outside awhile."

Tanner had brought out a couple of oversize bath towels, so he wrapped me in one, himself in the other. We settled on the chaises, I sitting, he reclining with his head propped in his hand. I watched a trickle of water as it dripped from hair to hair on his shins and then disappeared into the cushion.

Our silence began to feel awkward. "Uh"—I tried my voice— "I'm sorry I put a damper on things."

"Don't be nuts." God, what a smile. "You're here. *We're* here."

"At least for tonight."

"*And* tomorrow night."

I returned his smile, but it faded fast as my thoughts leapt to Tuesday and to Tanner's departure.

Reading my mind, he said, "I'll be just up the road. LA is two hours from here. I'll be back."

"Sure," I said, sounding chipper, "and I'll get over to Los Angeles now and then." Fat chance. Having left New York and having begun a new life in the desert—with its easy pace, clean air, and serene, natural beauty at every turn—the allure of urban sprawl was now nil.

"Besides," he said, "all my friends are here."

Leveling with him, I noted, "You'll have new friends, Tanner."

He began to protest.

But I continued, "A phase of our lives is drawing to a close. There's no point in denying it—better to deal with that reality than to kid ourselves into thinking that nothing will change. Otherwise, later, when we realize that everything *has* changed, we'll be festering with disappointment and, just possibly, bitterness."

He sat up. "Bitterness? That's impossible, Claire. I could never—"

"Tanner, dearest"—I shook my head gently—"reality can't be wished away by lofty intentions."

"This has nothing to do with 'lofty intentions.' It's about love. Don't you get it, Claire? I *love* you."

"And I love you, Tanner." I moved to his chaise, sat at his side, and held his hands. "But we entered this relationship fully aware that it was not a conventional romance. Sure, from the beginning, we've both had deep feelings for each other, but beyond that, we've both understood that our relationship has served other needs—namely, my theater program and your career. We've *benefited* each other."

After a moment, he asked, "Like . . . traders?"

I pinched his cheek. "Yes, like *Traders.*" We were speaking of the thematic concept that was at the heart of my play.

He drew his knee up onto the cushion, turning to face me. "You mean, we've been using each other." His words carried no tone of disillusionment, for he had come to understand the philosophy embodied by the play.

I nodded. "We *have* used each other. But here's the important part—we've used each other with each other's knowledge and consent. We've traded purposes, and in doing so, we've both accomplished other goals."

"And along the way, we fell in love."

"We did." I held him tight for a moment. "I think we both understood that our initial attraction was mere infatuation, partly fueled by those other goals and purposes. But sure enough, along the way, we came to love each other. And that's what lasts."

He eyed me askance. "Not two minutes ago, you told me that a phase of our lives is drawing to a close, that everything will change."

"True enough. What's ending is our shared life as lovers; that's a huge change. What's not ending, though, is our love. I will always love you, Tanner. Once your film career is up and running, we may resume some sort of relationship; maybe not. But we will always be loving friends."

"Ahh," said Tanner, " 'loving friends'—that sounds so chaste and proper, doesn't it?"

I chortled. "Depends on the friends."

Not whining, truly curious, he asked, "Will there still be room for intimacy?" He slid a hand up my thigh.

"Who knows? If you marry, which you probably will—someone your own age, I might add—then, no, there'll be no future intimacy between us."

"And what about *you?*" He laughed softly. "What about marriage? What about . . . Glenn? Someone *your* own age, I might add."

"Whew!" I backed off a few inches. "I should've seen *that* coming."

Tanner laughed louder, telling no one, "She can dish it out . . ."

"Okay, okay"—I gave his hand a playful slap—"your point is well made. It's just that I've never quite seen myself in the role of a, of a . . . wife." I nearly choked on the word.

"You might consider it, Claire." His tone was serious. "You deserve that security."

"You think I'm insecure?"

"Hardly. But Glenn has a *lot* to offer, and—"

"An egotistical billionaire shopping for a third wife may have a lot to offer, but I doubt if there's much security in *that* dowry."

"You're being kinda tough on him, aren't you? He worships you."

"He does." Ho hum. "But I just can't deal with Glenn and his doting—not now, not yet." I paused, adding, "Not while you're here, Tanner."

He leaned and kissed me. "My time here isn't long. I suggest we make use of it." He nuzzled my ear.

"Mmm." I slid my hand down his back and under the waistband of his shorts. His skin felt warm and comforting against my fingers. "What'd you have in mind?"

"For starters," he said into my ear, "I think we should move indoors."

"Bedtime?" I asked coyly. "It's barely ten."

"We can while away a few hours till you're sleepy. I'll think of something to amuse you."

"I'll bet you will."

"Shall I carry you?" He wasn't kidding. Tanner occasionally carried me indoors from a midnight dip, providing a seamless fantasy that moved from the lapping of water to the rumpling of bed linens. Was this dreamy, or what?

"Uh"—I wavered, but my practical side won out—"my clothes." I had left them in a heap near the pool, and I didn't want them lying there till morning.

Equally practical, Tanner suggested, "While you take care of that, I'll set up the coffeemaker for tomorrow."

"Deal."

So we both got up from the chaise and set about our domestic chores, readying for a romp in the bedroom. Within no time, we had moved inside and locked the doors. I slipped out of Tanner's T-shirt and added it to the bundle of my own clothes. Tanner was turning off the music and I was switching off the lights in the living room—when the phone rang.

We both froze, unsure of what do to.

I shook my head. "Let the machine get it. People shouldn't be calling at this hour."

"But they are," Tanner noted as the phone rang again, "so it might be important." He was very likely correct; I had almost forgotten that a murder investigation was now in the works.

I dropped the wad of clothes on the leather bench near the fireplace and crossed to the pass-through bar, where the phone rang a third time. Before the answering machine clicked on, I picked up the receiver. "Yes?"

"Hi, Claire. Larry Knoll. Sorry to disturb you so late."

"No bother at all, Larry." I must have been a sight, standing there stark naked, gabbing on the phone, because Tanner stifled a laugh as he scooped up our clothes and took them back to the bedroom. I said into the phone, "What can I do for you?"

"I spoke to Rebecca Wallace, and I'm planning to visit her late husband's house in the Movie Colony tomorrow morning at ten. I want to get a general feel for the place, but more to the point, I need to take a good look at Wallace's darkroom. I sent the evidence techs over there today to seal the room. With any luck, no evidence has been disturbed—if there even *was* any evidence."

"You sound skeptical that the poisoning was related to Spencer's photography."

"At this point, I don't subscribe to *any* theory. I have an open mind, but what I don't have, just yet, is evidence. Tomorrow morning, the real hunt begins."

I reiterated my earlier offer: "I'll help any way I can."

"That's why I called, Claire. Since you're familiar with the house in Palm Springs and actually worked with Wallace in the darkroom, I'm wondering if you could come along. I think you could be helpful."

"Sure, Larry," I answered, trying not to sound too eager. "I need to spend some time on campus tomorrow and check in at the theater, but I don't have any Monday classes, so my day is wide open. I'm at your disposal."

"Great. I appreciate it. I'll pick you up at a quarter to ten."

"It's a date," I said, almost chirping. Then, toning down my enthusiasm, I added, "Let's hope we find some answers."

Larry seconded that wish; then we both said good night and hung up.

" 'It's a date'?" asked Tanner, standing in the bedroom hall. "I thought *we* had a date." With a single, fluid motion, he unfastened the top button of his khaki shorts, unzipped them, let them fall to his feet, and stepped free of them.

I didn't bother explaining Larry's call. Crime solving could wait. First things first.

9

Despite the troubling events of that weekend, I slept like a baby on Sunday night; Tanner had made good on his promise to "amuse" me before bed. Monday morning, I was raring to go.

As planned, Larry Knoll picked me up in his unmarked cruiser at a quarter to ten. He wore one of his usual business suits that day with a freshly laundered white shirt and neatly knotted tie. Though lacking his brother Grant's sartorial flair, he looked professional and authoritative, ready to take on a busy week. While driving northwest, up valley, from Rancho Mirage to Palm Springs, he updated me on the case. "I visited Coachella Catering yesterday. I was able to track down the owner Sunday morning, and we met at their office in the afternoon."

"Is the owner Thierry? He seemed to be in charge at the party on Saturday."

"Right, Terry Armand." The French pronunciation eluded Larry, making me wonder again whether Thierry was indeed French. Perhaps Canadian. Or was he corn-fed American, christened with a distinctive family name?

Larry continued, "Terry was helpful and cooperative, shocked by the news of what had happened. He checked his records and even opened his books for me, giving me complete information on everyone who had worked at your party. The bottom line is, we found no suspicious connections between the deceased and any of the catering staff."

I recalled, "But Coachella had done some catering for Spencer, correct?"

"Right. They'd worked several events for him. Erin Donnelly had said as much on Saturday night, and Terry confirmed it yesterday. I saw the records of those bookings; everything looked routine." This meant, in effect, that Larry had no new potential suspects for Spencer's murder. Which further meant that he would be focusing his investigation more closely on my party guests—and me.

I thumped my forehead. "Gosh, Larry, I just remembered—I promised to give you my guest list, but I'm afraid it slipped my mind."

He laughed. "Glad you brought it up. I neglected to ask for the list when I was at your house yesterday with Rebecca."

I muttered, "She *was* a bit distracting."

"Can you pull that list together today? I do need it."

"Of course." I crossed my heart.

Larry made a turn and glanced ahead through the windshield. "We must be getting close."

"It's just a few more blocks," I told him.

The initial boom period of development in Palm Springs took place during the late 1920s, when Hollywood discovered the then remote desert oasis and fell in love with its warm weather, spectacular scenery, and sparse population, which offered an ideal getaway from burgeoning Los Angeles. Indeed, many westerns of the era were filmed against the surrounding backdrop of craggy desert mountains, but more significant was the migration of studio moguls and stars to the resorts and spas that were being built. When the El Mirador Hotel opened in 1928, it quickly became the favorite of Hollywood royalty, many of whom decided to stay awhile, building second homes in the surrounding neighborhood, which came to be known as the Movie Colony.

The houses built in the Movie Colony were not, by and large, palaces, but quiet weekend retreats where the famous could escape the trappings of conspicuous wealth while at leisure in tasteful seclusion and relatively modest surroundings. The entire Palm Springs area was, until that time, essentially undeveloped, so it presented architects with a clean canvas against which they could create a style that was both playful and uninhibited.

The early wave of stars' homes, built in the thirties and forties, was generally of a design vernacular that was ornately Spanish, borrowed from the style that then dominated homes being built in and around Hollywood. Another early favorite, which evolved from the Spanish style, was the true California ranch, with ready access to the outdoors from virtually every room. Later, in the fifties and sixties, modernism—whether fanciful or minimalist—would take hold and become the trademark style of the desert.

"Here we are," I told Larry as Spencer Wallace's home came into view. It was a charming California ranch, originally built in the forties by another producer, then famed, now a footnote.

From the street, the low, rambling house was discreetly unpretentious, mostly hidden by well-manicured vegetation. Curious eyes were given no clue that the homey, casual-looking entrance (it might have been a spiffed-up bunkhouse) led to a sprawling labyrinth of rooms and wings that surrounded a private courtyard with an Olympic-size pool, replete with diving boards, high and low.

"Glad to have you along," Larry said with a quiet laugh. "I would've missed it." Other than an unassuming house number on the mailbox, there was no visible hint that this had been the home of Megahit Wallace, Mr. Blockbuster himself.

We got out of the car and walked the winding brick path to the front door. A sheriff's van was already parked in the motor court, hidden from the street by a high wall of oleander in full, white bloom. A sleek, black Porsche was parked in the shade of an arbor. I presumed it belonged to either Rebecca Wallace or her attorney, Bryce Ballantyne, but the car's standard-issue California plates did not suggest which one.

Stepping to the front door, Larry hesitated, given the choice of announcing our arrival by either a doorbell or a knocker. Choosing the knocker—a large, squeaky contraption of curlicued wrought iron—Larry thumped the door as gently as possible, but each stroke seemed to rumble and reverberate within the house. I felt like one of those angry, torch-wielding peasants making a ruckus outside Frankenstein's castle.

Moments later, the door inched open with a prolonged creak. I half expected to find a hunched Igor peering at us from the other side, and I wasn't far off. Rebecca Wallace looked like hell that morning.

"Ah," she croaked, "hello, Detective." She squinted into the sunlight as if roused from the grave. Then she noticed me, standing in Larry's shadow. "And Miss Gray. Good morning."

"Please," I said, offering my hand, "it's Claire."

"Of course, Claire." She took my hand and wiggled it listlessly. "Do come in." Opening the door wide, she stepped back as we entered, adding, "I hope you'll forgive me—I'm a fright this morning."

If she expected polite rebuttals, she was disappointed, as I simply couldn't bring myself to deny her unflattering self-assertion. When she had visited my house the previous day, she had been the picture of well-groomed dignity in the face of sudden loss. Now she looked like something not even a cat would drag in. Her steely hair, before perfectly coiffed, was now limp and tangled; her attire, previously pert, trim, and razor-edged, was now replaced with a slovenly pink terry-cloth bathrobe that looked not only slept-in, but eaten-in. Near the lap, there was a large stain that I hoped was orange juice. I didn't mean to stare, but I could barely take my eyes off the woman.

Sidestepping the topic of her appearance, Larry said, "It was good of you to open the house to our investigation."

She asked, "Did I have any choice?"

"You made the choice to cooperate. That's easier on everyone."

"And why *wouldn't* I cooperate?" Her question rang with insinuation, daring Larry to tell her that he held her under suspicion. Which I hoped he did.

His answer was more diplomatic than mine would have been. "There's no reason *not* to cooperate with the investigation. We share the same goal; we both want to determine how and why your husband died."

"Of course we do." The flat tone of Rebecca's agreement verged on cynicism.

Larry continued, "I'm most interested in your late husband's darkroom."

"So I understand. Your other men are already back there. It's at the far end of the house"—she flung an arm in the general direction. "If you don't mind, Detective, I really ought to try to put myself together." Taking her leave, she retreated down a nearby hall.

Larry called after her, "But I don't know where it's—"

I touched his arm. "I know the lay of the house, Larry. I'll take you."

Rebecca had by now disappeared, so we made our way through her late husband's home unobserved, pausing to gawk at the various rooms we passed. The living room, though not grandiose, was wonderfully spacious and comfortable, decorated in a laid-back western style suggestive of television's old Ponderosa set, except that the Cartwrights' living room did not open to a swimming pool, which the Wallaces' did.

"It's quicker to cross the courtyard," I told Larry, leading him out to the terrace, around the pool, and into another wing of the house. "The darkroom is beyond the library."

The leather-upholstered, brass-studded, book-lined den was in the same manly, cowpoking style as the living room. Giddyup. Between two floor-to-ceiling bookcases, a narrow hall led back to a windowless room; perhaps it had been a storeroom or large closet. This was where Spencer had set up his darkroom, and today, yellow police tape hung limp from the doorway. I could hear the evidence technicians conversing within.

Larry greeted them as we entered, then introduced me, adding, "Miss Gray learned the basics of photography from the deceased in this darkroom. I thought she could help us make sense of what's here."

Though the darkroom had felt roomy enough when Spencer and I had worked in it, today it was cramped and hot. Larry, the two deputies, and I could barely move without risking greater intimacy than decorum allowed. A dim work light reinforced the feeling of claustrophobic unease.

"Everything is just as we found it," one of the techs told Larry. "We checked everything for prints, and we've been busy making an inventory of the room, especially the chemicals."

"I don't suppose you found a big, incriminating vial of cadmium chloride stashed away somewhere."

The deputy chuckled. "No, Detective. No such luck."

"So, then"—Larry looked about—"what've we got here?"

The deputy suggested, "Since Miss Gray is familiar with the equipment and the chemicals, maybe she could give us *all* the Cook's tour."

"Good idea." Larry turned to me. "Claire?"

"Well," I began, trying to keep it terse, "Spencer processed his film on *this* side of the room, adjacent to the sink. The film is developed in a lighttight canister"—I pointed to it—"so the process doesn't require much space. Prints are a different matter." I directed everyone to turn toward the opposite side of the room. "The exposed film is projected and focused onto photographic paper, using this enlarger"—I patted the sizable piece of equipment—"then the paper is submerged and gently agitated in a series of three trays containing chemical baths: developer, stop bath, and fixer. A fourth tray allows the finished print to rinse in clean running water. Each step is timed to the second, and the entire process takes place under a 'safe light,' which is amber; black-and-white photo paper is not sensitive to light of that color." I demonstrated how a large timer on the wall was set and reset, and I flicked the safe light on, work light off, to give the investigators a better sense of what it was like to print photos in near darkness.

Switching the work light on again, Larry said, "From what we know of chronic cadmium poisoning, the deadly compound, a powder, could be dissolved in any acidic solution, then inhaled by the victim slowly, over time. That lends itself to these photo baths." He indicated the three empty trays, asking me, "Can you show us which chemicals are used in these?"

Spencer had arranged the bottles of concentrated solutions, in order, on a shelf above the trays, so I had no difficulty recalling, "Spencer used conventional Kodak chemicals, available from any photo-supply store. He preferred Microdol developer for its fine grain. Ektaflo stop bath, which halts the process and prevents overdeveloping, is favored by many photographers and was always Spencer's choice. And he'd been using a Polymax fixer, which preserves the printed image after it's exposed to light. There's nothing the least bit unusual about the setup or the chemical solutions."

"Detective?" said one of the deputies, taking the bottle of concentrated stop bath from the shelf. "The label warns that this contains acetic acid."

"Yes," I affirmed, "the stop bath is corrosive and highly acidic. The concentrate is deep yellow and has a piercing vinegar smell. You dilute it with care and keep your hands out of it. But I don't mean to imply that it's dangerous, not when handled properly and used for its intended purpose."

Larry nodded. "But *any* acidic solution—tomato juice, for instance—could be used to dissolve cadmium chloride, so the stop bath could *become* dangerous, even lethal, if spiked with cadmium."

"I'm no chemist, but that sounds reasonable, yes."

"Once the concentrated chemicals have been poured from their bottles and diluted in the trays, how long do they last?"

"With open trays, the rule of thumb is twenty-four hours. But that can be stretched, and I know that Spencer often did, simply replenishing the trays after they'd sat overnight." Sensing where Larry's reasoning was headed, I added, "Given that scenario, someone could have spiked the tray of used stop bath, perhaps during the night, leaving Spencer to inhale the fumes during his next session in the darkroom."

Larry directed the deputies to impound the trays, equipment, and concentrated developing solutions for evidence. "Take special care with the chemicals. Have all the bottles analyzed to confirm whether their contents are consistent with their labeling. And needless to say, check scrupulously for trace elements of cadmium anywhere in the room."

The evidence technicians got down to work. By now, they were sweating.

So were Larry and I. He pulled a handkerchief from his hip pocket and mopped his brow.

I said, "There must be an exhaust fan in here. Let me try to find the switch." With the walls, switch plates, and ceiling all painted flat black, the task was more difficult than one would suppose.

"Uh, Miss Gray?" said one of the deputies. "It doesn't seem to be working. There's an exhaust system, and we found the switch, but it won't kick on."

Larry and I exchanged a glance. He told the tech, "We need to get to the bottom of that. Figure out what's wrong with the fan."

"Yes, sir."

Larry asked me, "Do you recall if it was working before, when you were here with Wallace?"

"Sorry, I don't. I *presume* it was working, because I never noticed the heat. But then again, there were never four people in the room, just the two of us."

Larry paused. "Let's get some air."

I needed no further prodding. We slipped out of the darkroom and passed through the library, then stepped out to the courtyard. Dazzling sunlight ricocheted in bursts from the rippling surface of the pool as my eyes adjusted from the dim interior. Through a squint, I asked Larry, "Now what?"

"Well"—he slipped on a pair of dark glasses that gave him a vaguely sinister mien, a bad-cop air—"I plan to visit the clinic where Wallace got a checkup last week. The doctor who examined him is expecting me in a half hour. I can drop you off at home, or you can tag along with me."

"I suppose I have time." Of *course* I wanted to go. "Besides, I've been meaning to tell you about something, a strange encounter."

Readily interested, he suggested, "Tell me now."

"Let's sit down." We were near the deep end of the pool, where a tall palm happened to cast a circle of shade around the anchored end of a diving board. A foot or so off the ground, it made a handy bench, so we both settled on it. I told Larry, "Remember yesterday morning, when you were trying to reach me and you called Grant's cell phone?"

"Yup. My hunch was correct. You were with him."

I nodded. "Since he'd spent Saturday night at my house, he took me out for Sunday brunch—at the Regal Palms Hotel."

"Nothing but the best for Grant. He has *fabulous* taste." Larry grinned, removing his glasses and pocketing them.

"That's where we were when you phoned, out on the terrace."

"A table with a view . . ."

"Yes, his usual table."

"So? What was so strange about the encounter?"

With a soft laugh, I shook my head. "The encounter with *Grant* wasn't strange. It was the bunch of hotel guests at a nearby table. They were having a good time and being conspicuously loud. I didn't think much of it—it was a champagne brunch. My mood was on the sour side because of what had happened, but I couldn't expect total strangers to share my dumps over Spencer's death. As far as I knew, they hadn't even heard about it."

"It was all over the TV news yesterday morning."

"I hadn't realized that; I was thinking of newspaper deadlines. Later, during a trip inside to the buffet table, I heard them gabbing merrily about Spencer's death—they'd heard the news. I also heard someone mention my name—they'd seen the interview in the *Tribune*. Most important, I realized that Gabe Arlington was among them."

Larry scrunched his brow. "Who?"

"Gabe is the director Spencer had hired for the filming of *Photo Flash*."

"Ah, sure. Gabe Arlington—I know the name."

"He used to be big, but according to Spencer, he was practically washed-up in Hollywood, so *Photo Flash* represented a golden opportunity for Gabe to stage a comeback and rekindle his faltering career."

Larry looked confused. "Then you'd think he'd show some remorse over Wallace's death."

"Precisely. Spencer Wallace had given Gabe a much-needed break. But according to both Gabe *and* Tanner, the film production is still on schedule and the buzz surrounding Spencer's murder will actually *help* the picture with added publicity."

Larry shook his head, musing, "And I thought *police* work could be a cold, brutal business."

"I just don't get it," I said with a frustrated sigh. "*No one* seems the least bit fazed by Spencer's death. In fact, most of those who ought to be grieving seem downright giddy that Spencer fell victim to such an awful twist of fate."

"It wasn't fate," Larry reminded me. "Circumstances suggest that his death was not only intentional, but carefully premeditated." He got out his notebook and turned to his schedule for the day. "It sounds as if I should have a chat with Gabe Arlington."

"God, Larry, I suppose so, but I'm not sure you can trust *my* instincts anymore. *Everyone* looks suspicious to me."

"I was thinking the same thing myself." As he scribbled a note, I wondered how suspicious he found *me* at that moment. Taking the cell phone from his belt, he asked, "Do you think I can reach Arlington at the hotel?"

"Not sure. He planned on driving back to LA today. Maybe he hasn't checked out yet."

Larry got busy on the phone.

I stood, pacing a few steps along the side of the pool, away from the shaded diving board. Another tall palm, I noticed, was casting the shadow of its fronds directly into the pool, making a dark, wavy blob beneath the water. Again I was reminded of Spencer's body drifting in the depths of my own pool. Blinking away this morbid image, I marveled at how easily I had transformed icons of paradise—swimming pools and palm trees—into symbols of death. This is nuts, I told myself, and I knew I had all the more reason to help Larry solve the murder. I wanted to return, and quickly, to a paradise unthreatened by shadows.

"Claire," said Larry, covering the phone with his hand, "I caught Gabe Arlington. He can meet us for lunch at the hotel. I don't even know the guy, so I'd appreciate it if you could join us. Can you make it?"

"Are you buying?" As if I cared. Without waiting for an answer, I told him, "Sure, Larry, count me in."

Larry finished on the phone, wrote a note, then rose. "It's good of you to give me so much time."

We stood at the pool's edge, gazing over the water. I recalled, "Yesterday you said that by any objective measure, I had to be considered a suspect in this case. So I have a vested interest in helping you prove that anyone but me was responsible. My time is your time." I paused, adding, "Except I *do* need to get over to campus this afternoon."

He smiled. "I'll drive you there myself, if necessary. Now, then—shall we visit that doctor?"

"What's his name?"

Larry filled me in as we stepped around the pool, crossed the courtyard, and entered the main wing of the house, heading for the front door.

Arriving in the entry hall, Larry and I paused and looked about. We were capable of letting ourselves out, but we were inclined to announce our departure and thank our hostess for her "hospitality" and cooperativeness.

"Maybe she went back to bed," Larry told me.

I muttered, "For her sake, I hope so."

Just as Larry was reaching for the door, I noticed, from the edge of my vision, a pink bathrobe whisking past an adjacent hall. I called, "Oh, Rebecca?"

Larry and I paused at the door as Bryce Ballantyne retraced his steps, appeared again in the side hall, and strode forward, barefoot, to greet us. His robe not only resembled Rebecca's, it was the same slovenly cover-up. I recognized the orange-juice stain.

"Detective. Miss Gray," he said, extending his hand. In the opposite arm he cradled a hot bag of popcorn, fresh from the microwave, still steaming. The heady smell filled the room within seconds. I felt suddenly famished; my mouth watered.

We exchanged terse greetings, explaining that we were just on our way out.

I couldn't help asking, "Popcorn for breakfast?"

"Not really. We're watching a movie. Oh—have some?" He proffered the bag.

Larry declined.

I hesitated, but reached for a fistful, thanking Bryce.

Then Larry and I left. Walking to the car, I munched kernels of popcorn from my palm.

"Huh," said Larry. "Interesting—movies on Monday morning."

I swallowed, nodded. "And when Bryce said, '*We're* watching a movie,' I assumed he meant he and Rebecca. Did you notice? They were sharing more than popcorn."

"Yup. They were sharing the same bathrobe."

"Huh," I echoed Larry's earlier observation. "Interesting."

10

Shortly before eleven o'clock, Larry drove into Palm Desert and found the side street off El Paseo where Sunnyside Medical Center was located. Despite its lofty name, the "medical center", was simply a walk-in clinic consisting of several doctors' offices. A uniformed car parker stepped forward the moment we pulled to the curb, leading me to conclude that Sunnyside served a well-heeled clientele.

"Do you have an appointment?" he asked while assisting me out of the car. Perhaps I looked sickly.

Larry told him, "Doctor Jandali is expecting us."

"Very good, sir. Please step inside." He slid behind the wheel of the car, doubtless surprised to find the bland sedan equipped with police radio, flashers, and a DMV computer. When he touched the accelerator, he was also surprised by the souped-up engine that propelled the car into the street with a fearsome lurch. Larry barely took note of this; it happened all the time.

We stepped under an awning, through the door, and into a small but tastefully appointed reception area—no fish tanks, no play area for the kiddies. A smartly dressed woman, not a nurse, sat behind a marble counter, flashing us a well-practiced smile. "Good morning . . . ?" she said with a lilt, as if to ask what we wanted.

Larry introduced himself, produced his badge, and explained, "We have an eleven o'clock meeting with Doctor Pradeep Jandali. Is he available?"

Flustered—apparently not aware that the police were expected—the woman flipped a few pages of her appointment ledger and answered, "I think so, yes. He's finishing with a patient right now, and I don't see any others scheduled till afternoon. Let me check." She got on the phone. When the other party answered, she swiveled away from us and conversed in a whisper.

Larry caught my eye and drummed his fingers on the counter.

"Yes, Detective," the receptionist said, hanging up the phone, standing. "The doctor can see you now. If you'll follow me . . . ?"

I expected to be led into a cramped doctor's office, an examination room, but the room we entered was large and inviting, resembling a clubby lounge. French doors opened to a tranquil garden with a fountain. The receptionist had no sooner left us when a door on the opposite wall opened and in walked the doctor. He carried several oversize files.

"Good morning, Detective. I hope you weren't kept waiting." A dark little man with intense eyes, a caring smile, and no trace of an accent, he shook hands with Larry and introduced himself to both of us.

Larry introduced me as a friend of the deceased.

"I was so very sorry," the doctor told me, "to learn of Mr. Wallace's untimely death."

Larry suggested, "Might we sit down?"

"Of course." Doctor Jandali gestured toward an oblong library table, not quite a desk. He set down his files, offering us chairs on one side facing him on the other.

Settling next to Larry, I explained to the doctor, "Mr. Wallace was at my home on Saturday night when the, uh . . . accident occurred."

Jandali nodded. "I can appreciate how upsetting that must have been, especially when it was determined that the tragedy was other than an accident."

I sighed. "Yes. I still can't believe it."

Larry said, "As I told you on the phone, Doctor, the medical examiner has determined that when Mr. Wallace drowned, he had been weakened beyond the point of saving himself, suffering from chronic cadmium poisoning."

The doctor tapped his pile of folders. "Since we last spoke, Detective, I've done some research on cadmium poisoning. You're probably aware that it's very rare. When Mr. Wallace visited these offices last week—it was Wednesday—he mentioned complaints ranging from fatigue and sour stomach to irritability, weight loss, and yellow teeth. These vague, seemingly unrelated symptoms at first led me to a cursory diagnosis of constellation syndrome—a catchall term for conditions that don't seem to add up, medically or logically. But *something* was wrong, and he was most distraught. Unsure of where to start, I thought a chest X ray might prove helpful, as we could perform the test here on the premises and read the results at once. I've brought it along."

From the files on the table, Doctor Jandali removed a large sheet of X-ray film and held it up at an angle that allowed us to see it backlit by the room's fluorescent lighting. "I was easily fooled. As you can see"—he swirled his finger on an area of the film—"the X-ray results suggest bronchial pneumonia."

The foggy patches of light and dark meant nothing to me; I could barely discern the rib cage. I asked, "Did you tell Mr. Wallace that you suspected bronchial pneumonia? On Saturday night, I encouraged him to see a doctor. He implied that he had done so, concluding, 'It's nothing.'"

Jandali raised a brow. "Really? I assure you, Miss Gray, I discussed my diagnosis with Mr. Wallace at length and put him on a course of strong antibiotics. I also prescribed Xanax, as he needed something to calm his nerves. He seemed to fully understand this plan of treatment, grousing that he wouldn't be able to drink for a while."

Larry surmised, "Tranquilizers and alcohol don't mix."

"Not at all."

I recalled, "Spencer was drinking Virgin Marys on Saturday night, so he must have been taking your advice seriously, Doctor."

"The diagnosis of pneumonia was tentative, of course. I planned to see Mr. Wallace again this week to determine if the antibiotics had provided any relief. If there was no improvement, I would have moved on to other theories and other tests. Blood work would surely have revealed his liver damage, but to be perfectly honest, even then I would not have associated the symptom with cadmium poisoning—it's so very rare, and almost never accidental."

"No," agreed Larry, "there was nothing accidental about Spencer Wallace's death."

"Just out of curiosity," said the doctor, "did he ever express fears or concern that someone was out to harm him?"

Larry turned to me. "Claire?"

I thought back for a moment. "No, never. Except for his mounting concern about his health, Spencer didn't seem to have a fear in the world. Emotionally, he was very strong. As a friend, I found this an appealing trait in him. Many others, I've since discovered, regarded him as overly aggressive and egotistical."

The doctor asked, "Then he did have enemies?"

"Before Saturday, that's not the word I would have used. I'd have said that Spencer had competitors or business rivals or perhaps even artistic adversaries. Now, though, it's abundantly clear that he had at least *one* real enemy. Did he express such fears to you, Doctor?"

"No. I wish he had. If he'd walked in here last week complaining of so many disparate symptoms while confiding fears that someone meant him harm, I would have instantly suspected *some* sort of poisoning and would have researched the possibilities. With any luck, I might have zeroed in on cadmium."

Larry wondered, "Would you have been able to save him? Or was it already too late?"

"We'd have *tried* to save him," Jandali assured us.

I asked, "But the chances?"

The doctor heaved a frustrated sigh. "I'm afraid we'll never know."

11

When Larry and I arrived at the Regal Palms Hotel, we crossed the lobby to the main dining room and announced ourselves to the hostess, explaining that Mr. Arlington was expecting us to join him for lunch.

"He stopped by a few minutes ago," she explained, "and asked me to let you know that he's waiting for you in the lounge." She gestured across the lobby to the hotel bar.

Recalling that Gabe Arlington had been boisterously feeling his champagne the previous morning, I wondered if he had a little problem. The pitfalls of alcohol had ruined more than one career in the theater; the movie business, I reasoned, was no different. Had Gabe's once spectacular directing career been scuttled by booze? It was a reasonable explanation. Still, if Gabe wanted to drink his lunch today, he could do it in the dining room as easily as in the bar. He'd been staying at the hotel for a few days; maybe he wanted a change of scenery.

"Ah! There you are." Recognizing me as I entered the lounge with Larry, Gabe rose from a corner booth and stepped in our direction. At least I assumed it was Gabe; my eyes had not yet adjusted to the room's subdued lighting.

When he drew close enough for me to discern the crop of silvery hair, I greeted him in turn, then introduced Larry, who thanked him for making time for us.

"Anytime, Detective." Gabe shook Larry's hand heartily, telling him, "I hope I can be of use to you—though I'm not sure how." His tone was bouncy, his manner backslapping, as if meeting old pals at the club for a rusty game of golf. Gabe continued, "Hope you don't mind eating in the bar. The bill of fare is lighter than the dining room's, and the service is quicker."

"This is fine," said Larry. "In fact, this room seems better for conversation. Nice and quiet."

"Exactly." Gabe led us to his table, which was set for three. Near the middle place setting sat a half-empty highball.

At that hour, the cushy lounge was indeed quiet. A couple of well-dressed women sat at the bar, drinking and chatting, fortifying themselves for an afternoon of shopping. A bartender fussed with glassware; his natty uniform resembled a tuxedo, except that he wore a vest instead of a jacket with his pleated shirt and black bow tie. The thick carpeting and dark wood paneling gave the room a muffled intimacy—perfect for imparting secrets or arranging assignations.

Some maneuvering was required for the three of us to get settled at the small round table in the corner booth. Gabe took my hand and assisted me as I slid into one of the end positions; my rump squeaked on the polished oxblood leather of the crescent-shaped banquette. Then Gabe entered from the other side, jostling to the center position, also squeaking up a storm (the ladies at the bar turned, looked, and tittered, then returned to their whispered gossip, nose to nose). Larry slid in next to Gabe, across from me. We unfurled our linen napkins, spreading them in our laps.

The bartender stepped over and took drink orders. Gabe was still nursing his Tom Collins (I hadn't seen anyone drink such a concoction in years); Larry asked for iced tea (he was on duty); I opted for a glass of well-chilled chardonnay (why not?).

We avoided serious conversation while the drinks were prepared, discussing instead the several lunch options listed on a card at the table. Club sandwiches, hamburgers, hearty salads—everything was priced at twenty dollars even. Cheese on the burger was an extra five.

When the drinks arrived, we ordered lunch. When the bartender left us, we raised our glasses.

Sobered by the moment, Gabe said earnestly, "To the memory of Spencer Wallace."

"To Spencer," Larry and I seconded.

We tasted, set down our drinks, and fell silent.

As it was time to get down to business, Larry took his notebook from his jacket pocket and opened it on the table. Squinting to read his own writing in the dim pool of light cast by an ornate overhead lantern, he asked Gabe, "Can you tell me about your relationship to the deceased?"

Gabe leaned back in the booth, eyeing the dark ceiling for a moment. "Well," he said, uncertain where to begin, "we had lately entered into a working relationship—on his new film, *Photo Flash*—but beyond that, I wouldn't say we had a 'relationship' at all."

"Somehow," said Larry, "I was under the impression that the two of you were old friends."

Gabe shook his head. "We rubbed shoulders in the same industry for many years, but no, we rarely socialized, never one-on-one."

Larry tapped his notes absentmindedly. He hesitated, then asked, "Am I mistaken, or has your career been . . . 'inactive' for a while?"

Gabe broke into a grin. "I appreciate the sensitivity with which you worded that question, Detective. Truth is, my directing career ground to a halt some years ago. Pictures are a tough business—it can be merciless and unforgiving."

Entering the conversation, I recalled, "Spencer told me you'd had the misfortune of directing a picture or two that didn't quite set box-office records."

"Claire," said Gabe, beading me with a get-real stare, "if Spencer said that, he was being uncharacteristically softhearted. Let's call a spade a spade—after a promising start, I directed a string of flops. My glory days were over, and my career was washed up." Gabe was correct; Spencer had used essentially the same words to describe Gabe's fall from grace.

"I don't recall how Spencer phrased it," I fibbed, "but he obviously held you in high regard. After all, he wrote *Photo Flash;* he doted over that script and had great expectations for the production. He wouldn't have signed you on for such a high-profile film if he hadn't respected your talents."

Gabe fingered his icy cocktail glass, agreeing with a slow nod. "That's what he said. When he first approached me and tried to recruit me for the project, I asked him bluntly, 'Why me?' I mean, he could've had the pick of Hollywood's elite. Why settle for a has-been?"

"You are *far* from a has-been," I told him.

"You're kind. But the fact is, I haven't directed in ten years, so Spencer's offer came as a surprise, to say the least."

"Then why *did* he come to you?" asked Larry. "I don't mean to sound crass, but I'm grasping at straws. Did he get you cheap?"

"Hell, no." Gabe laughed, taking no offense. "In fact, he offered far more than I'd have dared to ask. He *paid* for top talent, so he must have thought he was *getting* top talent." Gabe's mood slackened as he added, "Of course, I hadn't yet learned all the details."

It was my turn to grasp at straws. "Hmm. Don't tell me. No sooner had you signed with Wallace than you found out he'd really wanted someone else—someone 'bigger' who was unavailable because of other commitments."

"No. To the contrary, I found out that both Spielmueller and

Wertberg had *wanted* the picture. According to friends, they were waiting around for the phone to ring. Spencer could've had either of them if he'd wanted them."

I concluded, "So he wanted *you*."

"Indeed he did. He paid top dollar and offered me a comeback opportunity to boot. In return, I offered a known name, a once-illustrious track record, and a publicity opportunity for buzz about the comeback. When the contract arrived, I didn't hesitate to sign it. My agent had combed through the fine print and assured me it was all standard boilerplate. Only later, when Spencer and I got into initial discussions regarding budgets and production schedule, did I realize that he had retained complete artistic control over the picture."

Larry looked up from the notes he was taking. "Pardon my lack of insight, but is that unusual?"

Gabe explained, "Depends. The producer and director often work as a team; sometimes it's the same person. In a battle of wills, the moneyman generally wins—except at a certain level of talent where artistic control is presumed absolute. Can you imagine Spielmueller deferring to anyone's wishes? I don't *think* so." Gabe snorted, then continued, "Spencer had lured me into the project with vague—not specific—promises of artistic autonomy. He gave the *impression* I was being hired under those terms, and such an understanding would be expected in a high-budget picture like *Photo Flash*. So it came as a rude awakening when I realized that my artistic concept of the film didn't matter. Essentially, I was hired to aim the camera for Spencer Wallace."

I gave a long, low sigh. "I'm so sorry, Gabe. That must have hurt."

Larry asked, "Why didn't you quit? You could have gotten out of the contract; you'd been misled."

Through a soft laugh, Gabe said, "Do you honestly think I'd

give up a deal like this? It's the chance of a lifetime to reestablish myself. If I walked out on it, I'd end up even lower than I'd been before, a true pariah. Besides, I need the money. The loss of artistic control was a disappointment, a major one, but I quickly learned to live with it."

"I must say"—I smiled—"your approach to this difficult situation is stunningly good-natured and practical. I'm not sure *I'd* be able to show your forbearance."

"Perhaps your artistic integrity is greater than mine, Claire."

"Don't be unfair to yourself. You found yourself in a dilemma not of your own making. You dealt with it the only way you could." I sipped some of my wine, which had gone warm.

"Perhaps." Gabe paused. "Besides, it doesn't matter now."

"Oh?" Larry's eyes slid toward mine.

Gabe explained, "With Spencer gone, so is his artistic control."

I nodded. "I suppose that makes sense."

"I assure you, it makes perfect sense. I spent yesterday afternoon on the phone with my agent and my lawyer, and *they* spent this morning with the production company's legal team. They first determined that the picture is not in jeopardy—the show *will* go on. Second, and just as important, they confirmed that artistic control over the production now rests solely with me." With a satisfied nod, he drank the last of his Tom Collins.

"Hmm," I said, swirling my wine, "then everything's dandy."

"It is, isn't it?" agreed Gabe. He hadn't caught the chilling subtext of my idle pronouncement: Gabe Arlington's artistic ego had been tremendously bolstered by Spencer Wallace's death.

The bartender arrived with our lunch just then—thank goodness, as I didn't enjoy the direction our conversation had taken. Larry finished the note he was writing, then closed his pad and set it aside.

"Excellent," Gabe told the bartender, rubbing his hands

together. "I'm famished. Perhaps another Tom Collins as well. Everyone else happy?"

Larry and I declined second drinks; then all three of us began to eat. A minute or two passed as we sampled our first bites, pausing to sigh with satisfaction.

At the back of my mind, however, a memory of Saturday evening scratched at my consciousness and distracted me from the pleasures of a twenty-dollar sandwich. Dabbing my lips with my napkin, I turned to Gabe and said offhandedly, "I presume you won't be filming *Photo Flash* in black and white."

Gabe nearly choked. With a chortle, he replied, "Are you kidding?"

Larry looked confused. He asked me, "Why would he do that?"

I was about to explain that Spencer had openly considered that option at Saturday night's party, but Gabe answered for me, "Now and then, Detective, some artsy-fartsy filmmaker gets the notion that cinema needs to 'connect with its roots' or whatever, and presto, you get some epic shot in grainy black and white. It ends up looking experimental and low-budget, and the ticket-buying public finds it annoying at best. Spencer was a devoted amateur photographer—black and white, naturally—and he was flirting with the idea of doing *Photo Flash* in monochrome. I tried to dissuade him, but I knew very well that if Spencer Wallace had a brainstorm, there was likely no stopping it. If you ask me"—Gabe laughed—"the guy must have been sniffing his photo chemicals."

Larry and I glanced at each other. It escaped neither of us that Spencer may in fact have died from inhaling toxic fumes from his photo baths. This detail of the investigation was not generally known, but Gabe Arlington was intimately familiar with Spencer's screenplay, which had spelled out a precise formula for murder.

The director continued, "Thank God *that* battle's behind us."

Though his opinion was already clear, I decided to draw him out some, asking, "Did you see no merit at all in filming *Photo Flash* in black and white? The idea struck me as inventive and daring."

"Claire," he said, resting his fingers on my arm, "I admire your artistic sense greatly, but it stems from the theater, which is intrinsically symbolic and interpretive. Film, on the other hand, is reality; at least that's how audiences see it. Hell, film is rarely even *film* anymore. Many pictures are now shot on high-definition video, then *transferred* to film for projection in theaters."

"Is that so?"

"Yup. Bottom line: the movie-going public simply has no appetite for such retro affectations. You never see a new *television* show in black and white, do you?"

"No," I admitted. But I thought, So what?

"So the same applies to films. Why risk it? Spencer was boss of this project, but I wasn't going to let it go black and white without a fight. Fortunately, saner ideas have prevailed." Gabe gave a self-satisfied nod, then hungrily returned his attentions to his half-eaten club sandwich. The bartender brought his second Tom Collins.

We avoided further discussion of the deceased producer until the meal's end, when our plates had been cleared and coffee was poured. Larry opened his notebook again. "You've been very candid, Mr. Arlington, and I appreciate that. Plain and simple, can you tell me—did you like Spencer Wallace?"

"Hmmm." Gabe nudged aside his cup and saucer. "There's no point in window dressing, I suppose."

"No, there isn't."

Gabe weighed his words. "I think it's safe to say, Detective, that *no one* in the film industry truly 'liked' Spencer Wallace, myself included. That said, everyone did respect the man; his accomplishments were legendary, and his power was self-evident. Because of that power, most of his associates also felt a measure of fear. Wallace was capable of ruining careers—in a heartbeat, on a whim—and he sometimes did."

Larry asked, "Your previous career slump, did that have anything to do with Wallace?"

"Nothing at all. I blame only my own poor judgment for those dark years. Wallace handed me the opportunity to turn everything around again."

"And still, you say you didn't like him."

"As a person? As a friend? Certainly not." Gabe turned to me. "Sorry, Claire. I realize that you and Spencer had gotten close. Evidently, you saw something in the man that I didn't."

"I *did*," I insisted. "I'm sorry he's gone."

Gabe couldn't bring himself to voice sympathy for my sense of loss. Instead, he noted, "What an *exit*. At least Spencer's dramatic departure will serve the best interests of *Photo Flash*, and I know how deeply he cared about the project. The buzz is already starting to build. You can't *buy* that kind of publicity."

"So I've heard." Finishing my coffee, I felt an acidic knot grip my stomach.

When the bartender returned to present the check, Larry signaled that he wanted it, but Gabe piped in, "Nonsense, Detective. I'll take that. Let the production company pay for it—it's nothing." He signed the bill to his hotel tab.

The three of us rose and walked to the lobby together. Preparing to part company, we paused under a large, graceful chandelier. I thanked Gabe for lunch; Larry thanked him for his time.

"My pleasure entirely," he told us, glancing at his watch.

I did the same; it was nearly one o'clock. I asked Gabe, "Checkout time? Ready to head back to LA?"

He nodded, but looked unsure. "That was the plan. But the day seems to have slipped away already." He yawned—doubtless the effect of his two cocktails.

I suggested, "Stay another night. Tanner isn't driving out till tomorrow morning. I understand the preproduction meeting isn't till Wednesday, correct?"

"Correct." Gabe shrugged. "Maybe you're right. Why rush back?"

We exchanged a few pleasantries. Then Gabe strolled off toward one of the guest wings; Larry and I went out to the portico, where we waited for his car.

It was Larry's turn to check his watch. He seemed perplexed.

"Late for a golf game?" I asked with a twisted smile.

"Right." He laughed. "I'm supposed to meet my brother at three—we have a little business matter to take care of—but the logistics have me stumped. He has a two o'clock in north Palm Springs, but I have an appointment down in Indio." They would be at opposite ends of the valley.

As Larry's car circled up the driveway, I offered, "You can meet at my place if you like. It's about midway, and I should be back from campus by then."

Cocking his head, considering my proposal, Larry asked, "You don't mind?"

"Of course not. You and Grant are always welcome."

"Then I think we'll take you up on that."

When we were settled in the car, Larry phoned Grant, told him the plan, and drove me home so I could pick up my own car.

12

Driving my silver Beetle across the valley toward the campus of Desert Arts College, I attempted to clear my head of the murder and to concentrate on matters relevant to the school. I was on Glenn Yeats's payroll, after all, not Larry Knoll's, and it seemed only fair to give my employer an hour or two of my time as we entered the final few weeks of the school's first academic year.

I needed to drop in at the theater and check on the crew's progress at striking the set of *Traders*. By now, I assumed, there would be little or no evidence of the show that had closed on Saturday. A clean stage would await the theater's next production.

Also on my brief agenda: I wanted to stop at Glenn's office and inform him that I would commit to conducting a theater workshop that coming summer. This decision would doubtless be greeted as wonderful news, which I hoped might lessen his transparent annoyance that I had, once again, gotten myself—and the school—mixed up with a murder investigation.

Finally, I planned to spend a few minutes in my own office, checking my files, re-creating the party guest list that Larry had requested. This last task, I realized, was hardly school business; I marveled at how quickly circumstances had thwarted my good intentions to earn an honest day's pay.

The campus now lay dead ahead, an instant landmark rising from the sand-swept valley floor. I. T. Dirkman's collection of buildings punched the severely blue sky in calculated confusion, but the one structure that dominated this fanciful backdrop was my theater. The mere sight of it was enough to freshen my mind and energize my thoughts. Flooring the Beetle, I tore through the main entrance to the campus and sputtered to the faculty garage, where I parked in the prime space that Glenn had reserved for me on the day when Dirkman had first unveiled his plans.

The campus was built around a large paved plaza called College Circle. One o'clock classes had begun, and I had the entire space to myself. Walking through the lushly landscaped common, with its palms, pools, and fountains, I momentarily dismissed the vexing questions of an unexplained death, contemplating instead the sheer beauty of the setting and the day. A warm early-afternoon breeze hinted at the planetary slide from spring to summer. An unseen mockingbird trilled with ecstatic abandon.

I preferred to think of the plaza as an enormous entryway built solely to lead visitors to my theater's facade. My pace quickened as I approached the building's angular shadow. With heels snapping on the stone pavers, I strutted through College Circle as if I owned the place.

Arriving at the lobby doors, I paused, wondering if they were locked, wondering if I had thought to bring my key. But then I noticed lights at the box office in the lobby, where a few patrons hunkered over seating diagrams, choosing tickets for various events. Stepping inside, I felt an instant sense of calm, as if arriving home—truly home. Then, crossing the vast, plush expanse of carpet, I felt my pulse rush in anticipation of entering the auditorium itself. I had walked into theaters surely thousands of times. Each time, it was new again. It was magic.

Passing through the double doors from the lobby to the theater, I saw that the strike crew had nearly completed its work. The *Traders* set had been completely removed, as had most of the furniture; an odd chair or two remained. Striding down the aisle, I hailed the crew foreman, "Yoo-hoo! Morgan."

"Howdy, Miss Gray." He waved to me from the edge of the stage. "Just finishing up." With a hearty laugh, he added, "Bring on the next one!"

"Soon enough, Morgan. Soon enough." I climbed a set of rehearsal stairs that led from the auditorium floor to the stage apron.

Hearing my voice, Kiki appeared from the wing, stage right. "Claire, darling, I hope there's no rush—I've barely recovered from *this* production." Though she was joking, she did seem frazzled that afternoon. She carried an armload of costumes that I didn't recognize, period dresses that would have looked absurdly anachronistic in the contemporary setting of *Traders*. She handed them off to a student assistant, explaining to me, "Amazing how things pile up. I found a whole rack of misplaced gowns from the Christmas choral program." With a grand flourish, she directed the student, "To the costume vault!"

The kid lumbered away, lost in a heap of flounces and petticoats.

Morgan helped one of the lighting technicians move a tall ladder offstage, and suddenly, the job looked complete. He asked me, "Do you want those chairs put away?" Without them, the stage would be empty.

"Thanks, Morgan, but just leave them." A bare stage has always struck me as sad and lifeless.

Morgan and his remaining crew stowed some tools, locked their storage bins, switched off the backstage work lights, and left through a freight door, closing it with a thud that echoed through the empty theater.

I turned to Kiki, who stood alone with me onstage. "Well," I told her with a shrug, "another shining moment in theatrical history . . . is history."

She heaved a big, dramatic sigh. "Blood under the bridge, dar-ling."

I put my arm around her shoulder and gave her a squeeze. "It's good to be with you, Kiki. Need to run?"

She checked an oversize wristwatch with a mile-wide black patent-leather band. "Not yet. My practicum class starts at two."

"And they can't very well begin without you."

"They dare *not.*" Kiki laughed. "Ah, how I love teaching—like playing God." She plopped herself onto one of the two armchairs, center stage.

"Teaching isn't a power trip, Kiki. It's about molding young minds. At least it's supposed to be." I sat in the other chair, near her.

"Yeah, yeah, yeah." She was unconvinced.

I mimicked her nasal tone. " 'Yeah, yeah, yeah'? Not very sophisticated—*dah*-ling."

"Why, Claire, I hardly need to keep up pretenses with *you.*"

I wondered aloud, "Why keep up pretenses with anyone?"

"Hmm?"

"Nothing." I reached and patted her hand. "I'm grateful for the company. Keeps my mind off . . . you-know-what."

Kiki whirled a hand, stabbing at an answer. "Murder?"

I nodded. "The investigation intrigues me, but I never thought it would take *this* particular turn. I'm an *active* suspect."

She flicked a wrist dismissively. "In a *technical* sense. *Maybe.* But Larry won't be giving you the rubber-hose treatment—at least I doubt it."

Grimly, I observed, "That's reassuring."

"Claire—forget the murder. He'll figure it out. It had nothing to do with you. Case closed."

"Hope you're right."

"Of *course* I'm right."

I stood, took a step downstage, and looked out over the empty rows of scarlet velvet seats. With a contented little sigh, I said, "We should do this more often—take time to talk."

"Just like the old days."

I turned to her. "Did you ever think, thirty-odd years ago, when we met at Evans College, that we'd end up *here*—today—thick as thieves?"

"Ah," she said wistfully, "we've come a long way from idyllic little Evanstown."

"Mm-hm," I agreed. "Three thousand miles."

"That's not what I meant," said Kiki, wagging a hand. "I mean . . . life. The 'journey.' "

"I know." With a warm smile, I sat next to her again.

"Now here we are again, full circle, back at college together."

"Except, now, we're on the opposite coast."

"And," Kiki stressed, leaning near, "we're running the show."

Laughing, I asked, "You really do love it, don't you?"

With matter-of-fact innocence, she replied, "Absolutely. It's my life."

"Mine, too."

"No, Claire." Kiki's look turned serious. "Your life is *theater.* Mine is academia. I'd be utterly adrift without it, and my position here is the fulfillment of a fantasy. But you, Claire—this was never what you had in mind."

Mulling her assertion, I realized she was largely correct. "Still," I said, "now that I'm here, I have no regrets. When I made the decision to suspend my career on Broadway, I saw it as an adventure, not a goal. I guess I was lured by the prospect of starting over." With a soft laugh, I added, "At *my* age . . ."

Kiki rapped my hand. "At *our* age. But, hey"—she sat erect, with mock defensiveness—"*we're* not old."

"Hell, no!" I said, miming her tone and posture.

She sat back. "My point, Claire, is that *you* have options; you always have. Good God, gal, you're at the top of your profession. You've not only established a rock-solid reputation as one of the greatest directors in American theater—enough in itself—but you've written a top-notch play of your own, you've launched countless new actors' careers, and I can't even *guess* how many times you've had featured interviews in Newsweek, The New Yorker, you name it."

I named, "The *Los Angeles Tribune.*"

"Ugh, well, forget that one. All I'm saying is this: if things don't work out for you here, or if you simply get *bored* with it, you'll move on to something else. And you'll knock 'em dead again and again." She leaned forward. Her tone turned flatly realistic, not whining. "I don't have those options, Claire. For me, being here, now—this is what I do. This is *all* I do. And it's all I've ever *wanted* to do."

I repeated her earlier assertion: "It's your life."

"But getting here . . . well, it wasn't easy." She flumped back in her chair, dangling one arm.

I didn't intend to sound condescending, but perhaps my tone was too kindly as I told her, "Let's just say you hit a rough spot along the way. That's behind you now. It was a long time ago, Kiki."

"Not long enough. It never will be." She fidgeted with her empty hand, picking at her nails. "Aarghh! Why *did* I quit smoking?"

Pointedly, I answered, "For the same reason that you battled your way out of those *other* bad habits."

She rose, strolling downstage. "Yeah, yeah, yeah . . ."

Through an exaggerated, nasal twang, I echoed, "Yeah, yeah, yeah . . ."

With a little spit of laughter, she turned to me. "I hardly ever talk about it, but with you, it's easy."

"What are friends for?"

Kiki paused, turned to the imaginary audience, and delivered a gossipy spiel, as if giving a tell-all interview on a TV talk show. "Well, ya see," she began, sounding chatty, "it was back in the seventies—the *sizzling* seventies. Everyone was doing it, and I developed this little *problem*. Designer drugs were all the rage, and—never one to miss out on a trend—I was *there*, baby. Drugs were big among the theater crowd back then; still are, I guess. And they *never* went out of style on campus, so I got the proverbial double whammy. I'd just returned to Evans, my alma mater, as a lowly instructor in the costume shop, and well, I was having a ball."

She took a breath. When she continued, her tone was less glib. "I was having a ball—I thought. Until one night when things got out of control at a party. It wasn't on campus, but there were plenty of faculty there and some students, too. Somehow, the notion of a 'raid' seemed absurdly cliché and remote. But sure as shit, it happened."

Kiki's shoulders slumped. Her flat inflection turned sober and pensive. "The local cops issued some fines, and they were happy. The school, needless to say, was *not* happy, and they made noises about a mass dismissal, but there were simply too many faculty involved. So we were formally 'censured,' whatever that means. Eventually the whole hoo-ha seemed to go away, buried in the dusty files of the halls of ivy."

I rose and stepped to her, saying gently, "Meanwhile, you confronted your demons and managed to escape a self-destructive spiral."

Kiki turned to me, lifted her chin, and struck a flamenco pose. "No worse for wear, I daresay." Her wacky appearance belied her statement.

"The jury's still out on that." Seriously, I added, "The point is, dear, what's done is done. You can't undo the past, so live for the future. Besides, those ancient indiscretions hardly strike me as all *that* grievous. If everyone who'd ever experimented with drugs at college were 'brought to justice,' half the nation would be behind bars."

"You're right, I imagine." Kiki slowly turned away. "And I appreciate the moral support. But I'm afraid there's more to this story—a trifling footnote I've never had the nerve to confide in you." She stepped from the stage and down the stairs to the auditorium, settling in one of the first-row seats.

I followed down the stairs. "If you're trying to pique my interest, you've succeeded."

"This isn't easy." Kiki swallowed. "The night of the party and the drug bust, a young woman died—of an overdose."

"How horrible," I mumbled, sitting in the seat next to Kiki's.

"It's worse," she told me. "The kid was a student—of mine. She was a senior theater major with an emphasis in costuming, extremely talented, with a promising career ahead of her. That fall, we had clicked instantly. Throughout the year, she thought of me as a mentor."

Wide-eyed, I asked, "Good Lord, Kiki, you weren't trafficking drugs to her, were you?"

She shook her head vehemently. "*No,* Claire, absolutely not. She had her own habit, her own source. But still, she looked up to me. She saw me as a role model, and I made a poor one. That night at the party, she lost all sense of judgment. *Lots* of us lost control, including me, and she followed my example. To this day, I often wonder if—in some sense—I killed Jennie." Kiki bowed her head, clarifying, "That was her name."

I touched my friend's arm. "I'm so sorry, Kiki. Why haven't you shared this with me before?"

"It's just not the sort of thing you 'share.' I could barely deal with it myself."

"Was there any . . . fallout?"

"There was. With so many people at the party, lots of them knew that Jennie and I were student and teacher—and close friends. Rumors started flying that I *had* been pushing drugs to her, that I was responsible for the overdose. There was a police investigation."

"Oh, no," I groaned, utterly deflated.

Kiki stood, moved toward the stage, and turned to me. "Nothing came of it. I'd played no direct role in what happened to Jennie, so there was nothing to prove. There were never any charges. The incident was noted in my school records, then buried."

I promised, "The secret's safe with me. Don't give it another thought."

She breathed a weak sigh. "Denial is a marvelous self-defense mechanism. And I did a fairly decent job of repressing the whole mess—until this past January. That's when I went to Cabo."

"Uh-oh."

"Mm-hm." Kiki nodded slowly. "Spencer Wallace and I had some chemistry, as you've noted, and he enticed me down to his vacation home in the Baja for that lost weekend. It was spectacular—the house, the setting—and it *might* have been naughtily romantic. But there was a problem." She paused, then told me bluntly, "It was you."

With a dumbfounded gasp, I rose. *"What?"*

"Spencer wasn't interested in *me,* Claire. He was interested in you."

Pacing past the front of the stage, hand to head, I recalled, "And his widow said he was after *Tanner.*" I turned to ask Kiki, "How do *I* fit into this picture?"

"Tanner?" asked Kiki, herself confused. "Spencer must've wanted *him* for sex. But not you, Claire."

I stepped face-to-face with Kiki, exasperated. "Am I supposed to be relieved—or *insulted*?"

She tsked. "Spencer was far too old for you. You wouldn't have enjoyed him."

"But you *would* have? Kiki, you and I are the same age."

"Oh."

Reining in my emotions, I paced again, thinking aloud, "I'm no sweater girl, far from it. And I can live with that; my life has other priorities. But now and then it *is* difficult not to feel the slightest bit—shall we say—insecure?" I turned back to Kiki, expounding, "My own *mother* once called me 'handsome,' and now—"

Kiki gasped. "She *didn't.*"

"She did. And now *you're* telling me that Spencer Wallace, a shameless womanizer, a notorious lech, was more interested in my *boyfriend* than he was in *me*?" The pitch of my voice had slid beyond its normal range; I wasn't so much speaking as squeaking.

Stepping toward me, Kiki spoke in soothing tones. "Spencer was *very* interested in you, Claire. But not 'that way.'" Meaningfully, she added, "He had other plans for you."

Tossing my arms, I asked, "What on *earth* are you talking about?"

Kiki sat again in the first row, patting the cushion of the seat next to her. "Sit down, dear."

Warily, I did so.

Kiki looked me in the eye. "Spencer admired you tremendously."

Hangdog, I recalled, "His wife told me that if he didn't invite me to Cabo, it was a sign of 'respect.'"

"Yup." Kiki nodded knowingly. "That was the very word he used. The entire weekend I was in Mexico, he yammered nonstop about his 'respect' for you. He felt your talents were being wasted here—in the desert—teaching college."

"*Well.*" I was suddenly huffy. "It's good to know that *someone*—other than my own mother—saw fit to correct the course of my misguided life."

"Spencer felt your true destiny was still further west . . ." Kiki paused. "In Hollywood."

"Oh, Lord." I laughed, but I was hardly amused. "How many times have I heard *that*? People who make movies seem so convinced that they've answered the ultimate calling, that anyone in his right mind would hotfoot away from legitimate theater at the first possible chance, joining the ranks of the glitterati who 'do pictures.'" With a derisive snort, I added, "Have you ever noticed that? They *never* call a movie a 'movie.' It's *always* a 'picture.' So self-important . . ."

"And Spencer Wallace was the most important of them all. He *wanted* you, Claire—in his production company, in his studio. He wanted to make you a star director—of 'pictures.' He said you could make a fortune—for both of you."

Skeptically, I noted, "He never mentioned it to *me*."

"He was afraid to. He'd read your interviews. He knew only too well that you could be a tad defensive about"—Kiki cleared her throat, placed a hand over her bosom, and completed her statement with a highbrow delivery—"about the *legitimate theater*."

"Good." I crossed my arms, smugly self-satisfied.

"So his plan was to recruit *me* into helping recruit *you* for *him*."

"*What?*"

Kiki nodded. "Spencer didn't give a damn about *me*. The only reason he took me to Mexico was to brainwash me into advancing his scheme."

I patted her hand. "Well, I'm glad you refused." As an afterthought, I asked, "You *did* refuse, didn't you?"

"Yes, of course. But that wasn't the end of it. A few weeks ago, Spencer phoned me, wanting to meet for drinks at the Regal Palms. I was skeptical, but he assured me his only purpose was to apologize for his presumptuous behavior on the trip. So I went."

"And . . . ?"

"And he'd reserved a quiet corner booth in the hotel lounge, where he was waiting for me."

I wondered if it was the very booth where I'd lunched with Gabe Arlington only an hour earlier.

Kiki continued, "As soon as we'd ordered our drinks and the waiter had left, Spencer made it apparent that his purpose was *not* to apologize, but to ratchet up the pressure. First he tried friendly persuasion, but when that failed to sway me, he took another tack. He produced a manila file folder, placed it on the table before me, and opened it. Even in the dim light of the bar, I knew at once what it was."

Apprehensively, flatly, I told her, "I don't believe it."

"Believe it, Claire. Spencer had had me *investigated*. He'd done a complete background check and had managed to dig up copies of my files from Evans. In short, I was about to be coerced—*blackmailed*—into snaring you for his production company."

I couldn't help thinking of Glenn Yeats's similar campaign, two years prior, to recruit me onto his future faculty. He'd been aggressive, but he hadn't been ruthless. "Christ," I muttered. "Or else . . . ?"

"Or else," said Kiki, "Spencer would expose my past problems, very likely putting an end to my teaching career. He was in thick with various board members at Desert Arts College, which has a strict, zero-tolerance policy for drug offenses. Oh, I know, it's mere posturing at best, a nod to the ruling conservative element, but no two ways about it—*drugs* is a far dirtier word today than it was thirty years ago. If Spencer revealed my previous arrest, coupled with Jennie's death, there's not a college in the land that would let me within a mile of its students. I'd be totally, irreversibly sca-*rewed*."

I heaved a big sigh. "God, Kiki. What'd you do?"

She stood, recounting, "I begged—no soap. I pleaded—get real.

At best, Spencer would only give me a little while to think things over and decide. So I was buying time."

I stood, grasping her arms. "Why didn't you *tell* me about this? I could have played along, helped you, then backed out on Spencer—screwing *him*."

Kiki shook her head. "Nice thought, but Spencer was too savvy. He stressed that he'd settle only for *results,* not appearances of cooperation. My other option was to go to the police, and I was tempted. But that would bare the very details I needed to keep hidden."

Looking into her eyes, I wanted to cry. "Oh, Kiki, I'm mortified to know that I played some role in this—even unwittingly. I can't *imagine* what you must've been going through. I'm remorsefully sorry."

"Oh, well," she said with unexpected breeziness, "all's well that end's well."

"Huh?"

"He's *dead,* Claire. And I, for one, couldn't be happier." Kiki gave me a brisk nod, checked her watch, then headed for the stairs that led up to the stage.

Following, I sputtered, "You, uh . . . didn't . . . ?"

Standing on the bottom stair, she turned to tell me, "Of *course* not. But somebody did, thank God, and that's all that matters to me."

"I can understand your relief. And I appreciate that you've shared this with me. But don't you think it's time to fill Larry in?"

"The police?" she asked, aghast, stepping down to the floor. "Whatever for?"

"This is a previously unknown aspect of Spencer Wallace's background; it could be important to the case. If he stooped to blackmail *you,* Kiki, there's no telling how many others he'd victimized. As it stands, *I'm* on the suspect list, probably near the top, and I'd like to give Larry a little more to work with."

Kiki tossed her head. "It *sounds* as if you're angling to substitute *my* name for *yours* on that list!"

With equal umbrage, I retorted, "That's nonsense. I merely want to give Larry a helpful new direction for his investigation."

Kiki planted a hand on her hip. "While deflecting suspicion from yourself . . ."

I struggled to keep my anger in check, but just barely, telling her, "Sure. Why not? I *know* I didn't kill the man. Why shouldn't I nudge the police toward the same conclusion?"

Kiki blew. "While pinning the murder on your best *friend*? Oops, sorry, I forgot. I'm *not* your best friend, am I, Claire? No, I'm your *OLDEST* friend!" She huffed up the stairs.

I followed her to the stage. "Kiki," I said, mustering a conciliatory tone, "please, let's try to keep everything in perspective. We go back too far together to be divided by misunderstandings and unfounded suspicions."

She spun toward me. "Then don't expect me to . . . to 'take the rap' for you."

I grinned. "For heaven's sake—I'm asking for no such thing."

She returned my grin with the slightest little pout, a moue. "Then don't betray the confidence I shared with you. I have the right to expect that, if only out of friendship."

I paused before acceding, "Very well. If you insist."

"I do," she said firmly.

The thump of a backstage door provided a timely interruption to our conversation, which had grown tiresome and upsetting. As the door opened, a shaft of daylight spilled across the black floor. "Miss Gray?" called a voice, Morgan's. "You still here?"

"Yes, Morgan," I answered, stepping off to the wing.

He closed the door. "I thought I'd shut down all the lights, but if you ladies—"

"No, Morgan, that'll be fine. We're finished here."

Kiki told me, "I really do need to run—that practicum class."

"And I have errands that shouldn't wait."

We stepped to each other and, uncertainly, exchanged a good-bye kiss on the cheek.

Then Kiki went her way.

I went mine.

My bouncy mood had soured considerably by the time I crossed College Circle again. Heading away from the theater, toward the administration building, I wasn't listening to the birds and going gaga over the weather. This time, I struggled with my mixed feelings about Kiki. I was angry, sorry, suspicious, and defensive; my thoughts were adrift in a jumbled stew of conflicting emotions.

Entering the circular office building, I decided to keep my meeting with Glenn Yeats brief, spend a few minutes in my own office reconstructing my guest list, then go home to think things through. After seven months on campus, I had at last learned to navigate the confusing curved floor plan of the administration building without getting lost or retracing my steps, so moments after leaving the plaza, I found myself outside the gleaming mahogany doors that led to Glenn's luxurious suite of offices—the inner sanctum.

Stepping inside his reception room, I was struck, as always, by its understated elegance—and the arctic chill of its air-conditioning. I don't know whether Glenn Yeats had some neurological problem with his body thermostat (I wasn't brazen enough to ask), but I never managed to enter his windowless domain without fighting off a crop of goose bumps.

"Ahhh, Ms. Gray," cooed Glenn's executive secretary, Tide

Arden, a tall, ferocious-looking black woman with an incongruous voice of honey, softened further by the trace of a lisp. She had stepped out from her office, which in turn guarded the entrance to the holy of holies. "Always such a pleasure. What can I do for you?"

"I'd like to see Glenn. Is he in?"

"He is, Ms. Gray, but I'm afraid he's occupied right now." She frowned an apology for delivering such crushing news.

I suggested, "Perhaps you could give him a message."

"Of course. Let me write it down." She led me to her desk, prinking atop spike heels that made her appear all the more Amazonian. As she moved, the long, ropy muscles of her thighs flexed beneath a tight leather miniskirt. As usual, she wore a halter top adorned with chromed studs and grommets, exposing a good deal of flesh—but no goose bumps. Was she, I wondered, warm-blooded? Or had she simply adapted to her boss's frosty environment? When she had settled at her keyboard, flexing her mannish fingers with French-manicured nails, she asked, "And your message?"

Recalling the last time my words had been transcribed, Saturday night by Kemper Fahlstrom, I paused to rehearse my message before Tide could commit it to paper. I then told her, "This is in regard to the summer theater workshop." She pecked away, nodding, as I continued, "After due deliberation, I have decided, in the best interest of the school and of my program, that—"

A nervous buzz interrupted us, issuing from Tide's telephone, a many-buttoned instrument of titanic proportions. A red light blinked. We both halted.

"Excuse me," she said. She didn't need to explain who was calling. Lifting the receiver, she answered, "Yes, sir."

I listened idly as she scratched a few notes and voiced one-word replies to various questions.

Then she flipped a page of her gilt-edged desk calendar, saying,

"No, Mr. Yeats. No other appointments this afternoon, but Ms. Gray does happen to be standing here right now." She winked at me. "Of course, sir. I thought you'd want to see her." Tide hung up the phone and stood, offering a huge smile.

"Don't tell me I've been admitted."

"Yes, Ms. Gray." Her breathy tone carried such pride, one would have thought she'd cracked the gates to Oz. "This way, please."

I knew the way, but she seemed to take pleasure in escorting me, so I followed as she crossed the room, gripped the knob (I had no doubt she could have ripped the door off its hinges, if so inclined), and led the way to the inner office. She announced me: "Ms. Gray." Then she slunk out, closing the door behind her.

With a beaming smile, Glenn rose from behind his semicircular, granite-topped desk. Rows of computer monitors flickered behind him, set into a curved wall of creamy travertine. The Oz metaphor again traced through my mind. *"Claire,"* he gushed. "What an unexpected surprise."

"I'm delighted you're so easily pleased."

"You know Lance Caldwell, of course." Glenn gestured to one of the buttery-brown leather sofas that formed a U in front of his desk.

As he did so, the faculty's composer in residence rose and turned to me. "Good afternoon, Claire." Forty-something, lanky, and long-haired, wearing a black turtleneck, he looked every inch the maestro at leisure. The sweater struck me as far too warm for April in the desert, but it struck me as just right in Glenn's frigid office; I wished I'd worn one.

"Hello, Lance," I said. A handshake didn't seem called-for—we were colleagues, and he'd visited my home on Saturday night—so we exchanged a casual nod. I told both him and Glenn, "I didn't mean to interrupt. It's really not important. I can come back."

"Nonsense," said Glenn. "Lance and I have been having a long

discussion—too long—and frankly, we're getting nowhere. Maybe you could help."

"I will if I can."

"Do have a seat, Claire. Make yourself comfortable."

As instructed, I settled on a second leather sofa, facing Lance's. Both the composer and the college president resumed their seats.

"Now, then," Glenn asked, "what can I do for you?"

Brightly, I answered, "I don't mean to sound egotistical, but it's more a matter of what *I* can do for *you*, Glenn." There was nothing egotistical about the message I had come to deliver, but the word seemed to pop from my lips. As soon as I'd said it, I understood why—Lance Caldwell had always struck me as the personification of an inflated ego. In all fairness, his musical talents were enormous, but so was his opinion of himself. This, coupled with his artistic leanings, gave him the air of the quintessential prima donna.

"Well, now," said Glenn, "isn't *that* enticing? So tell me, Claire, what can you do for me?" He chortled.

"It's the summer theater program, the workshop."

"Ahhh." His brows arched with interest.

"In a nutshell, Glenn, I'd like to do it. If you still have interest in running the program, I'll commit to it."

"Still have *interest*?" he asked, as if I were nuts. "Certainly, Claire. The more we can offer, the better; the more publicity, the better. I've wanted the workshop all along, but I'm amazed that you're willing to put in the extra effort."

"It'll be worth it," I said objectively. "I don't need to remind you, we're losing Tanner. He'll be hard to replace, but there's other talent in the pipeline. I'm especially impressed with Thad Quatrain, who's finishing his first year. He told me he'd attend the workshop if we held it, and that's what swayed me."

Glenn nodded. "You think he's the real deal?"

"He might be. And if he is, he'll be around for a while."

Slyly, Glenn said, "I like your thinking, Claire—so calculating, unflinching, and premeditated."

I laughed, asking, "That's a bit over the top, isn't it? You make it sound as if I *killed* someone." Then my smile fell. The last thing I needed just then was to plant *that* idea in anyone's head. I coughed, adding, "So if you want the program, you've got it."

"I want it. In fact, I've been planning on it. I asked Tide to draw up the contract rider this morning. You can sign on your way out if you like."

"I should have known—one step ahead of me." I rose.

The billionaire broke into a pouty frown. "Can't you stay?"

"For a few minutes, I suppose." I sat again.

Glenn smiled with satisfaction. "We need your advice." He turned to the composer. "Don't we, Lance?"

As if waking from a nap, Lance replied, "Sure, Glenn, sure. If you say so."

"I do." Glenn turned to me again. "When Lance wrote the incidental music for your production of *Laura* last fall, everyone agreed that it was a spectacular contribution to the overall effort."

Without hesitation, I concurred, "Lance's original score *made* that show. He perfectly captured both the mood of the script and the style of the production. Lance's music was every bit the equal of David Raksin's famed movie score. In fact, better." My words were true enough, but intentionally inflated for the sake of the composer's self-image. No doubt about it—Lance Caldwell thrived on adulation, and I hoped to cajole him into lending his talents to future productions.

"You're *far* too generous," he told me, lapping it up.

"Not at all, Lance dear." Turning to Glenn, I asked, "So what's the, uh . . . problem?"

"Let me back up," explained Glenn. "When your production of *Laura* opened, inaugurating both the DAC theater program and the theater building itself, you invited numerous theatrical luminaries to the gala, including, of course, Spencer Wallace. And what a launch it was! We garnered national press."

"Yes, Glenn." His unquenchable appetite for publicity went beyond boring.

"At the reception following the performance, Wallace met Lance, and—"

The composer picked up the story, telling me, "And Wallace took me aside to say that he'd absolutely *adored* my score—he *loved* the incidental music, which, in his words, 'made the show.'"

Though I myself had spoken the same words only moments earlier, I was galled to hear it attributed to Spencer and repeated by Lance. "Yes?" I asked patiently. Lance was oblivious to the steely edge my tone had taken on.

"Well," he continued, enjoying his own story with breathless excitement, "Wallace and I chatted for some time that night, and after a drink or two, he casually mentioned that I might compose the score for one of his future film projects. Needless to say, this struck me as a marvelous suggestion—to enhance the prestige of the school, I mean." Lance smiled at Glenn.

Glenn returned his smile.

"So when I got wind of *Photo Flash,* I thought it would make an excellent vehicle for an original score. I phoned Wallace's office, inquiring if I might have a look at the screenplay. I wanted to study it before I began toying with a few thematic sketches. The secretary I spoke to didn't know *anything,* but when she checked and found out 'who I was,' she sent the script *immediately."*

I nodded knowingly. "I'm sure." Deciding to accommodate him with another stroke, I added, "I'll bet she's *still* bragging up a storm in the steno pool, telling about the day when Lance Caldwell phoned."

"Perhaps," he agreed. "So I studied the script, and I liked it—

solid plotting, good dramatic tension—but I saw at once that the film could be immeasurably improved by a first-class score. And I wrote one."

"Hm." I thought for a moment. "Really? I hadn't heard anything about that. Neither Spencer nor Tanner ever mentioned that you were doing the music."

Glenn told me, "That's where this story gets sticky."

"Oh?"

Lance continued, "I wrapped up my work about a month ago. The score requires full orchestration, naturally—it's lush, it's *me*—and that gets pricey. So for presentation purposes, I recorded a synthesized version of the music, burnt it onto a CD, and sent it to Wallace along with the written score."

This struck me as standard procedure. "It sounds as if the project is moving right along."

"Well, uh . . . *no,* it isn't."

Glenn leaned toward me, propping his elbows on the granite desk. Speaking softly, as if imparting something indelicate, he explained, "The project isn't moving along, at least with regard to Lance's score, because Wallace, in a word, hated it."

"Ah," I said flatly. "I see."

"Can you imagine?" Lance was now huffy. "I poured my musical heart and soul into that score, only to have some Hollywood philistine tell me, 'It's not right for my script. I had something altogether different in mind.' "

In recent days, I'd heard many unflattering assertions regarding Spencer Wallace's character, but I'd never heard anyone describe him as less than a genius when it came to the art and craft of filmmaking. If Spencer felt Lance's score was wrong for his script, it had surely missed by a mile. Softening this conclusion, I told Lance, "In the artistic realm, judgments can sometimes be highly subjective."

"But to reject it *out of hand,*" the composer blustered. "And then, to add insult to injury, he didn't even offer a kill fee, while informing me that someone else had been hired—'for the job,' as he so crassly put it." Harrumph.

"It was unconscionable," agreed Glenn.

"Hold on a minute." I could expect the prissy attitude from Lance, but not from Glenn, who was, first and foremost, a consummate businessman. I asked, "Did Lance have a contract with Spencer?"

"Well, no . . ."

Lance said, "It had been a gentleman's agreement."

From what I'd heard, this gentleman's agreement struck me as little more than cocktail chat.

"Yes," Lance conceded, "I wrote the score 'on spec,' so to speak, but given our mutual stature, it would have seemed almost *boorish* to sully our agreement with ironclad clauses and such."

To my way of thinking, there had been no agreement at all.

"It's not the *money,*" Lance insisted, "or the loss of valuable creative time. I'm not driven by such considerations. However, the affront to my talents and the smirch on my reputation are insufferable. Far worse"—Lance turned to Glenn—"rejecting the score belittles Desert Arts College and everything our founder has struggled to establish here."

I doubted if anyone even knew about the rejected score; this was the first *I'd* heard of it. So how could the misunderstanding possibly be construed as an insult to the school?

But Glenn was more than eager to buy into Lance's indignation. "I *never* liked him," he said through a disgusted shudder. "As far as I'm concerned, Wallace got what he deserved."

"Stop that." I was getting angry.

"Even after *I*—D. Glenn Yeats—phoned Wallace *personally* to ask him to reconsider, he flat-out refused. Now, I ask you—is that the sort of treatment a man in my position deserves? Don't I deserve greater respect than that?"

Oh, Lord. We'd previously battled over the semantics of *respect.* In Glenn's lexicon, it was synonymous with *ass kissing.*

Glenn's rant continued, *"I'd* read the script; Lance showed it to me. *I'd* heard the music; Lance played it for me. Why, the score was fine, just fine."

"It was *perfect,"* added Lance, tossing both arms.

"Perfect," echoed Glenn, rising from behind his desk.

There was no point in arguing the aesthetic merits of music I'd never heard, so I calmly voiced a practical and evident observation: "These artistic disagreements are history now. Spencer is gone. There's nothing to be done about it."

"But there *is,"* said Glenn, wide-eyed, swooping around from his desk to sit next to me on the sofa.

Uh-oh. "Glenn, dear, whatever are you talking about?"

"Gabe Arlington, the director."

"Don't you see, Claire?" asked Lance, leaning forward from his sofa. I'd have sworn the tight neck of his sweater stretched a foot. "With Wallace out of the way, we've got a second shot with Arlington." His eyes flashed, intense and catlike.

"I don't know . . . ," I said warily. "You probably shouldn't try—"

"Claire," said Glenn, leaning close, *"you* could approach him. You and Arlington seemed to hit it off at your place on Saturday. And you have ready access to him through Tanner." With a happy laugh, he asked, "Why not?"

I could think of several reasons, not the least of which was my complete lack of interest in Glenn and Lance's petty crusade. They were out of their element, attempting to influence artistic decisions in a medium they knew nothing about. For that matter, I myself knew zilch about filmmaking, and I wasn't about to embarrass myself by exposing my ignorance to Gabe Arlington while displaying the gall to meddle in his production.

I knew, however, that Glenn was beyond reasoning at the moment; he would be deaf to my protests.

So I told him vaguely, "I'll see what I can do."

The profuse, giddy thanks lavished on me by both Glenn and Lance was embarrassing—as well as unwarranted—so I extricated myself from their grateful hugs, offered a round of farewells, and escaped to the outer office.

True to Glenn's word, Tide awaited me with a contract for my summer services, offering a pen. There was no point in reading it; coming from Glenn, the terms of the agreement had surely been subjected to microscopic scrutiny by a roomful of lawyers, and there was never any question of Glenn's generosity to me. So I signed, told Tide good-bye, and left the presidential suite.

Walking the circular hall toward my own modest office, I began to mentally reconstruct the list of guests who had attended Saturday's party. Among them, of course, were Glenn Yeats and Lance Caldwell.

I now understood why they had both been in such ill humor that night.

What's more, I now was aware that they had both read Spencer's script.

Reconstructing my guest list took longer than I'd planned. During the final production weeks of *Traders,* I'd had a lot on my mind, and the mess in my office had gotten out of hand. So I now had to dig through the piles on my desk, as well as my files, to find the names of everyone I'd invited to Saturday's party. I put my own name at the top, as host, then listed the two guests of honor, Spencer Wallace and Tanner Griffin. Moving on to the other attendees, I first listed Lance Caldwell and Glenn Yeats. The names went on and on. My earlier estimate had been correct—about fifty guests. I knew, however, that the list was incomplete; there had been a number of people at the party whom I hadn't recognized.

Leaving my office, I needed to rush to make it back to my house by three o'clock, the hour at which Grant Knoll and his brother, Larry, had planned to meet there for some "little business matter." While driving through the flat, straight back roads of Rancho Mirage, I wondered what possible bit of business could bring the gay real-estate broker and the murder-minded detective together on a Monday afternoon. Their lives seemed to revolve in two distinct orbits.

When I turned onto my street, I saw that Grant was already waiting for me, parked at the curb in his hefty white Mercedes. What's more, he had a passenger with him, a woman. As I pulled into my driveway and drove into the garage, they got out of the car, and I recognized the woman as Brandi Bjerregaard, Grant's fellow broker and developer from Los Angeles.

"Sorry I'm late," I told them, greeting them in front of the house.

"No problem," said Grant. "Larry isn't here yet, and we're in no hurry." Tucked under the arm of my friend's nubby-silk sport coat was a zippered leather-bound folder.

Brandi said, "Thank you again, Claire, for including me at Saturday's party. What a bash." She breathed her languid laugh, looking pretty but bored—or disconnected—like an urban fish out of water.

"Any friend of Grant's is a friend of mine." I wasn't concentrating on my insipid phraseology; I was thinking about Brandi's odd behavior on Saturday evening. She, like so many others present, had turned peevish upon the moment of encountering Spencer Wallace.

The afternoon was getting hot. I suggested, "Let's go indoors. I'll get us something to drink." And I took them into the house.

Setting my keys, wallet, and guest list on the pass-through bar, I offered, "I could open a bottle of wine."

"Sure, doll, that sounds great." Grant had set his leather portfolio on the boomerang-shaped coffee table and drifted to the patio doors with Brandi.

She asked him, "And that's where it happened?"

"Yup," he answered, almost bragging, "the scene of the crime."

Having stepped into the kitchen, I called to Brandi, "Too bad you had to leave the party so early. You missed Grant's heroics."

"That *would* have been worth seeing." She lolled her head back again and emitted her barely audible laugh. A smart little purse dangled on a gold chain from her elbow.

Entering the living room with a bottle of chardonnay and a

corkscrew, I asked Grant, "Palatable?" He was a wine snob second to none.

"Very." He raised an approving brow. "Let me open it for you."

Handing him the bottle and the opener, I said, "I'll get the glasses."

"*I'll* help," Brandi insisted. "You relax, Claire." She stepped into the kitchen.

Grant and I sat on the cushioned bench. He got to work, squeaking the cork from the neck of the bottle, telling me, "I've got the most *delicious* dirt."

"Really? Is that the purpose of this visit?"

He frowned. "Actually, no. That's *too* dreary to discuss. Besides, you'll hear it soon enough, once Larry arrives." He popped the cork out of the bottle, then sniffed it.

Very well, I thought, the dreary part could wait. "So what's the dirt?"

"*Well,*" he began, setting the bottle on the coffee table, "you'll never—"

"Claire?" called Brandi from the kitchen. "I can't seem to find the wineglasses. Which cupboard?"

"Sorry, Brandi. I should have mentioned—they're underneath, next to the dishwasher." No doubt about it, my kitchen was still in greater disarray than my office. I reasoned that because everything in the kitchen was behind closed doors, it didn't warrant fretting over.

"*Well,*" Grant began again, "you'll never believe what *I've* just learned about the widow Wallace." He paused enticingly.

From his tone of voice, and from his promise of dirt, I had a hunch where his story was headed. Playing dumb, I said, "Poor woman. I know she and Spencer didn't have the happiest marriage, but it must be awful for her now, finding herself suddenly alone."

Grant was fairly bursting to tell his news; he looked as if he might wet his pants. "You *bet* it was an unhappy marriage," he said, fidgeting with the wine cork, "but there was more to the problem than Spencer's wandering eye."

"Hey," said Brandi, entering from the kitchen with four wine-glasses, two in each hand, "this is *my* story." She set the glasses on the table near the bottle, then settled in one of the three-legged chairs. Removing the purse from her arm, she set it on the floor.

Grant began pouring a few fingers of wine for the three of us, telling Brandi, "I acknowledge, sweetest, that you are indeed the source, but you gave me this information on an insider basis, broker to broker. Telling it to Claire, however, constitutes gossip, and I don't think it would be terribly professional of you to spread gossip regarding your own clients." Setting down the bottle, he begged, "Let *me* do it."

Brandi leaned to ask me, "Has he always been so persuasive?"

"Yes, he has." I picked up a glass.

"There, now, all settled," Grant told Brandi. He handed her a glass and picked up one for himself, saying, "Cheers, gang."

We touched glasses, then tasted the wine.

Turning to me, Grant continued with his story. "I've learned some *juicy* details regarding the Wallaces' rocky marriage. This information comes to me from an unimpeachable source, a colleague in the real-estate biz." He turned briefly to give Brandi a big, obvious wink before elaborating, "My friend handles a lot of high-end properties in the Los Angeles area—she's *very* well connected. It happens that she was a passing acquaintance of Spencer Wallace, and she knows Rebecca quite well. In fact, my friend brokered the deal when the Wallaces bought the house in Brentwood. So she also knows the lawyer, Bryce Ballantyne, because he handled the closing. Well! Here's the dirt: Rebecca and Bryce have had

more than just a 'professional' relationship for some time now."
Grant beamed.

"Do tell." I had deduced as much that very morning, but it was
intriguing to hear Grant's gossip, which seemed to confirm the
conclusion I'd already reached.

"In fact," Grant added, "they're practically *living* together."

"My, my, my," I mused. I might have added that I'd already seen
Rebecca and Bryce sharing a bathrobe, but I didn't want to spoil
Grant's fun in delivering the unsavory news.

Grant set down his glass. "So Spencer wasn't *entirely* responsible
for the loveless marriage with Rebecca—or their separate lives."

I sighed. "Ah, what tangled webs the wealthy weave."

From the side of his mouth, Grant told Brandi, "Say *that* five
times fast."

"You're right, Grant." I tweaked his cheek. "That *was* delicious
dirt."

"I thought milady would like it."

"Like it? I love it." Leaning past Grant, I said, "Thank *you*, too,
Brandi. I had a hunch there was something going on between
Rebecca and Bryce."

"So," Grant asked me, "you know what this means?" When I
failed to respond quickly enough, he said, "I'll give you a clue:
motivation."

"Ahhh." I swirled my wine. "The wealthy widow had a possible
motive for wanting her husband dead—that much was clear from
the get-go. But now we know that the widow had a lover, so he
also had a motive."

Brandi leaned into the conversation. "A *double* motive, if you
think about it. First, the money. And second, Spencer's death has
freed Rebecca to marry someone else."

Grant amplified, "Namely, Brycey-boy."

With finger to chin, I told Grant, "I like the way you think. When did you get so devious?"

"*Moi?* I'm not devious—merely suspicious. And I learned that from *you.*"

"Perhaps you did." With a pensive laugh, I rose from the bench, stepped to the patio doors, and gazed out upon the pool for a moment. Then I returned to the coffee table. "Grant, now that you've tattled on Bryce and Rebecca, are you aware that Bryce himself did some tattling yesterday?" I raised a brow.

Grant looked confused. "Bryce tattled? On Rebecca?"

"No, love. On you."

With mock shock, Grant sat ramrod stiff. "Why, that snip! He *swore* he'd never kiss and tell." Then, with his features twisted in thought, Grant allowed, "He's all right, I guess, but not my type. I barely know the man. Other than our *very* brief encounter here yesterday, I've never even met him." Then, as an afterthought, Grant asked, "Just what *did* he tell you?"

"Nothing to do with romantic interests—his *or* yours." I cleared my throat. "No, when he realized that you were Larry's brother, he connected the names and recalled that you and Spencer Wallace had been working on a real-estate deal—a mountainside golf-course development?"

"Oh." Grant's shoulders slumped. "That."

"Yes, that. The way Bryce tells it, Spencer pulled out at the wrong moment. Word spread, other investors fled, and *you* took a bath."

Grant took a sip of wine, swallowed, and looked at me over the rim of his glass. "That would be the gist of it, correct."

"Actually, Claire"—Brandi leaned forward in her chair and set her wine on the table, placing both hands on her knees—"Grant wasn't the only one to get stung. The golf-course development was mine. *I'm* the one who put together the consortium, so *I'm* the one who looked like an idiot in the eyes of other investors. On top of which, I lost a bundle."

My eyes slid to Grant. "How much did *you* lose?"

"Well"—he tossed a shoulder—"despite what Bryce told you, I wouldn't quite call it a 'bath.' That has such a pejorative ring of overstatement. I'm surprised; lawyers are usually more precise. Yes, the deal fell through with Wallace, but I've chalked it off as a . . . a mere mixup." He sipped more wine.

I persisted, "How *much* of a mixup?"

He paused to calculate. "About a half. Well, a little over half."

"Half?" I crossed my arms. "Half *what?*"

Setting his glass on the table, he mumbled, "Half a million."

My eyes bugged. "Good Lord, Grant. I'm impressed. I didn't know you had a half million to *lose.*"

He stood, telling me, "When it comes to investments in California real estate, the numbers do sound inflated—like Monopoly money—but that's the name of the game here, and I play it quite well. The Coachella Valley is a hotbed of development; I'll recoup my losses on the next deal. Win some, lose some. I happened to *lose* on this particular venture."

"Because of Spencer Wallace."

Grant took a measure of solace in my statement. "That's right. *Wallace* blew the deal. He was a nervous Nellie about the risks, pulled out at the wrong time, and was inept in the way he handled it. The result was, I lost a bundle."

"So did I," seconded Brandi. "And so did several others."

"Hmm." I paced toward the bar, set down my glass, and turned to ask both of them, "So how do you feel about Spencer's death?"

With a tsk, Brandi said, "Need you ask?"

I must have looked dismayed.

Grant asked me, "How would *you* feel? Look, murder is inexcusable, period. I'm sorry he was poisoned, I'm sorry he drowned—or *however* it happened. But am I sorry he's gone?" With a sharp nod, he answered, "Not one bit."

An awkward silence fell over us. Noticing that Grant's glass was empty, I offered, "Uh, more wine?"

"No, thanks. That's enough." Having vented his bitterness, he was chipper again. Stooping to lift his glass from the coffee table, he said, "I'll just give this a rinse." And he carried the glass to the kitchen.

Brandi replenished her glass from the bottle on the table. She called after Grant, "Considering how you felt about Wallace, it was good of you to try to save him Saturday night."

Grant's voice carried over the sound of running water. "I didn't know who it *was* down there. I couldn't get a good look at him till I had him out of the water. Had I known, I wouldn't have been so quick to ruin my clothes."

I assured him, "You did the right thing."

The doorbell chimed. Recognizing the tune, Brandi looked up from her wine. Lamely, I explained to her, "The previous owners . . ." Stepping toward the door, I told Grant, "That must be your brother."

Appearing in the kitchen doorway, Grant intoned, "The law never rests."

I opened the front door. "Hello, Larry." Before he could speak, I asked, "Is it true you never rest?"

"Huh?"

With a laugh, I told him, "Do come in. Grant's here; so is his friend Brandi."

"Yes, I saw the car," he said, still sounding disoriented by my queer greeting.

"Hello, Detective," said Brandi, rising briefly.

"Miss Bjerregaard," he acknowledged her, and she sat again.

"Hey, bro," said Grant, stepping forward. "How's it going?"

"Fine, Grant, fine." Larry turned to me. "How about you, Claire?"

I shrugged. "Just trying to keep one step ahead of the law." Stepping to the bar, I retrieved the guest list I had reconstructed for him.

Grant took his brother aside, telling him facetiously (I think), "Arrest her, Larry. Lock 'er up."

Ominously, Larry quipped, "All in due time . . ."

I shot them both a dirty look. "I'm not too sure I like the sound of that." Then I smiled. "Here's the list I promised you, Larry. Hope it helps, but my instincts tell me it will only muddy the waters."

He took the list, glanced over it, and slipped it into a pocket. "The more information, the better. I appreciate it."

I suggested, "Do sit down. Can I pour you some wine? Just opened it; there's an extra glass waiting."

He crossed to the bench and sat where Grant had been sitting, telling me, "Thanks, but I'm on duty. I don't need anything."

"How about some iced tea? Made some this morning."

"Sure. That'd be great." He took a pen and notebook from inside his suit jacket and set them on the coffee table near Grant's zippered portfolio.

"Back in a flash," I told them, moving to the kitchen to get the tea.

A minute or two later, I returned with a small tray bearing the glass of tea, a saucer of lemons, and a sugar bowl. Grant was now seated on the bench with Larry; Brandi still sat in the nearby chair. All three leaned toward the coffee table, huddled over Grant's portfolio, which had been zipped open to disgorge a sheaf of papers. Brandi was saying, "It's only pennies on the dollar, but at least it's something. It's the best I could do."

Grant sighed. "Sorry, Larry."

The detective also sighed. "It's not a total loss—but almost."

Their somber tone suggested that this "little business matter" wasn't so minor. And with Brandi involved, I had a sudden insight regarding what had happened. "Oh, no," I said, setting my tray on the table. "Don't tell me you got roped into that golf-course deal too, Larry."

He looked up at me, chagrined. "My gut told me this deal was too good to be true. At the same time, it seemed too good to pass up." His mouth sounded dry. He reached for the tall glass of iced tea and took a sip.

I now understood why Larry had reacted so oddly—pinched brow and forced smile—when Bryce Ballantyne had first mentioned the deal on Sunday afternoon.

Sounding defensive, Grant explained, "I didn't pressure him, Claire. Honest. I happened to tell Larry about the prospects for the development, and I guess I was overly excited. I would never steer my own *brother* wrong, but he wanted in."

"Grant warned me of the risks," Larry admitted. He lifted the sugar bowl's lid, glanced inside, then closed it again, looking forlorn.

I was certain that Larry—a cop with a family, a dog, and a station wagon—did not have his brother's financial resources, so I hoped he had not taken similarly high risks. I ventured to ask, "How bad was it, Larry?"

Making light of his losses, he answered, "Nowhere near as bad as it was for Grant. I don't have that kind of money."

Grant told me quietly, "He used part of his kids' college funds."

"Grant, don't," said Larry.

"I'll help you out. It's still a few years off. We'll make it happen."

"Let's just drop it, okay?"

Brandi tried to lighten the conversation. "At least we're all getting *something* back. There's a conservancy dedicated to the preservation of bighorn sheep. This group presented our greatest obstacle to development all along, so now that the golf course is dead, our consortium is selling the tract of mountainside land to the sheep huggers."

"Pennies on the dollar," Grant repeated wistfully.

"Take it or leave it." Brandi nudged a pile of papers in his direction.

Grant uncapped an exquisite fountain pen and scrawled his signature on several flagged documents. Then he turned to Larry, offering the pen. "Bro?"

"Sure," Larry answered without enthusiasm. He silently added his signature to the papers.

As they were finishing, I extended feeble sympathies for everyone's misfortune (everyone's but the sheep's, that is). My comments were accepted gratefully, and I continued to mouth hackneyed assurances that clouds would part and tides would turn. It didn't matter what I said. I simply felt the need to keep talking, hoping the noise would mask a horrifying notion that had popped into my mind, demanding consideration: Larry Knoll, detective in charge of the investigation, had lost a nest egg because of Spencer Wallace and could therefore have nurtured the most base of motives for the victim's extinction, spite.

I grasped for any topic that would distance my mind from this idea, but it was Grant who finally shifted the conversation to safer ground. "Oh!" he said to his brother, returning his pen to his pocket. "Brandi and I have reason to believe that Becky-baby and Brycey-boy are an 'item,' if you catch my drift."

"Yeah, I sorta got that impression myself."

Brandi was collecting the signed papers and returning them to the portfolio. "Do you think it has a bearing on the case?"

"Maybe." Larry nodded. "But first things first."

I asked, "Meaning . . . ?"

"Meaning, the darkroom. We're waiting for the results of tests to determine if any of Wallace's photo chemicals had been tainted. But *my* guess is that the killer wouldn't be clumsy enough to leave evidence of cadmium there in the darkroom." Larry picked up his glass of iced tea, then set it down again without drinking.

I asked, "How long will the tests take?"

"Maybe a few days. But don't forget—we've already made an important discovery that suggests we're on the right track. The ventilation system wasn't working, and it may have been tampered with."

"You have *got* to be kidding," said Grant. "Why, that's just like the screenplay—the faulty vent system increased the toxicity of the fumes in the darkroom."

"Correct." Larry touched his glass again, then withdrew his hand.

"Uh, Larry," I said. "Don't you like it—the tea?"

"It's fine, Claire. Great, thanks." He hesitated before telling me, "But I could use some sugar, and there isn't any." He removed the lid from the sugar bowl and showed me that it was empty.

"Oh, Larry, I'm sorry." I stepped forward, took the sugar bowl from him, and moved toward the kitchen.

Grant skittered after me. "Stay put, milady. I'll take care of it. My pleasure to serve." He took the sugar bowl from my hands; then, with a flourish and a bow, he charged off to the kitchen.

Brandi told Larry, "It sounds as if everything is starting to line up."

I added, "Exactly as detailed in Spencer's own script."

"Uh-huh," agreed Larry. "But I don't think Wallace meant to send us a 'message from the grave,' so to speak. This has none of the earmarks of suicide—no note, no motive, no history of depression."

I averred, "Which leaves under suspicion anyone who'd read the script."

Larry tapped his notebook. "Precisely. So the next step—"

"Aowww? Hwat's this?"

Larry, Brandi, and I exchanged a quizzical glance. I called to Grant in the kitchen, "Finding everything?"

"I'll say!" Grant returned to the living room. In one arm, he cradled my open kitchen canister of sugar. With his other hand, he held the top of a brown bottle he had apparently pulled from the canister. It was flask-shaped, with a typewritten label and a black screw top, the generic sort of bottle that a druggist might use for cough syrup. I noted at once that it was small enough to be concealed in a pocket or handbag. Grant repeated, "Hwat's this?"

Larry, Brandi, and I had already rushed to surround him. Peering close at the label, I sputtered, "I don't . . . I can't believe . . . How could it possibly . . . ?"

With hand to chin, Larry nodded. "Cadmium chloride."

"Hidden in milady's sugar canister." Grant arched his brows.

Larry said, "Don't touch it, Grant."

His brother quipped, "What am I supposed to do—levitate it in midair?"

"I mean, have you handled the bottle?"

"Just the cap."

Larry asked me, "Got a plastic bag?"

"Sure, Larry." I dashed into the kitchen for a moment and got one.

When I returned, Larry had his notebook open and was asking Grant, "This is how you found it, buried in the sugar?"

Grant nodded. "Just below the surface."

Writing in the notebook, Larry mumbled, "Not very subtle . . . unless . . ." He closed the notebook and pocketed it.

"Here, Larry." I handed him the plastic bag.

"Perfect." Using the bag as a mitt, he took the bottle from Grant, then turned the bag inside out, containing the bottle. Tying the neck of the bag, he said, "I want to get this down to the lab right away. First, we'll verify if it actually contains cadmium chloride, not just, say . . . baby powder . . ."

"Or sugar," Grant suggested, licking his fingertips.

Larry continued, "And second—"

I interjected, "Fingerprints?"

"Right. Let's see if someone got sloppy and left us a clue."

"Larry"—I hesitated—"I know this sounds lame, but I'm really getting worried. I feel I've been . . . well, 'framed.' "

The detective acknowledged, "Could be a setup."

"Either that," joshed Grant, "or I've stumbled upon milady's stash."

"That's not *funny*," I said with a foot stomp.

"Hold on," said Larry. His tone was calm and sensible. "Time out. Let me take this over to forensics, and we'll see what we've got." He began moving to the front door.

I followed, then halted, snapping my fingers. "Larry."

Halting, he turned to me. "Yes?"

"I'm not naive, Larry. I understand how incriminating this appears for me. Jeez, you might as well have found a bloody dagger in my trash. I also understand that you would fully expect me to deny any knowledge of where it came from. Before, I was merely mystified by the circumstances surrounding Spencer's death. Now, I'm feeling threatened, which makes me not only frightened—but angry."

Grant prodded, "You go, girl."

Ignoring him, I continued, "So it seems to me that the simplest, most direct means of exonerating *myself* is to name the *real* killer."

"Logical enough," Larry agreed. "So tell me, Claire: Who did it?"

"I don't know—*yet*—but I damn well intend to find out." Having vented my ire, I felt more levelheaded, and a fresh thought occurred to me. My tone changed abruptly as I asked, pleasant as pie, "Do you happen to have plans this evening?"

Larry shrugged. "What'd you have in mind?"

I tried not to sound *too* scheming as I told him, "A party. A little cocktail reception. An intimate gathering of friends."

"Oh, goody," said Grant, "a party. On a Monday evening, no less. My calendar's wide open, doll."

"Wonderful"—I tweaked his ear—"because you're most definitely invited, Grant. You too, Brandi. Shall we say six-thirty?"

"Fine with me," said Grant.

Brandi nodded her acceptance, returned to the chair where she'd been sitting, and picked up her purse from the floor.

"Me, too," said Larry, stepping to the door and opening it. "I'm curious to see where you'll take this. Until then, if you'll excuse me . . ." And he walked outside.

"We ought to run as well," said Grant, leading Brandi to the door. Handing me the sugar canister, he leaned to peck my cheek. "Thanks for the chardonnay—enjoyed it. See you tonight, love."

"Good-bye, Claire," said Brandi. "We'll be back at six-thirty." She stepped outside with Grant.

I called after everyone, "Don't be late." My wry delivery had an ominous ring that sounded more comical than foreboding.

Closing the door, I paused in thought, planning the evening that lay ahead.

Then I realized that I was still holding the sugar canister. Feeling foolish, I carried it to the bar and set it down near the phone. Thumbing through the little black book I kept there, I found the number of Coachella Catering, lifted the receiver, and dialed.

When a man answered, I said, "Good afternoon. This is Claire Gray in Rancho Mirage. Ah, Thierry, it *is* you; I thought so. Yes, that's right, it was dreadfully unfortunate, thank you. The reason I'm calling, Thierry—I've decided to throw another little get-together this evening. I know it's short notice, but I'll need help with the bar and serving appetizers."

He asked for a few details, and I explained, "That's right, just drinks and hors d'oeuvres, starting at six-thirty. Some ten or twelve of us, no more. What's that? No, Thierry, it's not another going-away party."

I paused, then added, "This will be more of a . . . a cat-and-mouse party."

PART THREE

photo finish

Sometime after six, I sat at the dressing table in my bedroom, primping for an impromptu cocktail party, wondering about the uncertain evening that awaited me and my guests. Whatever its outcome, the night was sure to bring developments of consequence, so I had no difficulty picking an outfit for the occasion. Red, some might say, was too festive a choice for a night that would focus on solving a murder. But red carries overtones beyond those of mirth and celebration. Red is primal. It's commanding and sensual. It's in-your-face. I hardly need add, red is evocative of blood, which itself is metaphoric for death as well as life.

It would be disingenuous of me to claim that the silky scarlet blouse I wore that night was meant to convey anything more symbolic than my affection for the color. If, however, my guests chose to interpret it as an assertion of authority in my own home, I would not quibble, for my purpose that evening was not to play the congenial hostess. I intended, rather, to unmask a killer.

Standing, I checked myself in the mirror. The red blouse draped smartly over plain black slacks. The only adornment it needed was a simple gold chain. Opening a drawer to find the necklace, I spotted Tanner's wristwatch, a dressy one he rarely wore; he'd missed it while packing his other things. I took it out and placed it on the dresser, where he would be sure to spot it later. He'd had a busy day, meeting the movers at his apartment and tidying up some loose ends on campus, so he would arrive at my house like any other guest this evening. Unlike the others, he would spend the night here—his last with me.

I was tempted to get soppy, to lift the watch reverently and slip it around my wrist, as if this action would somehow bind us, attach us, secure us with a slim strap of crocodile hide, but I reminded myself that Tanner, like every other visitor who was soon to arrive, was possibly responsible for the mystery I sought to solve. The likelihood of Tanner's guilt struck me as infinitely remote, but still, I needed to remain objective because, objectively speaking, my own innocence was questionable.

Congenial hostess, indeed. I held *all* of my guests under varying degrees of suspicion that evening. And these suspicions, I now realized, were focused on couples—or more precisely, "pairs"—which made it all the more difficult to sort through the motives and the likelihood of guilt.

Rebecca Wallace and Bryce Ballantyne, for instance, were a couple. Semisecret lovers, they had both taken satisfaction from the abrupt end to Rebecca's unhappy marriage to the powerful producer. Rebecca was now a wealthy, independent woman, and Bryce was now free to watch movies with her all morning, lounging in a shared bathrobe while feeding her hot popcorn. They had both read Spencer Wallace's screenplay, which was a virtual guidebook to his own demise.

Another pair, not a couple, motivated not by avarice or romantic passion, but by spite, was Glenn Yeats and Lance Caldwell. Glenn's bruised ego, combined with Lance's artistic pique, could have been sufficient to impel deadly payback for a rejected movie score. I had previously entertained notions that Glenn's self-conceit cloaked a sinister edge, only to be proven wrong. So my suspicion now gravitated toward Maestro Caldwell, whose vengeful instincts may have been bolstered by Glenn's resentment. Both men had read the screenplay.

Base revenge provided a feasible motive for another pair who'd been wronged by Spencer. Grant Knoll and Brandi Bjerregaard had lost a great deal of money—and a great deal of face, professionally—when Spencer had turned their high-stakes golf-course project into a worthless sheep pasture. Grant had become my closest friend, so I was loath to consider him a killer. I had no reason to extend my kindhearted thinking to Brandi, however. To the best of my knowledge, she hadn't read the script, but Grant had, and he may have unwittingly told her all she'd needed to know.

Similarly, Grant was half of another motivated pair, which consisted of him and his brother, Detective Larry Knoll. The circumstances were identical to those with Brandi—financial loss—but I was terrified by the thought that Larry could conceivably be hunting for a suspect to cover his own crime.

Equally unsettling was another pair with a shared motivation—Gabe Arlington and Tanner Griffin. Both the washed-up director and the rising-star actor had movie careers riding upon the success of *Photo Flash*. Both Gabe and Tanner were keenly knowledgeable of the screenplay. After Spencer's death, both had spoken matter-of-factly of the publicity boon that the film would reap from the tragedy.

Even more disturbing was Rebecca Wallace's revelation that her husband had voiced an aggressive sexual interest in Tanner. Whether Tanner had been aware of this, I simply didn't know, and I didn't even want to consider whether Spencer's lechery could have driven my young lover to an impassioned crime. It may have been wishful, defensive thinking, but my suspicions of the movie pair—Tanner and Gabe—fell squarely on Gabe.

Finally, there was Kiki. Not a couple, not a pair, she and she alone represented the most strongly motivated of those who now found a silver lining in Spencer Wallace's untimely death— untimely, that is, except in the eyes of Kiki, who'd faced a deadline for salvaging her career, her reputation, and her life in academic theater, the only life she'd ever known or cared about.

On the one hand, I was mortified that she had faced this dilemma as the result of Spencer's scheming with regard to *me*. The whole plan, frankly, struck me as ridiculous, but Spencer had taken it seriously, and so had Kiki. So I felt a measure of guilt. On the other hand, I felt a measure of anger because Kiki had refused to divulge to Larry's investigation this important insight into Spencer's modus operandi. I was all the more irked because Kiki had secured my collusion in this secrecy by invoking our past friendship.

Tonight would put that friendship to the test. Tonight would also test my sense of ethics. Tonight I would have to ask myself, When does a promise "not count"?

It was nearly time. Within minutes, my crowd of guests would arrive. I'd managed to reach everyone that afternoon, and when I'd explained my purpose, no one had dared decline to attend. At that moment, Kiki, Rebecca, Bryce, Glenn, Lance, Grant, Brandi, Gabe, Tanner, and Detective Larry Knoll were on their way to my home for an evening of iffy fun and ructious games, not to mention cocktails.

Music—bouncy, upbeat party music—now drifted through the hallway from the living room. Thierry had arrived earlier from Coachella Catering, before I had retreated to the bedroom to don my hostess garb. Still shaken by the outcome of Saturday's party, he wanted to be on hand for my follow-up soiree to ensure that everything would go smoothly. He had begun setting up in the kitchen and would tend to duties there; a server was to join him, passing appetizers and tending bar. Hearing the music, I surmised that Thierry's help had arrived.

I paused for a final spiff in the mirror, then left the bedroom, following the music through the short hall.

Emerging into the living room, I saw that all was ready. The bar had been set up, a few candles had been lit, and nibbles had been set about. Even the view from the terrace doors had cooperated. The sky glowed orange near the horizon; the day had begun its slow slide toward a perfect desert evening. Ripples of blue light from the swimming pool were reflected from the underside of a surrounding canopy of palms.

"Good evening, Miss Gray. My, what a beautiful blouse."

My gaze returned from the pool to the living room. Erin had entered from the kitchen, wearing the same black, formal maid's uniform she'd worn on Saturday night. Moving to the coffee table, she set down a tray of small plates and napkins.

I adjusted my necklace. "Thank you, Erin. Nice to see you again." In truth, I hadn't been expecting her, not after she'd seen fit to tell Larry about my threat after Saturday's party. Perhaps Thierry hadn't heard this detail when he'd scheduled her for tonight. I asked pleasantly, "Everything under control?"

"Yes, Miss Gray, all set. The hors d'oeuvres are still in the kitchen; I'll pass them when your guests arrive."

"Sounds reasonable. Very good."

Erin gestured toward the bar. "Can I get you something while you're waiting?"

I checked my watch. "Still a bit early, thanks." Then I reconsidered. "Well, just a taste of wine, please."

"Yes, ma'am." She stepped to the bar.

Moving to the fireplace, I realigned a few of the framed photos that hung there—just so—and noticed Erin behind me, reflected in the glass, pouring my wine. Picking up the Cabo photo, I studied it for a moment before positioning it on the mantel. It caught the image of Erin crossing the room toward me with the wineglass. Presuming herself unseen by me, she grooved to the music while walking, almost dancing. Ah, I mused, the carefree days of youth.

When I turned, she instantly switched to a more sedate, decorous gait, completing her cross. "Here you are, Miss Gray." She extended the glass.

"Thank you." Taking the glass, I air-skoaled the girl, then sipped. She remained stationed at my side, watching as I swallowed. "That's all for now," I told her, nodding once with a stiff smile.

"Yes, Miss Gray." She made an awkward stab at a curtsy, then hesitated. "Uh, Miss Gray?"

"Yes, dear?"

"I was sort of surprised when they told me I was working here tonight."

My thoughts exactly. Avoiding the real issue, I told her, "I realize it may seem strange for me to entertain so shortly after Saturday's tragic turn of events, but I—"

"Oh, no, Miss Gray, that's not what I meant. I'd never question your reasons for having the party. I only meant, I'm surprised you'd allow me on the job."

With a chortle, I told her, "After what happened Saturday, I'm surprised you'd take the job." Graciously, I added, "Why wouldn't I want you back?"

"Uh," she said, ambling from the fireplace, toward the bookcase that housed the sound system, "this is sort of awkward." Indicating the stereo, she asked, "May I?" The peppy music was ill suited to the uncomfortable topic she meant to broach.

"Please do." I moved to the leather bench and sat.

She switched off the music, then turned to tell me, "It's not what happened in the pool Saturday. But after."

Reading the evident concern in her voice, I suggested, "Do sit down, Erin. Tell me what's troubling you." I set my wineglass on the coffee table.

She chose the three-legged chair nearest the bench. "Thank you, ma'am."

"You're welcome to call me Claire, you know." I smiled.

"Oh, no, no"—she shook her head vigorously—"that doesn't seem right. You see, Miss Gray, I just wanted to apologize for telling Detective Knoll what you said that night." Needlessly, she clarified, "About wanting to kill Mr. Wallace."

Leaning toward her, I peered into her eyes. "You didn't think I was serious, did you?"

"No. I mean, not when you said it. But then, later, when Mr. Wallace turned up dead, well, it was hard not to wonder. So I told the detective. Now I'm afraid I've gotten you into trouble. I wish I hadn't mentioned it."

With a short breath of laughter, I agreed, "I wish you hadn't also. But you did what you thought was right—can't blame you for that."

She gave me a weak smile. "Thank you, Miss Gray. That means a lot to me. You're the *last* person I'd want to rub the wrong way."

I informed her, "I hardly think you've 'rubbed' me—*either* way."

"It's just that I *respect* you so very highly."

"I keep hearing that." Thinking aloud, I wondered, "Whatever have I done to inspire such awe?"

"Well, your *career,* Miss Gray."

"Erin, sweet thing, I was asking the question rhetorically."

"Oh," she said with a blank look. Then, with sudden enthusiasm, she continued, "It's just that, well, you're the greatest director *alive,* and now you're *here,* at Desert Arts College, and there's no one else on the *planet* who I'd rather study theater from."

Pedantically, I corrected, ". . . from whom I'd rather study theater."

With a bright-eyed, energetic nod, she agreed, "Yeah!"

"A-ha. I thought so. A would-be actress. I might have guessed—that was a *marvelous* stage scream you delivered on Saturday night."

Flattered beyond measure, she flopped a hand to her chest, gushing, "*Thank* you, Miss Gray. I've worked on it. But I know—there's *so* much more to learn. Do you think there might be a chance, any chance at all, that I could enroll in your program at DAC?"

I shrugged. "It's worth a try. I've decided just today to conduct a summer workshop, so at this point, enrollment is wide open. Go over to campus, pick up an application, and send it in. You'll get a call when auditions are scheduled. I can't promise anything, but—"

"Of *course,* Miss Gray," she interrupted. "I'm just grateful to know I have a chance. Theater is *everything* to me." She sat back. With a big sigh, she added, "It's my dream."

"Join the club—and it's a large one. Competitive, too." Leaning to her, I said earnestly, "I wish you success, but I must warn you: if you're intent on dedicating your life to theater, you'll find room for little else. Few professions are so demanding. You might want to start a family first, then decide if your priorities have shifted. Not that I myself have any regrets, but sometimes, it's difficult not to wonder about other paths."

Softly, seriously, the girl told me, "Miss Gray, you made the right decision. As for me, well, I won't be starting a family, either." Her head dropped. "Circumstances made the decision for me. It's not going to happen."

Though tempted to ask her to elaborate, I didn't know her well enough to pry, and in truth, I preferred to maintain our distance. With quiet sincerity, I told her, "I'm sorry, Erin."

"But in a way," she continued, perking up, "that's just fine. I mean, it lets me focus on my dream."

"Hold on to that dream, dear."

She gave me a warm smile. "I will, Miss Gray."

"So, then,"—I stood—"ready for a party?"

"You bet." She stood as well. "Let me check on Thierry in the kitchen." And she left the room.

I surveyed the well-stocked bar, the polished glassware, the flicker of candlelight. How festive. The corners of my mouth twisted with a crooked grin.

"Miss Gray?" called Thierry from the pass-through. "I just saw headlights in your driveway."

"Curtain going up," I told him.

Let the games begin.

As the door chimes sounded, I glanced at my watch. It was not quite six-thirty.

"Shall I get that?" asked Erin from the kitchen doorway.

"No, thanks, dear. This ought to be Detective Knoll. I'm expecting him first."

Erin bopped back into the kitchen as I crossed the living room to the front door. Opening it, I found my hunch confirmed. "Evening, Larry."

"Hello, Claire." The detective stepped inside, closing the door behind him. "Hope I'm not *too* early."

"Not at all," I told him, strolling him into the room. "Just thought we should have a few minutes to compare notes before the others arrive."

"Brought mine," he said, showing me the notebook he withdrew from an inside pocket.

Tapping my noggin, I assured him, "So did I." As we were standing near the bar, I offered, "Care for something?"

"Still on duty. Iced tea, maybe." With a laugh, he added, "No sugar."

"No problem." I laughed as well. As Larry seated himself on the leather bench, I called to the kitchen, "Erin, could you get the detective—?"

"Yes, ma'am." She appeared at the pass-through. "I heard."

I joined Larry, sitting near him in one of the three-legged chairs.

Flipping through his notes, he looked up to ask, "So, then. Who's coming?"

"Everyone. At least everyone of interest." I ran him through the list, concluding, "Which leaves Rebecca, the not-so-bereaved widow, and her pet lawyer, Bryce Ballantyne. Rebecca seemed downright mystified by my invitation when I phoned today. But when I told her *you'd* be here, she quickly decided to attend. I'm not certain, Larry, but I highly suspect the killer will be among us tonight."

"You suspect them *all*?"

"To varying degrees. I admit, it's hard to think of Tanner, Kiki, or Grant—people I love—in such a light. But *someone* murdered Spencer Wallace, and it wasn't I. So I can't afford to leave any stone unturned."

Larry nodded. "I admire your thoroughness—and your impartiality."

I thought for a moment, then told him, "Theater may be fiction, but life is real, and reality can't be wished away. We need answers—wherever the truth might lead us."

"Spoken like a true-blue cop. You seem to have a knack for this, Claire."

I wasn't sure how to respond, so I was grateful that Erin appeared just then.

"Good evening, Detective. Your tea."

"Thanks, Erin." He took the iced tea, tasted it, and set it down as the girl returned to the kitchen.

I reached for my wineglass, which was still on the coffee table. "Your turn, Larry. Your notes?" I sipped the wine.

"Let's review. We know that Spencer Wallace had wealth, power, and few real friends. We know he died of drowning, already weakened by chronic cadmium poisoning. We also know—"

The doorbell interrupted him.

"Sorry." I rose.

"Just as well—saves me the trouble of repeating everything later." Returning his notes to his pocket, he sipped his tea.

Excusing myself, I crossed to the door and opened it. Surprised to find not one guest waiting, or two, but four, I said theatrically, "And so the onslaught begins—greetings, all."

Kiki rushed in, followed by Tanner, Grant Knoll, and his colleague Brandi Bjerregaard. Kiki pecked my cheek. "I've been called many things, darling, but never an onslaught."

In spite of the evening's heavy purpose, the arrival of my friends lightened my spirits and gave our gathering the feel of a party. Everyone had dressed for the occasion, looking their best, though they had instinctively worn dark colors; my red blouse fairly shrieked, pleasing me no end.

Larry had risen and stepped forward to greet the group of arrivals, shaking hands with the men.

Tanner kissed me on the lips. He wore all black—dress slacks, oxfords, and a knit shirt that nicely displayed his physique.

"Grrr," I said, giving him the once-over, "aren't *we* looking devilish tonight?"

"You're the one in red," he noted with a laugh. He then explained, "We just happened to pull up together—we didn't all *ride* together."

Grant gave me a quick hug, cheek to cheek. He wore a beautifully tailored dark suit, probably Armani. "Actually, love," he told me, "the rest of us *did* ride together. I gave Kiki a lift from the condo; then we picked up Brandi at her hotel."

"Yes, darling," Kiki said vacantly. "Saves gas, you know. Just doing our bit for humanity or the environment or whatever." She whirled an armload of bracelets. Her getup that evening was one of the more fanciful I'd seen her wear, which took considerable effort, as she could not easily outdo herself. Her costume of the moment, all black and gossamer, made her look like the Queen of the Night from *The Magic Flute.*

Tanner lectured, "That's called 'carpooling,' Kiki, but I doubt if it applies to a five-minute ride to a cocktail party with your neighbor."

While Kiki and Tanner traded a few amiable barbs, Grant pulled me aside. Eyeing Tanner, he told me, "Good *God,* you're one lucky woman."

Brandi said, "See, Claire? There he goes again." She wore a classic little black dress. With a smile, she added, "Thanks so much for inviting me."

Obliquely, I told her, "Our gathering wouldn't be complete without you."

Larry had fallen into conversation with Kiki, escorting her away from the crowd, into the room, where she sat regally on the end of the bench near the fireplace. Larry took his iced tea from the coffee table and stood nearby.

Entering from the kitchen, Erin offered to get drinks for the ladies. Brandi asked for white wine. Erin turned to Kiki. "And you, Miss Jasper-Plunkett?"

"Something light, I guess. Perhaps wine . . . or kir." Kiki rattled her bracelets again in thought. "Oh, hell, let's call it a martini. Breathlessly dry. Up, of course."

"Of course." Erin retreated to the bar to prepare the drinks.

Grant asked me, "May I serve milady?"

"All set, Grant, but thanks." I crossed to the coffee table, picked up my wineglass, and joined Larry, standing near the fireplace.

Grant nudged Tanner. "Then I guess it's up to us boys to fend for ourselves. Come on—I know where she keeps the good stuff." And he led Tanner off to the kitchen. I heard him greet Thierry with a burst of campy laughter.

From the bar, Erin looked over her shoulder to ask Kiki, "Would you like an olive with that?"

"No, thank you, dear—takes up far too much room in the glass!" She barked a loud laugh.

"Here we go." Erin brought the martini to Kiki, who accepted it with a grateful nod, tasted it, and cooed. Erin then took a glass of wine to Brandi, who settled with it on an oblong hassock near the coffee table, across from the bench.

Returning to the kitchen, Erin passed Grant and Tanner in the doorway. Bottles clanged in their arms as they stepped into the living room and moved to the bar, then rearranged the liquor.

Slapping Tanner's back, Grant said, "I'm mixing, lad. What'll it be?"

"Scotch'll be great."

"Rocks? Soda? Twist?"

"No, thanks. Neat."

"What a man . . . ," purred Grant while pouring drinks for both of them.

There was such an easy conviviality among us, I was disappointed that our underlying purpose would eventually squelch the merry mood.

"Claire, love?" Kiki looked up at me from the bench.

"Hmm?"

"Who else is coming tonight? Or is it 'just us'?"

"No, it's not." I hesitated before telling Kiki, "Rebecca Wallace, Spencer's widow, will be joining us."

"Oh, ish. I'd rather not meet the woman. But I had a hunch

she'd be here—under the circumstances. I mean, it's a rather spe-
cious pretext for a party, isn't it?"

Still working at the bar, Grant asked over his shoulder, "What
about Bryce, the boy wonder?"

I answered, "He's coming as well."

"I have to admit," said Kiki, "I admire the woman's consis-
tency—she *never* travels without her lawyer."

Grant quipped, "Don't leave home without one—that's *my*
credo."

"Amen," seconded Brandi, raising her glass.

Kiki asked me, "Anyone *else* coming?" Her tone suggested that
Bryce and Rebecca were already two too many.

"Glenn Yeats said he would be here, and he's bringing Lance
Caldwell."

Everyone knew who Glenn was—everyone in the *nation* knew
of Glenn Yeats—but Lance's renown had not spread beyond the
arts crowd. Larry asked, "Caldwell?"

"He's DAC's composer in residence. He submitted a film score
for *Photo Flash,* which was rejected." Meaningfully, I added, "He
was here Saturday night."

"Ah." Larry nodded.

"Last but not least, the film's director, Gabe Arlington, will also
be joining us."

"Really?" said Tanner, standing at the bar. "I thought he was
driving back to LA today."

"Let's just say he had a change of plans." I sipped my wine.

Erin had returned from the kitchen, bearing a tray of appetizers.
Stopping first at the bar, she offered crudités, cheese things, and
stuffed, broiled mushrooms to Grant and Tanner. Grant plucked up
some radishes and carrot sticks while Tanner stepped briefly to the
coffee table to get a couple of small plates.

Kiki leaned toward Larry, asking, "Tell me, Detective. Is it true? The autopsy results were conclusive? Spencer Wallace was poisoned?"

Larry sat in the chair nearest her. "Yes, Kiki. The mechanism of death was asphyxiation by drowning, but toxicology revealed chronic cadmium poisoning that had seriously affected his kidney and liver functions. That, coupled with cardiopulmonary depression, left his health severely compromised. When he fell—or was pushed—into the water Saturday night, he was simply unable to save himself."

Grant and Tanner had finished arranging food on their plates, and Erin had moved to the coffee table. She asked, "Miss Jasper-Plunkett? Appetizers?"

"Ah." Kiki took a plate from the table and picked a few things from Erin's tray while telling Larry, "It sounds so much like Spencer's screenplay; I've read Claire's copy. The actual poison used, the compound, was it"—she whirled her free hand—"cadmium . . . fluoride?"

"No, ma'am," said Erin, who had just finished serving Kiki. Helpfully, she corrected, "Cadmium *chloride.*"

"*Well,* now," said Tanner, sitting on one of several stools at the bar. "It seems we have a chemistry wiz in our midst."

Erin blushed. "Gosh, hardly. Sorry, Mr. Griffin. The poisoning was discussed Saturday night after Detective Knoll arrived." Passing the tray to Brandi, she added, "Guess I've got an ear for detail."

I nodded. "Highly commendable—in an aspiring actress."

Laughing, Tanner ran a hand through his hair. "Now, *why* doesn't this surprise me?"

Grant, next to Tanner at the bar, playfully shook a finger. "I warned you before, young man—no flirting." And he pinched both of Tanner's cheeks. The irony escaped no one that it was Grant, not Tanner, who was flirting.

Tanner endured these attentions with good-natured ease. Standing again, he gave Erin a courtly bow. "My apologies, miss. I didn't mean to give that impression. My heart belongs to another."

Grant sighed theatrically. "And that 'other,' alas, is not I."

With mock relief, I told him, "I'm glad you added that!"

Erin turned to me with her tray. "Hors d'oeuvre, Miss Gray?"

"Yes, thank you."

Pleasant chatter filled the room as Larry took two plates from the coffee table, passing one to me, keeping the other for himself. We picked a few cold vegetables and hot appetizers from the tray; then Erin left to replenish it in the kitchen.

The doorbell chimed, and we all fell silent. It seemed the mood of our gathering grew instantly serious.

"Excuse me," I said, setting my plate on the mantel and crossing the room to the front door. When I opened it, I was hailed by jolly hellos from Glenn Yeats and Lance Caldwell, who had ridden together, and Gabe Arlington, who had encountered them outside the house. I couldn't help feeling that their friendly but loud greetings carried a note of vulgarity; they were well aware that this party was a guise for grimmer concerns, as evidenced by their dressy but dark attire.

Still, I had invited them in a spirit of camaraderie, so it seemed peevish of me to deny them the very pretext I myself had fabricated. *"Welcome,"* I gushed as they filed through the door. "So good of you to join us."

With the exception of Larry, everyone present had attended Saturday's cast party, so introductions were brief, and within a few minutes, the new arrivals had settled into conversation with my other guests, drinks in hand. Gabe joined Tanner and Grant at the bar. Lance ended up on the long hassock with Brandi. Larry took one of the three-legged chairs. Glenn stood with me near the fireplace. And throughout, Kiki remained firmly planted on the leather-cushioned bench.

At a lull in the conversation, Kiki said to Larry, "Forgive me if I keep obsessing about the murder, but—"

"That *is* why we're here," I reminded everyone.

Kiki continued to Larry, "—but I'm confused. If Spencer drowned, but had already been poisoned at home in his darkroom, how did the killer end up *here* at Saturday's party?"

All heads turned to Larry. He said, "That's a major sticking point of the investigation. We're all but certain that Wallace was poisoned, at least partially, by *inhalation* of cadmium fumes in his darkroom. But he was also affected by cadmium *ingested* here at the party, as revealed by analysis of his stomach contents. Now, cadmium chloride is easily dissolved in any acidic solution—"

Once again, we were interrupted by the doorbell.

"Hold that thought," I told Larry. Walking to the door, I added, "This party's not complete yet."

With a frown of disappointment, Kiki said, "And it was just getting good."

Grant heaved a bored sigh. "When *does* the dancing begin?"

Opening the door, I admitted the last of my guests. "Ah, good evening, Rebecca. So glad you could come."

Rebecca stepped inside with her lawyer, Bryce. I was relieved to see that Rebecca had put herself together since that morning; she was now as prim and well coiffed as when I'd first met her on Sunday. Tonight she wore widow's black, making a show of her mourning; her outfit included black hose, which I thought took the concept overboard. Bryce was looking especially handsome and severe in a black suit, white shirt, and silvery gray tie. As they entered, everyone in the room stood, except Kiki, who remained conspicuously seated, fussing with her food, avoiding eye contact with the bereaved Mrs. Wallace.

Rebecca gave me a stiff hug. "Thank you for inviting us, Claire." Wearily, she added, "Though I'm still not sure what you intend to accomplish."

"Soon enough, dear, soon enough." I turned to her lawyer and shook his hand. "Welcome, Bryce."

"Hello, Miss Gray. Most gracious of you." He closed the door behind him.

"Let's see," I said, taking charge of introductions, "you already know Detective Knoll, of course." Larry nodded politely from where he stood, exchanging greetings with the new arrivals. I then presented Glenn Yeats, making a considerable impression; wealth of such magnitude tends to raise the eyebrows of even the most jaded. Moving around the room, I also introduced Lance Caldwell. I could tell from Rebecca's reaction that his name meant nothing to her; I could tell from Lance's reaction that this blank reception made him bristle. Rebecca already knew Brandi Bjerregaard, from their real-estate dealings, and she seemed remotely acquainted with Gabe Arlington, from her husband's movie dealings.

Standing near Gabe at the bar was Grant. I told Bryce and Rebecca, "Although you got a fleeting glimpse of Larry's brother yesterday, I don't believe you've met him. This is my friend Grant Knoll."

Grant stepped forward to greet both coolly, then retreated to the bar, sitting on a stool.

"And *this*," I said, "is Tanner Griffin, the young actor who will be appearing in the film Spencer wrote, *Photo Flash.*"

Tanner stepped to Rebecca, took her hand, and held it. "My condolences, Mrs. Wallace. Your husband was a great man—and he was good to me."

"Your words are very generous, Mr. Griffin." The lilt of Rebecca's voice conveyed utter enchantment. "And I've heard wonderful things about *you*—all of them true, I'm delighted to observe." From the glint in her eye, I feared she might hitch her skirt, jump, and mount him.

Tanner turned to Rebecca's lawyer and shook his hand. "Good evening."

"Bryce Ballantyne. My pleasure."

I looked about, saving the best for last. "And, uh—oh! Kiki, love? Do meet our special guests."

Stone-faced, Kiki at last rose from the bench, holding her martini glass, which was now empty. Regally extending her free hand, she said without inflection, "I don't believe I've had the pleasure."

Stiff-jawed, the widow replied, "Mine entirely. Rebecca Wallace."

I explained to her, "This is Kiki Jasper-Plunkett, costumer extraordinaire, whom we're fortunate to have on the faculty at Desert Arts College." Turning, I told Kiki, "And this is Bryce Ballantyne, Rebecca's attorney."

Bryce said, "It's an honor, Professor Jasper-Plunkett."

No, it wasn't my imagination; Kiki was lucently charmed by the guy. With a dainty handshake, she told him, "There's no need to stand on ceremony, Bryce. Do call me Kiki." Primping, she added, "Did Claire mention? She's my *oldest* friend."

Bryce replied through a toothy, frat-boy smile, "Then you're both exceedingly fortunate."

Unnerved by this spark of mutual attraction, I said, "Rebecca? Please, have a seat." I indicated the cushioned bench. "Would you care for something to drink?"

Disinterested, she answered, "Oh, some wine, I suppose." She moved to the bench and sat in the spot Kiki had been warming. Kiki backed off a few steps, observing the new dynamics of the room. Larry sat in one of the three-legged chairs. Brandi and Lance sat again on the hassock.

Tanner offered, "I'll get Rebecca's wine." Noticing that Bryce did not yet have a drink, Tanner suggested that he join him at the bar. With a pleasant nod, Bryce did so, and they began pouring drinks.

Grant moved out of their way, stepping toward the terrace doors, where he stood looking out. Erin entered from the kitchen with a fresh tray of appetizers, stopping to let Grant pick from her tray.

Kiki seemed adrift. There were now only two empty seats—the spot next to Rebecca on the bench, and the three-legged chair nearest Rebecca, facing her. Kiki said, "Claire? Would you like to sit down?" She indicated the chair. "It seems everything's under control."

"I'll stand, thanks." I moved next to Glenn at the fireplace; he put an arm around my shoulder. Patting the back of the vacant chair, I told Kiki, "Please. Take it." Smiling sweetly, I added, "I insist."

Dryly, she told me, "Too kind of you." Then, with palpable reluctance, she settled into the chair, not two feet from Rebecca.

Erin plied the crowd with her tray, asking Rebecca, "Hors d'oeuvre, ma'am?"

"Thank you." Rebecca picked a tiny celery stalk, held it, but did not eat.

Bryce stepped from the bar with two glasses and sat on the bench next to Rebecca, handing her the wine, setting his cocktail on the table. Erin offered him appetizers; he took a few, arranging a plate for himself.

Grant, noting that Bryce had left the bar, moved back from the terrace doors, joining Tanner and Gabe, who all settled on bar stools.

Erin moved from the bench to the fireplace, where Glenn and I stood, behind Kiki's chair. She offered more appetizers, which Glenn accepted; I declined.

"There now," I said, surveying the room. "Is everyone comfortable?"

Kiki hoisted her empty martini glass. "I could use another . . ."

"Yes, ma'am." Erin plucked the glass from Kiki's hand, set it on her tray, and took it to the kitchen.

With finger to chin, I strolled, thinking, across the room. The others watched silently as I reached the front door, then turned back to them. The trace of a grin curled my mouth as I said, "I suppose you're all wondering why I've gathered you here tonight."

My comment was met by a roomful of blank stares.

"Sorry." I explained, "That was meant to be amusing. It's a stock line from the last act of every murder mystery I've ever directed."

"Of course!" blurted Kiki. "*Most* amusing, darling. Here we are, smack in the middle of the drawing-room scene from some tangled manor-house whodunit. How *very* Agatha Christie of you!" She heaved a huge, well-rehearsed laugh.

"Well"—my tone was pensive—"it *is* rather tangled, isn't it? The murder of Spencer Wallace, now two days past, has darkened my home and touched the lives of all present. For Spencer's sake, and for the peace of mind of those left behind, the riddle of his death must be solved."

Rebecca set down her wineglass and her celery stalk. Flicking imagined grime from her fingers, she said, "Don't make him out to be a saint, Claire. He wasn't."

"No, apparently not."

As I spoke, Erin entered quietly from the kitchen with a small tray bearing a cocktail shaker and a fresh martini glass. She moved to Kiki, leaned to let her take the glass, then poured from the shaker. When the glass was filled to the brim, Erin left with the shaker on her tray.

I continued, "It seems I'm the only one in this room who truly thought Spencer a friend. And yet, someone here tonight has gone out of his way to implicate *me* in this crime."

From the bar, Grant said, "They'd have to be nuts to think they could get away with it. We all know *you* didn't kill Wallace."

"Really? Do you?" I moved to the center of the room. "I was overheard on Saturday night *saying* I could kill him. I was quoted in Sunday's paper making fist-shaking threats against him. And just this afternoon, Grant, *you* discovered a stash of deadly cadmium chloride hidden in my sugar canister."

"How preposterous . . . ," Kiki sputtered over the rim of her drink.

Larry told us, "We ran the bottle through forensics. It did indeed contain cadmium chloride. As expected, it was clean of fingerprints, other than Grant's—he pulled it out of the sugar."

Tanner asked, "How would anyone get ahold of such awful stuff?"

I recalled, "Cadmium compounds have legitimate industrial uses. They're easily obtainable over the Internet, or even by mail order, using a fake letterhead. It's right in the script, as are so many aspects of Spencer's death. Don't you remember, Tanner?"

"Duh"—he thumped his forehead—"the screenplay."

"You're not the *only* one familiar with the script." Meaningfully, I added, "Everyone in this room has read it."

Brandi piped in, "*I* haven't."

"I stand corrected. Everyone *else* in this room has read the script."

Referring to his notes, Larry said, "And according to the profile we've developed, the killer had read the script."

Bryce raised a finger. "Remember, though: many others, not present in this room, have also read it."

Larry nodded. "Duly noted."

Seated at the bar, Gabe asked, "What else do we know about the killer?"

I enumerated, "We know the killer was present at Saturday night's party. We suspect the killer also had access to Spencer's darkroom. And I'm *sure* the killer has been inside my kitchen—at least once. What's more, it simply stands to reason that the killer had a strong motive to want Spencer dead. In short"—I moved toward the fireplace—"the killer could be anyone here tonight. Except Larry, of course." I patted his shoulder.

Looking up at me from his chair, he asked in an odd tone, "What makes you so sure of that?"

"Isn't it obvious?" I explained naively, "You represent the law, Larry."

"So do I," said Bryce, sounding left out and defensive.

"Do I hear you correctly?" said Glenn, stepping to my side. "You think it's possible that *I* killed Spencer Wallace?"

"Or *I*?" echoed Lance, sounding huffy.

Though tempted, I refrained from cracking a smile. "Perish the thought that either of you fine gentlemen would stoop to such an act. But is it possible? Of course it is. It's logistically feasible that either one of you was responsible."

"Just a moment, Claire." Rebecca straightened her spine. "If the killer was at Saturday's party, that rules *me* out. I wasn't there."

"Apparently, Rebecca, but I don't know that with certainty. There was a *crowd* here on Saturday, including a number of guests I didn't recognize. Spencer *would* have recognized you, so if you'd come for ill purposes, you might have worn some simple disguise—say, a wig and glasses."

She rolled her eyes. "Very well, that's a stretch, but I suppose it's plausible. However, I have *never* been inside your kitchen."

"Bryce *has*, though. When you arrived at the house yesterday, you asked him to get you some water."

"So?" asked Bryce. "Why would *I* be a part of this? I'm merely an *adviser* to Mrs. Wallace."

"Oh, *please*," said Grant with a loud tsk. "It's common knowledge that you and Rebecca are romantically involved. That would give *both* of you ample motive to want Spencer dead. And working as a team, you just might have pulled it off."

Bryce warned, "Watch yourself, Mr. Knoll. Your words could easily be construed as slander. And from you, of all people—you had your own score to settle with Spencer."

"So a deal fell through." Grant flicked a wrist. "What of it? It was nothing."

Brandi cleared her throat. "It was a half-million dollars, Grant."

Larry wagged his head, mourning his own losses.

"Why, *Grant*," said Tanner, turning to face him from his bar stool. "I'm impressed—I didn't realize you had that kind of money to play around with."

"You will too, lad, once that movie of yours goes into production." Grant sniffed Tanner lovingly, telling everyone, "I smell box-office gold."

"And," I noted, moving toward the bar, "as both Gabe and Tanner have pointed out, the publicity buzz over Spencer's death will only serve to hype the film, boosting the careers of everyone involved."

Gabe set his empty cocktail glass on the bar. "I hate to sound mercenary, but sure, that's true."

Tanner nodded. "A 'big film' just got much bigger."

Erin returned from the kitchen and began circulating with her tray of appetizers.

"If I'm not mistaken," Rebecca said coyly, "the young man may have had more than a *mercenary* motive to want my husband dead." She declined hors d'oeuvres with a wave of her hand, but Bryce took a few, arranging them on the plate balanced on his knees.

With an uncertain laugh, Tanner asked Rebecca, "What's *that* supposed to mean?"

"I *loathe* telling naughty tales," said Rebecca, not loathing it at all, "but Spencer made no secret of his lust for Hollywood's soon-to-be hottest heartthrob. Unless I'm mistaken, he was all *over* Mr. Griffin, which mortified our young hero, I'm sure. Did those advances *enrage* Mr. Griffin? Who knows?"

Grant stood. "Oh, for pity's sake. Tanner gets plenty of pawing from *me,* God knows. I've had *these* queer eyes trained on *this* straight guy for months, and he always takes it in good humor."

Matter-of-factly, Tanner told us, "I'm used to it."

"Of *course* he is." Grant gave Rebecca a brisk nod—so there. Then he grabbed several radishes as Erin passed by with her tray. Sitting again, he began munching one of them.

"*Really*, Rebecca," said Kiki, amused by the woman's lack of insight. "We theater folk are far more open-minded than that." She laughed airily. Then, catching Erin's eye, she tapped the rim of her martini glass, empty again.

With a nod, Erin returned to the kitchen.

Rebecca folded her hands in her lap. "Then we're at a stalemate. It seems everyone here tonight harbored something against my husband."

Returning to the fireplace, I said, "But *not* everyone here to-night has been to the Baja. Specifically"—I gestured toward the framed photo propped on the mantel—"Spencer's little getaway in Cabo San Lucas."

Rebecca looked away. "I'm sure I don't know what you mean."

Kiki cleared her throat with a nervous laugh, turning in her chair to look up at me. "Really, Claire. I thought we agreed we wouldn't 'go there.'"

Rebecca turned to Kiki, face-to-face. "You've *been* there?"

"That's not what I meant—not exactly." Kiki wriggled in her seat. Fortunately for her, Erin returned at that moment with the cocktail shaker and, blocking Rebecca, refilled Kiki's glass.

Taking my own glass from the mantel, I swirled the bit of wine remaining in it. "Spencer Wallace didn't mean to send us a 'message from beyond,' I'm sure, but the photo from Cabo tells us all we need to know."

As the others turned to whisper among themselves, speculating on the meaning of my words, Erin finished serving Kiki, who carefully raised her full glass to her lips and sipped. Noticing the empty glass in my hand, Erin stepped near and asked, sotto voce, "More wine, Miss Gray?"

"No, thank you, Erin, nothing else."

She nodded, turned, and moved toward the kitchen.

"Uh, Erin?" I said, reconsidering.

She stopped behind the leather bench and looked back to me.

"It was, uh . . . it was *you* who killed Spencer Wallace, was it not?"

Erin froze where she stood, wild-eyed. Larry instinctively rose from his chair. Simultaneously, Grant spit a whole radish halfway across the room, Bryce dropped his plate to the floor, and Kiki sprayed a mouthful of her martini, dousing Rebecca.

Kiki blurted, "You mean the goddamn *maid* did it!?"

Rebecca shot up from the bench, snarling and brushing gin from her dress. She moved toward the front door, followed by Bryce. Grant, Tanner, and Gabe rose from their bar stools and took a step toward Erin. Brandi and Lance rose from the long hassock, completing a loose circle around the girl.

"Miss Gray," said Erin, taking a tentative step in my direction,

"I . . . I don't . . . you can't possibly . . ." Stunned, she began to teeter near Kiki's chair.

Fearing that Erin might drop the martini shaker, Kiki reached up and took it from her hands, then refilled her own glass and set the shaker on the floor.

I moved toward Erin; Larry followed. Shaking my head gently, I told her, "I never would have guessed, but you gave yourself away tonight—it was such an innocent slip. When Kiki mentioned cadmium *fluoride,* you corrected her, telling her the poison was cadmium *chloride.* You said you recalled hearing it Saturday night, and your memory of this detail seemed plausible, as you've had some theatrical training. But so have I, Erin, and I recall with absolute certainty that you were not in this room on Saturday when Grant and I discussed cadmium chloride with Detective Knoll. So I could only conclude that you knew about cadmium chloride because you'd read the screenplay of *Photo Flash.* Then everything else fell together."

Kiki burbled, "Boffo, Claire. How clever." Then she cocked her head, confused. "Uh, *what* fell together?"

"Miss Gray," Erin pleaded, "you're jumping to conclusions . . ."

"Indeed I am," I agreed. "Perfectly logical conclusions, consistent with everything we know about Spencer's death. You see, I hadn't realized until tonight that you had an interest in theater. You seem to idolize me, so I assume you idolized Spencer Wallace as well—or at least saw him as an avenue to the career you dreamed of. You've worked at his home, at catered parties, and that's how you met. You ingratiated yourself, made your ambitions known, and he led you on—to the proverbial casting couch and then, I fear, to Cabo. That's you in the photo, correct? You've streaked your hair and played the dumb blonde, but otherwise, the dark-haired figure could easily be you."

She shook her head vehemently. "No, Miss Gray. I was never there."

Kiki looked up at me. "Nonsense, darling. I've already told you—that's *me* in the picture."

"What?" demanded Rebecca, hands on hips.

"Oops." Kiki slurped her martini.

I told Erin, "Regardless of who's in the photo, I'm reasonably sure Spencer had flown you to Cabo, where he arranged to take care of a 'little fix' he'd gotten you into. Did something go wrong in Mexico, Erin? You implied earlier that you can't have children."

Rebecca muttered with quiet disgust, "Oh, my *God* . . ."

I continued, "A few other details from Saturday night now make perfect sense. You served Spencer tomato juice all evening, which is acidic. You could easily have spiked it with the fatal doses of cadmium chloride. You've been in my kitchen more than *I* have, so you had ample opportunity to plant the incriminating compound in the sugar. What's more, during cleanup after the party, Tanner thought he knew you from somewhere. Grant dismissed this as flirting, but in fact, Tanner *had* seen you before—perhaps at a casting call for *Photo Flash,* or more likely, at Wallace's home in Palm Springs, where you were well acquainted with not only the bedroom, but the darkroom."

Tanner looked at her with fresh, unbelieving eyes. "That's it," he said quietly. "I should have realized . . ."

Erin's head dropped back as her mouth opened and disgorged a loud sob. Larry moved from behind me and positioned himself on the opposite side of Erin.

I told her, "The incident that should have tipped me off immediately, though, took place right after you'd 'discovered' the body in the pool. Grant dove in and made an attempted rescue, but before he'd gotten the body out of the water, you screamed, 'It's Spencer!' Grant himself didn't recognize him until after you'd said that, and just as damning, you referred to the victim by his first name. Detective Knoll, Tanner, and I have all invited you to use *our* first names, but you've been only too proper, steadfastly addressing us as Detective, Mr. Griffin, and Miss Gray. In the excitement of the moment, why did 'Mr. Wallace' become 'Spencer'? Because you'd been intimate with the man."

"That was his *name,*" insisted Erin. "What's the difference?"

"Finally, when my back was turned, while I'd gone into my bedroom to look for a copy of the script, you told Detective Knoll that I'd threatened Spencer's life. It was an empty threat, and you knew it. But you recognized a handy means of deflecting suspicion from yourself while steering the investigation down a false course."

Gaining some composure and starting to feel feisty, Erin challenged me, "Miss Gray, I'm sure this all makes sense in *your* mind, but it's pure speculation. You can't prove a word of this."

Bryce told me, "She has a point."

I'd heard about enough from Brycey-boy. "Oh, sure—I don't *have* proof, but we can easily *get* proof. If Erin was recently in Cabo, returning by air, presumably through Los Angeles, there will be passport records of her visit to Mexico. That alone should be sufficient evidence to prove the entire sordid scenario."

Knowing she was sunk, Erin heaved a long, low wail, buried her head in her hands, and slumped.

"You'd better sit down," said Larry, guiding her to the leather bench. Erin sat, looking out vacantly, as if beyond the walls of the room. Larry sat next to her, took out his notebook, and clicked his pen.

I stood directly behind the girl. Tanner stepped to my side and held me by the waist. Glenn moved to my other side and placed his hand on my shoulder.

Looking gaunt and drained, Erin began to speak. She seemed to direct her rambling words, her recollections, to no one but herself.

"I thought I'd struck gold. I thought I could skip a few hurdles along the road to stardom. It seemed like the easiest shortcut in the world when Spencer Wallace sort of fell into my lap—or should I say, I fell into his.

"Yes, he made promises; yes, he got me pregnant. He insisted on an abortion, but I refused. So he struck a deal with me: If I'd go to Mexico with him, he would have everything taken care of, safely and discreetly. Then, when we returned, he swore he'd cast me in his new film, *Photo Flash*. He even gave me the script to study.

"Well, things didn't go quite as planned. The doctor needed tequila—to calm *his* nerves—then botched the procedure, not in some back room, but right there at the house." Erin turned and looked at the photo on the mantel.

Becoming aware of her silent, gaping audience, she explained, "I was lucky to recover at all, but I'll never have another chance at motherhood. Then—I should have seen it coming—as soon as we got home, Spencer was 'terribly sorry' and all, but he just didn't think I was right for his picture. I was incensed, but what could I do?"

She paused, then grinned. "Well, he'd spelled out the plan for me in his own script. He still wanted to see me at the house in Palm Springs now and then, so I had plenty of time to explore his dark-room, spike the baths, and rig the fans. Then, on Saturday—Miss Gray was right about the tomato juice at the party. When Spencer staggered out to the terrace, the party was winding down and there was no one else out there. I saw my chance—and gave that fucker just the slightest nudge." Erin smiled. "That's all it took."

The girl looked Rebecca in the eye. "I wish I could say otherwise, but I'm glad he's dead."

Numbly, the widow told her, "So am I, dear."

"Erin?" Larry stood. "I think we should continue this outside."

"Yes, Detective. I suppose we should." Erin stood. Larry grasped her arm. She turned to me. "Miss Gray? I *do* regret dragging you into this. I'm sorry."

Stepping away from Glenn and Tanner, I moved to Larry's side and told Erin without rancor, "If you hadn't dragged me into it, I'd have merely *wondered* how Spencer Wallace died. Once I'd been cast under suspicion, I had to *prove* how it happened."

Larry began leading Erin to the front door. I followed. Rebecca and Bryce moved aside to let us pass.

Pausing at the door, Larry told me, "I'm glad you got involved, Claire. Cops generally frown on 'meddling laymen,' but I have to admit—your theatrical perspective on criminology, while unconventional, proved right on the money." He opened the door.

"Happy to help, Larry. Stay in touch."

With a wink, he assured me, "I will." Then he escorted Erin out into the darkness.

After a moment of dead silence, Rebecca moved to me at the open door, extending her hand for a curt shake. "I suppose I, too, should thank you," she said without emotion. "I'm not sure I appreciate the dirty laundry that was aired tonight—to say nothing of the innuendo targeting Bryce and me—but the case *is* closed now. That's all that matters. On balance, I'm a happy woman." She didn't sound happy.

"And I'm happy *for* you, Rebecca," I told her politely, but with a certain distance. "Good night."

Bryce said, "Good evening, Miss Gray," nodded, and escorted Rebecca out.

Standing at the open door, I watched them walk to the street. With no intended sarcasm, I softly wished them, "Pleasant dreams."

Closing the door, I then turned to the others. "Well. That was abrupt."

Kiki, the only one of us still seated, at last stood.

Looking a bit wobbly, she slurred, "I thought she'd *never* leave."

The party was over. Though I was finally able to relax and might have enjoyed a bit of reveling with friends, I'd lost my staff. Thierry had left in a panic shortly after Erin had ridden away with Larry Knoll, doubtless en route to the county jail in Riverside. It wasn't clear whether the catering boss meant to get a lawyer and try to bail out his errant employee or if he was simply chagrined that yet another of his parties at my home had ended like the closing scene from some gritty police drama.

My guests dispersed quickly. During the chitchat that followed the arrest, Brandi Bjerregaard seemed to hit it off with Gabe Arlington; as they were both staying at the Regal Palms, he offered to drive her there, and they left together. Lance Caldwell claimed the onset of a migraine, which he feared might impair the delicate cerebral balance that governed his composing skills, so Glenn Yeats agreed to drive him home at once, but not before exacting from me promises to lock my doors that night, stay out of trouble, and phone him first thing in the morning.

I had no trouble justifying my fibs of compliance as I waved good night and shut the door. Remaining in my living room were Grant, Tanner, and Kiki, the three who meant most to me.

"Alone at last," said Grant, moving to the bar to pour a glass of wine.

Tanner stepped toward me; I met him halfway. "Claire, you were wonderful," he said, wrapping his arms around me for a nuzzling embrace.

Grant offered me the wine. "Congratulations, doll. I had *no* idea where you were headed tonight—and I admit, you made me squirm once or twice—but what else can I say? Bravo!"

Accepting the glass from him, I sipped the cool chardonnay and enjoyed it thoroughly. It was the most carefree moment I'd experienced in days.

"Yes, darling, bravo!" said Kiki, setting her empty glass on the coffee table. With a burst of applause, she added, "You were a *triumph* this evening—a flat-out *triumph*!"

I bowed mechanically to both of them. "Thank you. Thank you." I paused, then added, "But I should probably restrict my *future* triumphs to the theatrical variety." Having expressed that intention on previous occasions, I knew better than to take myself seriously.

"Yes . . . ," said Grant, eyeing me askance, "my brother might appreciate that."

"I don't know, Grant." Tanner crossed the room to the bookcase that housed the stereo and began browsing for a CD to play. He continued, "The quick arrest will look good for Larry. He seemed *grateful* for Claire's involvement."

I raised a hand, pledging, "Be that as it may, my sleuthing days are done." Aware that I was fooling no one, I turned to Kiki, offering, "Nightcap?"

"I *couldn't,* darling, but thank you. I've had *far* too much already." She could barely stand.

"Besides," Grant told her, "we should skedaddle. I think milady would like to be alone tonight—that is, 'alone' with her studly protégé."

Kiki gasped, lifting a hand to her mouth. "I nearly forgot. This is your last night together. Tanner is off to LA tomorrow."

Tanner told all of us, "It's just up the road, a two-hour drive on the Ten. I'll be around." Ah, the best of intentions; I'd heard them before. Tanner punched a button on the stereo, and music began playing softly. The slow, jazzy melody set a pleasant, dreamy mood.

I set down my glass, telling Grant, "You don't *have* to leave. It's still early."

"You're just being polite. I know you're *dying* to get rid of us." His insight never failed to amaze me.

"Yes, dear," said Kiki, stepping close to peck my cheek. "I know an exit cue when I hear one. Ta, darling." And she moved to the door.

Grant followed. Opening the door, he flourished an arm, telling Kiki, "Madam's car pool awaits."

"Thank you, love." Kiki called across the room, "Good night, Tanner," then said to me, "Bye, dear. Call me tomorrow."

"Of course."

Grant glanced from me to Tanner and back again. Shaking a finger, he told us sternly, "You kids behave yourselves." Then he hooted, "Ciao, guys!" and whisked Kiki out of the house.

I waved good-bye. "Drive carefully!"

Closing the door, I paused, listening to the gentle sounds of Tanner's music. When I turned, he was still standing at the bookcase, on the far side of the room. We began a slow cross toward each other, speaking as we moved.

"Well?" I said. "It's 'just us.'"

"At long last."

"At least for a while—at least for tonight."

"I meant what I said, Claire. I'll still be around."

"No, you won't," I said with no bitterness. "You'll be busy."

Reaching me, he held my hands, facing me squarely. "That's nuts."

"That's *life*." I hugged him close. "But I have no intention of putting a damper on this evening."

"You bet." He growled in my ear, and we savored the touch of each other for a long, loving moment. When we stepped apart, Tanner took a quick look about the room. "Hey. Let me help you straighten up. Then we can relax." He grabbed a few things from the coffee table and carried them to the kitchen.

"You needn't do that," I told him, strolling to the fireplace, glancing at the wall of photos. "Oralia comes on Tuesdays. She'll tidy up."

"No trouble at all. I enjoy being helpful." He'd begun working at the pass-through bar, pulling bottles and glassware into the kitchen. "Uh-oh . . ."

I turned. "What's wrong?"

Stepping through the doorway and into the living room, he explained, "Protein bars. We're out of them."

Crossing to him, I twitched a brow. "Uh-oh is right. Wouldn't want you running low on protein—not tonight." I traced a finger down his chest.

"For *tomorrow*." He laughed. "I'll want a couple in the morning." He yanked a ring of keys from his pocket, jangling them. "Think I'll run down to the corner—only be a minute." Then a wrinkle creased his brow. "Do you mind?"

My brow wrinkled as well. "Of course not. Why would I mind?"

"Well," he explained awkwardly, "I don't want you thinking I've . . . abandoned you."

"Nonsense."

"But tomorrow—"

"I helped make this happen for you. How could I feel abandoned?"

"I mean," he said sheepishly, "I don't want you feeling . . . alone."

"Tanner. Sweetheart." I paused, looking into his eyes. Kissing the tip of my index finger, I told him, "I'm used to it." And I touched my finger to his lips.

Beaming, Tanner took hold of my shoulders for a moment, as if drinking in the sight of me. Then he dashed to the door, opened it, and rushed out, pulling the door closed behind him.

Watching him leave, I stood still and silent, then breathed a little sigh. Oddly, this quiet utterance carried no hint of longing or remorse, but seemed to signal a deep contentment. The feeling may have stemmed from the victory of a murder solved, or it may have simply acknowledged gratitude for the time I'd already spent with Tanner. Both of these emotional episodes in my life were now resolved simultaneously, and I felt not the slightest regret for either involvement. On the contrary, I felt that I had been both challenged and enriched.

Rebecca Wallace had called herself a happy woman, mouthing empty words. Charitably—perhaps condescendingly—I now wished she could feel some small measure of my own satisfaction.

Crossing the room to the bookcase, I notched up the music and drifted again to the fireplace, gazing at the mingled collection of photographs—mine and Spencer Wallace's. Feeling the music, I lifted the Cabo picture from the mantel and waltzed with it to the center of the room, studying it at arm's length. When I reached the bench, I dropped the photo facedown on the leather cushion and twirled gently once or twice, moving through the open doors to the terrace.

As the closing phrases of the music grew louder and reached their final cadence, I stopped near the edge of the pool, flung my arms toward the sky, and vented a loud, sustained sigh.

Like waning laughter, the sound of my voice vanished in the black desert night.